No Common War

Books by Luke Salisbury

Fiction

The Cleveland Indian
Blue Eden
Hollywood and Sunset

Nonfiction

The Answer is Baseball
First Class Times: Writing about New College's Charter Classes (with Lawrence Paulson, eds.)

No Common War

Luke Salisbury

Black Heron Press
Post Office Box 13396
Mill Creek, Washington 98082
www.blackheronpress.com

No Common War is a work of fiction. Except for historical figures, all characters that appear in this book are products of the author's imagination. Other than historical figures, any resemblance to persons living or dead is purely coincidental.

ISBN (print): 978-1-936364-29-9

ISBN (ebook): 978-1-936364-30-5

Black Heron Press
Post Office Box 13396
Mill Creek, Washington 98082
www. blackheronpress.com

This book is dedicated to
Sergeant Moreau J. Salisbury
Company G, 24th New York Volunteer Infantry Regiment
and
Private Merrick Salisbury
Company G, 24th New York Volunteer Infantry Regiment

Have you seen the elephant?
—Civil War inquiry about whether a man had been in battle

This is no common war.
—General William Tecumseh Sherman

Mason
Washington City
Christmas Day
1835

Prologue

In 1835, Colonel Thomas Meacham, the preeminent citizen of Sandy Creek, New York, recruited local men to take the world's largest cheese to Washington City. The Colonel made the fourteen hundred pounds of cheddar, with our help, right in the village. His mission was to present the cheese to President Andrew Jackson and give the village universal recognition. Filled with the prospect of adventure, my brother Lorenzo and I volunteered to accompany Meacham and his masterwork to Washington City. We had never been south of the Finger Lakes or out of New York State. The Colonel hoped his giant cheddar, dubbed the Great Cheese, would make him famous. I hoped it would make me famous. I thought there'd be important men, handsome women, superb opportunity in Washington City. I had not reckoned how a single day might so change a life.

Lorenzo and I saw slaves in Maryland. Neither of us had ever seen a slave. In Baltimore, Negroes unloaded freight and sang carols with a melancholy intensity not easily forgotten. I waved to a man with a sweat-soaked red bandanna and flax shirt that had no color. He just looked at me.

No crowds greeted the Great Cheese in Washington City. Christmas in the capital was a muddy, lonely business. We found no splendid balls, rich widows, or affable Senators. Everyone, it seemed, had somewhere else to be. The city was a disappointment. The roads were unpaved and the new government buildings far apart. Lorenzo said,

"This ain't a city. This is a hope for a city."

The President, we were told, was too ill to meet us. This was a severe disappointment, bordering on insult. We had brought the Great Cheese from the shores of Lake Ontario to the nation's wretched capital and weren't even to see Old Hickory, let alone find the doors of the best houses opened. A slave did tip his hat and say, "Welcome, cheese men," as the gigantic North Country cheddar disappeared into the back of the White House.

On Christmas Day, Lorenzo and I walked the deserted streets. I was ready to go home and visit a young woman who had been most sorry to see me go. We passed an empty slave pen and whipping post, and I said bitterly, "At least they don't sell human beings on the birthday of the Savior." We walked by the White House and considered stopping to inquire about the President's health. The day was gray and cold, though walking in the damp air felt less chilly than our drafty boarding house. We wore long coats. Lorenzo had a short-stocked shotgun under his greatcoat. He was rarely without it away from the farm.

We passed a whitewashed boarding house and heard screams and the sound of a whip. Lorenzo and I went around back to the stable where a heavy man, his white, collarless shirt stained with sweat, lashed a Negro. The Negro stood on an unpainted stool, his hands tied together and hung over a rusty hook in a joist. His neck, shoulders, back and feet were bare. His shiny black back was bloody and his ragged pants were bright with blood. Three stable hands passed a jug. One of them said, "Put your back into it, John." They wore soiled black coats and had red, sweaty faces.

I saw everything in an instant. A white mark on the forehead of a horse in a stall. The gap between the blackened teeth of the man swigging out of a jug. Rakes and bridles on the walls. A saddle in a pile of straw. The upraised hoof of a gray horse in another stall. A lantern on a chest whose varnished top was cracked. The crease in a slouch hat beside John. Manure on their the men's boots. A cowhide whip. The Negro's bloody feet on tiptoe on the rough stool. And most of all the red welts, blood flowing on the Negro's shiny back, muscles and tendons stretched so they might tear.

We stood in the door. Lorenzo put his hand under his coat.

"You got business?" said John, and spat.

We didn't answer.

"Costs to watch a cowhidin'," said the man with the jug. "A quarter."

"That ain't enough," said a squat man with big forearms and a bulging stomach, who leaned against a stall.

Lorenzo and I looked at each other. John gave the Negro two hard lashes and grunted with the effort. He evidently enjoyed inflicting pain. The Negro turned and I saw his face by the light of the lantern. The face was old, helpless, begging. Blood ran down to the man's feet and dripped off the stool. He screamed. John hit him again. The Negro's face begged us to do something.

I was humiliated, fascinated, furious. I couldn't watch; I couldn't not watch. I felt the raw satisfaction of the stable hands. They guffawed and swigged. I felt the hot arrogance of cruelty in John. The vicious pride. I took off my coat, walked past the hat, lantern, John, the whip. I put the coat over the man's bloody shoulders. The coat covered him to the ankles.

"Damn waste of a good coat," said John, and spat in the straw.

"He's cold," I said.

"Yankees," said the hand with big forearms.

"Yankees don't know niggers," said the hand with the jug.

"He's cold," I said again.

"Thank him," said John, touching the Negro's ear with the whip. Tears ran down the black man's face. He looked old enough to be my father.

"Do you call yourself a Christian?" I said, looking John in the eye.

The whip made a cracking, peremptory sound as it stung my face.

I doubled over, clutching my face. Lorenzo hit John on the side of the head with the barrel of the shotgun and in the stomach with the butt. John staggered and sat down on the straw. The whip dropped. John put his hand to his head, which was bleeding, groaned and fell to the straw. I watched him wriggle and jerk and cradle his head. I wanted the gun.

The squat hand reached for a pitchfork. Another picked up a rake.

"Don't," said Lorenzo. He didn't say it loud. No one moved.

"Give me the gun," I said.

"No," said Lorenzo.

The Negro sobbed like a child. The sound was unbearable.

"I'll kill him," I said. I felt a burning wetness from cheek to hairline.

"It's his country," said Lorenzo, glancing at John. Lorenzo moved back, gun leveled at the other men.

"For now," I said, and stepped on the hat.

We walked out of that stable. I didn't look back. Lorenzo didn't take his eyes off the men.

As we moved away, they strung that slave back up and beat him like they were beating us instead. They beat him so hard God could hear his screams. I hear them still and know I am a coward.

Mason

Son and Scar

Sandy Creek, New York

April 1861

1

April 12, 1861. Twenty-six years, four months and seventeen days after I was attacked, Fort Sumter was attacked. A generation of dithering over slavery became thirty-three hours of cannonade. The fort in flames, Union commander Major Robert Anderson, who once taught artillery to Confederate commander Pierre G. T. Beauregard at West Point, surrendered. Major Anderson was allowed to salute and remove his battered flag. His force of sixty-four men (One died in an accident after the bombardment ceased, none because of it) was allowed to leave. The commanders were gentlemen. War seemed decent and honorable.

Decent or not, it had come at last.

2

My son didn't want to go to war. He went because I made sure of it. I don't believe in atonement. Only explanation.

Moreau returned from seminary at Cazenovia after the attack on Fort Sumter. Mr. Lincoln called for 75,000 volunteers. The North Country, New York State, indeed the whole North, was united and inflamed. Everyone was inflamed, I should say, except my son. He seemed to be inflamed against being inflamed, or inflamed against me. Moreau followed the Lord and I was standing for election to the State Assembly in November. We argued mightily. Moreau said God's commandment against killing was unequivocal. I said slavery was an affront to God, man, and Jesus Christ. A time comes when words no longer suffice, even between father and son.

Two weeks after Sumter, a runaway slave found his way to Bob Chamberlain's farm by the bend in Little Sandy Creek, four miles from the Salisbury mill. I would help get the man to Canada, like I had helped several before him. I was often active in the work of the Cause. This was the chance to convert my son to Abolition. With deft maneuver, I might use this starving man for everyone's good. The runaway would get freedom and Moreau would get the opportunity to see why men should fight. The exchange was the perfect opportunity. I told Chamberlain to bring the man to the creek that afternoon to wait for me, then I took my son hunting.

The day was bright, the sunlight overpowering, flattening shadows to nothing. We watched Little Sandy run over broken layers of limestone, making hundreds of little falls as it winds through town, collects in millponds, and flows on to Lake Ontario. Our soil is fertile and watered by many creeks. Wind from the lake brings rain and we have two harvests. Winter brings snow that leaves ten-foot drifts, drops temperatures below zero, and may kill anyone caught in a storm. We live with extremes, but today was a spring gift of mildness. We paused in our walk.

I watched Moreau stare at the creek, no doubt pondering his future. He was the only son of a miller, a Baptist in a congregation where no less than forty people were Salisburys or married to a Salisbury, and the richest man in town had married into the family. His uncles had big farms on the Salt Road. I often told Moreau: *For unto whomsoever much is given, of him shall be much required.* He always answered: *The devil can cite scripture for his purpose.* Lately we hadn't been so civil.

My son wanted the Lord. Now President Lincoln wanted my son.

The spring creek was swift and swollen. I leaned against an oak and listened to the quick, clear water. Thick underbrush by the tag alders and willows had suffered a particularly hard winter. The buds on the trees were small and tight. Wild flowers that would be a riot of yellow and purple and blue were only a promise. Tangled vines on the moist earth were brown. Spring comes hard in the North Country—not an easy birth.

My son fiddled with his fowling piece as if it made him nervous. I started. "Why'd you go to seminary, Moreau?"

His usual answer was "To do right," and I intended to say, "Never in this nation's history has right been more obvious." However, this time he didn't say anything; this wasn't to be our usual conversation. Finally I said, "Did God whisper in your ear?"

Moreau crouched down on his haunches, Indian-style. He took

a breath and didn't look at me. "I went to answer for the Salisbury heads."

The Salisbury heads. The first Salisbury in America and his son killed an Indian, on a Sunday in Swansea, Plymouth Colony. Three days later, William and John and five other "soldiers of the King" were killed by Indians and their heads put on stakes over-looking the Kickimuit River. June 1675. The killings—by Salisburys, then Indians—started King Philip's War. To this day that war remains, *per capita*, the bloodiest on north American soil. By its end, one of every ten colonists—men, women and children— had been killed. Half the Indian population was dead or sold into slavery in the West Indies.

My son was obsessed by the tale. He used his "guilt" over his ancestors' act to glorify himself and puff up his "conscience." Moreau acted like repenting the sins of his ancestors provided a *gravitas* and moral depth unimaginable to his father. It must be easier to repent sins one hasn't committed.

It was, however, a hell of a story.

William, the first Salisbury in America, was a Welshman and Baptist. To the Puritans, that made him a Stranger, not allowed in Boston, so he made his way to Swansea on Narragansett Bay, by what is now Rhode Island. It took five years for life to turn sour. By June 1675, matters with Indians had gone so badly men took their guns to church. One Sunday, William and John returned to find three unarmed Indians pestering Mistress Salisbury for whiskey. William ordered John to shoot.

The Salisbury heads. Little Moreau had nightmares. Many nights his teary face appeared in the bed between me and Mary. The grown man had a "conscience." I suppose men become ministers for less.

I looked at slender willows, boxy tag alders, the glittering creek, at my son. Moreau stared at the swift-running water. He had his bearing-the-cross-for-his-ancestors look.

"Repenting other men's sins is vanity," I said.

"Sin is sin," Moreau said.

"America sins now!" I said hotly. "Don't lament! Act!"

"Tongues cut out, hands and scalps in trees." Moreau put down his gun. "Blood dripping down stakes." He rocked on his haunches and looked at the creek. High overhead a flock of Canada geese V'd their way north. "The heads started me praying. I never stopped."

"Don't you have enough sins of your own to pray over?" I said.

"Rash and bloody deeds," Moreau said, looking at the creek, as if the fast water transported his fancy to an age of slaughter and beheading.

"You were too young to hear the tale," I said.

"No one is too young to learn evil resides in God's world," he said.

"You know where evil resides!" I said, harshly.

The wind came up and half a dozen crows flew off the leafless branches of a cluster of tag alders.

"Slavery," said my son.

At least he knew that much.

Everybody in Sandy Creek and all the towns in Jefferson and Oswego Counties talked war now that this country's flag had been fired on. It might as well have been spat upon. That very Sunday, Deacon Enos Salisbury had roared from the pulpit, "This Union trembles like a stand of popples before a storm!" Enos meant the green and silver pointed leaves of quaking aspens by the lakeshore that shiver and tremble before rain. Enos finished the sermon shouting, "'For they have sown the wind, and they shall reap the whirlwind!'"

Amen.

"War," I said, looking at my son, who was looking at me now. I ran my hand down the barrel of a fowling piece that belonged to my father. He fought in 1812.

"'Blessed are the peacemakers,'" said Moreau. "Matthew 5:9."

"'The Lord is a man of war,'" I said. "Exodus."

"You're asking me to shoot, Father."

My son was no friend of slavery. He knew Lorenzo and I helped runaways get to Canada. The main route was through Syracuse to Buffalo and around Niagara Falls, but sometimes tired and frightened men and women came through Sandy Creek. We hid them in the mill among sacks of meal until I could get them to a lumber boat. Safety was eighty miles north and across the St. Lawrence, or a dangerous fifty miles across open lake. Mary and I had taken food and clothing into the mill for half-starved men, and once a shivering woman, who'd come the length of the country with rags for shoes.

I watched a patch of thick brown underbrush by a cluster of willows, oaks, and tag alders by the creek—the patch I knew concealed the possible herald of my son's calling. A living, breathing argument for war. Soon, I hoped, we would have no further need of talk. The fowling pieces rested against a log. Moreau stretched in the afternoon sun. He didn't notice the unusual agitation in the brush.

"You have a scar from a slaver," said Moreau. "I have the heads."

"We each found a calling," I said, sarcastically.

"You have anger," he said. "I have Jesus Christ."

I ran my thumb over my cheek. Yes, I have anger.

"Haven't Salisburys done enough killing?" Moreau asked.

"No," I said.

"'All they that take the sword shall perish with the sword,'" said Moreau. "Matthew 26:52"

"This strong sword shall devour slavery," I said.

"Christ said, 'Love your enemies. Do good to them that hate you.'"

"Jesus knew how to be a man," I said. "Look how He went to His death. He was no coward."

"'And a man's foes shall be they of his own household,'" said Moreau. "Matthew 10:36."

I scratched my beard. Words no longer sufficed.

Amen.

The rustling in the bushes broke the silence. The embodiment of my plan— Moreau's future savior—could no longer keep still. It was time. My son was up first, gun in hand. Moreau was tense, alert, no preacherly posing. In this swift moment, he didn't move like a preacher.

"You won't need that," I said, hoping the sight of a man who'd walked out of the house of bondage would touch my son to his soul.

Moreau, bent low and cautious, approached a clump of saplings, brush and willow trunks. He shouted what I might. "Come out, man! You'll be covered in poison ivy!"

A man in rags came out of the bush, dirty and so thin it looked like he hadn't eaten in weeks. His eyes darted between us like an animal expecting to be whipped.

Moreau took a quick half-step back, stood up, dropped the gun, and said, "By the Lord." Reflexively, he took off his coat and draped it over the man's shoulders. Another coat, another man's shoulders, another emergency. The runaway flinched at the contact. Neither of us had ever seen a human being so thin or so dark, even I with my experience of runaways. The whites of his eyes were so bright they seemed to banish the rest of him into shadow. He was dreadfully thin and dreadfully dirty. I blinked. To be so wretched was to be naked. The man's broad forehead looked stretched like the head of a drum. His mouth worked like he meant to speak, but fear or exhaustion got the better of him, and he was silent. He stared at us, then sat on the ground.

I told Moreau to run home and fetch the buggy, blankets and food. There wasn't time to wait for dark. Moreau ran off, brimming with excitement, shirt open, holding his hat and hoping, I suspect, someone would see his urgency. I was thrilled. Finally the struggle had entered my son's world. If a runaway couldn't make Moreau a soldier, he was born to preach. I was testing him. If Moreau could look this shivering man in the eye and say, "Forgive them, for they know not what they do," I would have no quarrel. I waited with the man, sure, absolutely sure, the kingdom of this world had laid hands on my son.

3

Our visitor, Mr. Gib Watkins, stayed with us for a week to recover. During that time, we watched a man emerge from the shaking skeleton we'd found by the creek. My wife said it was a miracle. I didn't tell her I had arranged it. The miracle I wanted was two men finding new lives.

I let Moreau bring meals to the stable where Gib stayed day and night. Sandy Creekers might all be Abolitionists, but we still had to be careful. Moreau and I barely talked, but I watched him. If ever a man had earthly purpose put in his path, it was my son. Let him pray to God or dream of the heads, Moreau had another chore now. No more chapter and verse.

Two days after finding Gib, Moreau told me he would delay his return to seminary. I tried not to show my delight, but I would have been surprised if my son had not been moved by a human being so miserable in his earthly life that he would travel by night eating roots, berries, even dirt, and kneel in the freezing April lake, thanking God he'd found the northern border. Other runaways we had sheltered in the mill had been in the hands of the Underground Railroad. No one would say they were overfed, but they weren't starving. Gib Watkins came to us close to death. This man was six feet tall and didn't weigh a hundred pounds. He lay in the stable for a week, regaining strength. Moreau sat by him, waiting for him to talk.

After a few days Gib said he was from Stafford County, Virginia.

He was twenty-four years old and not yet married. He could tend and shoe horses, and as soon as he could get up, insisted on grooming John Brown, the dappled gelding who drew the Salisbury buggy. Gib slept in the hayloft and said he felt "de water," Lake Ontario, in the night wind.

One morning when Moreau and I brought cheese, eggs, coffee and sourdough bread to the stable, Gib was washing himself with a rag and bucket. I was about to apologize for not bringing hot water when we caught sight of Gib's back in the dim light. Dark, raised scars crisscrossed his skin. Scars far worse than the one that graces my face. I had known about those too. Bob Chamberlain, who found him, had told me. Moreau almost dropped Gib's breakfast.

"Thank you, friend," said Gib. He took in our faces. "Seen my back?"

Moreau winced. I believe he felt he'd seen the man's soul. Or perhaps his own.

"Ain't as bad as gettin' separated from my woman. She got sold, so I run. Some day I git her back." Gib buttoned the shirt we'd given him and said, "It all done and gone. I ain't never goin' back."

Moreau set the food down and took the curry brush to John Brown. Gib sat on a stool and put his plate and cup on the old steamer trunk. He ate and looked at a beam of morning sun coming through the loft doors, which caught dust in a single, gleaming stream of light.

"Mr. Salisbury, I only seen my mother but four times. She come after dark when I small. She live on a neighbor plantation and walk seven miles. She hold me and cry. I can't have no family till we free."

Moreau stared at the beam of light, perhaps thinking of his mother, who was in the house eating breakfast in the warmth of the dining room hearth. "Let's pray," he said, and my son and the ex-slave went to their knees. It seemed the most natural thing. I lowered my head. Moreau said The Lord's Prayer, and Gib joined in. Then Moreau intoned: "Please God, give me the strength to be a soldier, and if I must kill, it is to free men like this Christian beside me and their wives and children. Please Lord, give me this strength. Amen."

Moreau's voice cracked on Amen.

Moreau

The Road to the Elephant

May 1861

4

The day before the Volunteers said goodbye to Sandy Creek, I left early with the buggy and John Brown to pick up Helen Warriner. Father excused me from the mill, saying every soldier needs a "girl I left behind me," as the song put it. Father and I weren't fighting anymore. The long, smoldering matter between us was gone. At least he thought so.

I was satisfied with my decision to enlist. I had come to love Gib Watkins. He was the most remarkable man I had ever met. Certainly he was the bravest. However, I despised Father's delight in my decision to leave seminary to go to war. I didn't make the decision for him. Father's scar and Father's anger were Father's business.

I knew Miss Warriner only slightly. I knew she defied her parents by leaving the Methodist church to become a Congregationalist. The girl was a funny mixture of gentleness and fixedness. At seventeen, she wasn't as easy to read as most girls her age. Two days before, she came into the mill twirling a pretty green parasol, but otherwise empty-handed. I blushed and asked what she wanted.

"A lesson."

"I'm no professor, Miss."

"But you studied to be a preacher, Mr. Salisbury. So did my father. He also went to seminary and chose not to follow the Lord."

"I follow the Lord, Miss, as I can."

"There's nothing the Lord says about enjoying a spring picnic, is there?"

I answered slowly. "Not that I know."

She twirled her parasol and smiled. "Tomorrow, then?"

I looked at her smooth brown hair and pert smile and said yes.

A young man and woman with a large basket covered by a blue blanket, a green parasol and familiar horse was an unusual sight for a Wednesday morning, even a fine morning in May. Tongues would have wagged if it were any Wednesday but this Wednesday. A man going to war was indulged, at least for a day.

Miss Warriner wore long black gloves and a violet Sunday dress carefully buttoned at the throat. Her hair was parted in the middle and two green ribbons that matched the parasol hung from the plaits. She had a broad face with a high forehead, prominent cheekbones, very brown eyes, and no apparent upper lip, like a cat. Her nose was her best feature—straight, prominent, well-shaped—a nose to meet the world on equal terms. I wore a black coat, white shirt and bow tie. I didn't look as good as Helen. She was three years younger than I, and I regarded her as a girl. The Warriners went to a different church, and though my parents knew her parents, our families were polite rather than friendly, perhaps because of the emphasis Helen's mother put on the Warriner who played the fife for Washington's army when it besieged Boston. The Warriners were strict Methodists, so Helen's defection to the Congregationalists at the tender age of thirteen, was, in my mother's view, punishment for family pride. I thought it brave, and a bit amusing. Even then Helen showed spirit, a force which not even her formidable mother could subdue.

It was ten sunny miles to the south branch of Big Sandy Creek, where the War of 1812 battle took place. I knew a fair bit about it—like the fact the battle took place in 1814—and hoped to impress Helen with such spots of knowledge. When I mentioned the battle, she laughed.

"I know too much history. My mother never stops talking about the Revolution, though it's my father's grandfather who played the fife. But I've never seen the actual battle site."

"I didn't know girls liked history."

"We just aren't supposed to show it, unless it's family history, which is supposed to help us get married."

"How?" I was impressed and taken aback by her forthrightness.

"Who's suitable and who's not. The sort of thing mothers, or my mother at any rate, specialize in."

"And who's suitable in Sandy Creek?" I said, smiling and lifting an eyebrow. It was going to be a good day.

"Well, the mighty Salisburys, of course." Helen burst out laughing and I couldn't help laughing too. John Brown snorted. We looked at each other and laughed again.

I could understand why Miss Warriner, pretty as she was, wasn't engaged. She scared boys silly. But I had recently come to think of myself as a man.

"You're not horrified by me?" said Helen.

"Of course not." I wasn't horrified, just a little nervous.

"I'm not usually this bold," Helen said. "But you're going away…"

I nodded and pressed her arm. These weren't ordinary times.

As the sun climbed higher, we drove west on bumpy roads past large farms, woods and open pastures. Men worked the fields and cows grazed and stared at whatever cows stare at while flocks of seagulls, loathed by farmers, traversed the freshly planted fields, and crows, big and night-black, circled or congregated in trees. The Canada geese had already gone north in their big V-shaped formations, traveling farther in a day than most men in a lifetime. My nervousness passed and I was happy. The morning was beautiful, and so was the girl beside me. Men waved straw hats as we passed. Plowing and planting—the backbreaking dance of men and earth, which, like war, sends men to the field.

In Woodville, we stopped to water John Brown by the McTavish place. The old man graduated Hamilton College and bred the best red cows in the state. Father says when men are in bondage, who has time to breed a finer shade of cow? McTavish's barn was white instead of red and meticulously kept, maybe to a fault.

The creek was high and a hundred little waterfalls splashed over narrow limestone shelves. I was quiet, which Helen noticed. The horse drank and whinnied. I looked east up the creek at the willows and the tangled box alders and splashing, clear water and remembered I was leaving tomorrow and might not see the creek or fields or Woodville again. I must have shuddered because Helen touched my arm. I looked into her face. Her eyes were full of tears and I felt a sharp twinge in my belly. I wanted to say it will be all right, but didn't. We stood by the creek while John Brown drank his fill.

"I'll wait for you," said Helen.

That's when I leaned down and kissed her cheek.

In an hour, John Brown was tied to a box alder by an S in the creek less than a quarter-mile from Lake Ontario. To our right was marshland, brown and yellow, touched with green, where cows grazed at their own peril; to the left was the creek, no longer full of splashing clear water, but moving slowly between muddy banks and thick clumps of trees and bushes. Helen spread the blue blanket a few feet off the path. In a month the vines and sumac and ash and wild grass would be thick enough to ambush British ships, but today we saw the creek and wetland through a thick tracery of branches. Trees slanted out over the water for sunlight, oaks felled by lightning rotted on the ground, odd holes where mice had burrowed for winter marked the edge of the path. We ate pork sandwiches and pickles and preserves put up last summer in jars.

Helen squinted into the sunlight at the water.

"Is this where our boys fought?"

"I think so," I said. "No one's exactly sure." The sandwiches were delicious, and the sarsaparilla too, still cool from being shaded in the buggy. If it weren't for Helen, I would have been so lonely, so ready to miss the fields and cows and creek, even the damn crows. As it was, I felt only contentment and didn't want it to end.

I lay back against the soft blue blanket, feeling the prickle of new grass poking through. "Father used to tell me, when you don't know something, mill it. Mill that theory. Grind that supposition between facts. Well, Americans ambushed the British here, but where? Let's mill the notion." Helen's eyes followed my finger as I pointed at spots along the creek bank. "Where could you hide and be protected? See the middle of that S? I think they waited right there. The British ships went slow. It was June, so the crick banks were solid with elms and tag alders and those vines that look like wood ropes. The Americans were commanded by Major Appling, a Georgian. His regulars were joined by local militia and two hundred Oneida Indians."

"Was a Salisbury with them?" Helen tilted her head, and the green ribbon touched her shoulder. My stomach fluttered.

"No, my grandfather Reuben was a lieutenant, but not here. Salisburys weren't here until 1823. They came from Vermont."

"The Warriners came from Herkimer County," said Helen. "I was born in Frankfort, New York. I'm glad we moved here." She gave me a long, knowing look. My stomach moved again.

"There's something I want to ask, if I might?" I looked into Helen's fine brown eyes.

"Yes, Mr. Salisbury?"

"Why did you leave the Methodist church?" I wanted to hear Helen tell it. I wanted to know Helen.

"I went to a Congregational service, Mr. Salisbury. In Adams. Congregationalists believe in deeds, not merely prayer. And I believe that too, that a person can change the world. Not just by prayer, but through his actions. God gave us minds and hearts and two hands. It's so simple to use them to make the world better. Christ won't return to a world like this."

I hadn't considered His return so imminent. "Are God and Caesar's things so similar?"

"Should religion be only mystical?" said Helen. "The Bible is more than poetry."

"Father's talked and reasoned his whole life. I don't think it's made him happy." I was sorry I said it. I never spoke about the family, but felt such tenderness for Helen I wanted to share my thoughts, even rank ones, with her.

"Is that why you left seminary—so your life would be more than talk?"

I nodded.

Her eyes were shining. "I don't know anyone like you."

We didn't kiss again. We held hands. We were proper and being proper made our feelings stronger. We were proper, as the sun slipped toward the lake and a chill breeze came over the marsh and rippled the creek. We wanted to be the best people we'd ever been.

"You *do* believe in deeds more than words," Helen said.

I touched her cheek, silkier than the finest-ground flour. "I was lonely in Cazenovia. I missed Sandy Creek. It's mixed up with Father. I went to try to talk to God, but wasn't ready. My prayers were just talk."

"You helped a runaway escape to Canada," said Helen. "You fed and nursed him. You *are* more than talk."

"I am now," I said, and hugged her.

The sun got low and the creek got black, winding through high, dark banks, obscure trees and invisible flowers to Lake Ontario. The hourglass of our day was running out. Crickets and peepers, the little frogs that wake up in the evening, started up, and a sliver of moon already hung over the horizon. Helen squeezed me hard. It was getting cold.

"I feel like a child putting off bedtime," she said.

I started to get up. I tried, but how could I take those warm arms from my shoulders? I looked at Helen. "I must tell you something that I've never told anyone before." She remained sitting, looking closely at me. "My ancestor, William, the first Salisbury in America and his son killed an Indian. The killing started King Philip's War, a terrible and bloody war. The populations of Massachusetts Bay and Plymouth Colonies were decimated. Do you know the word?"

"Decimation means kill one in ten. The old Roman punishment."

"You *do* know things," I said. "Half the Indians were killed or sold into slavery in the West Indies. My ancestors, we, us, Salisburys started the war."

"I didn't know Indians were sold into slavery," said Helen.

"New Englanders sold them."

Helen shook her head.

"William and John Salisbury killed an unarmed man who asked Mistress Salisbury for whiskey. The father ordered his son to shoot."

Helen looked at me carefully. "Is this your family secret or family fate?"

"By the Lord," I took her hand and felt a closeness I'd never felt, "you understand deeply. Three days later, William and John were caught by Indians, killed, and mutilated. Their heads put on stakes." I paused and looked into Helen's questioning, sympathetic eyes. "When I was little, I thought the heads watched me. I was frightened and wet the bed. I thought the heads spoke. I thought they asked a question I couldn't understand. A question I must answer or die before morning."

"How awful for a child," said Helen. She squeezed my hand.

"Oedipus and the Sphinx," I said. "Damned if you're right, dead if wrong."

Helen kissed me. "You're not a child now."

"A father tells a son to shoot, and heads on stakes watch the generations until someone answers the question."

"Have you learned the question?" Helen asked.

"I tried at seminary, but did not."

"And now?"

"No, but the answer is Gib Watkins," I said, suddenly feeling brave that I had an answer. It was easy to feel brave in the presence and warmth of Helen.

"Then I know the question," she said, taking my face in both her hands. "They ask, 'Are you like us? Or do you fight for another cause?'"

"I fight for another cause," I said. "And I love you."

Mason

Goodbye

May 1861

5

Our boys left on May 9th. Lorenzo and I would go with them as far as Utica. His boy Merrick, two years older than Moreau, had also joined the 24th New York Volunteers. Both were in Company G.

The train chugged slowly into Sandy Creek station, belching smoke and cinders from a wide funnel and filling the air with the smell of burning wood. The engineer slowed so everyone could hear the Ellisburg and Belleville bands which had gotten on with Company K at Pierrepont Manor. Men hung out the windows and waved to the crowd which cheered wildly. As Company G got ready to board, they were swarmed by mothers and fathers and girlfriends and relatives and friends. Suddenly it was time to go and tears mingled with manly hugs, desperate kisses, slapped backs and shouts of "You'll whip them rebels and be home 'fore hayin' time." Pies and sandwiches and carefully packed baskets appeared from everywhere and were given to men on the train and men getting on. Mothers and girlfriends climbed aboard for a last goodbye and squeeze. Pride and loss struggled in many faces, even the soldiers'.

Moreau and Helen parted by the train. They trembled, aware they were watched by parents, friends, soldiers, me. They embraced. Her green bonnet got pushed back; his tussled hair disappeared under the parasol. For the briefest of moments they had each other, and kissed—cheek—mouth—goodbye. So careful and public. So full of longing.

It hurt to watch.

I glanced at Mary. Her tears glistened in the sun. She wiped them quickly. They weren't for show.

Moreau gave Helen a white stone from the creek. Heart-shaped. Polished by eternities of water running to Lake Ontario. A stone to symbolize the constancy of his feelings. Helen gave Moreau something small. He kissed it, held it to his chest, and had it in his hand as he got on the train.

"It's a button," Mary told me. "A tintype, with her picture on the metal. It's the latest thing."

I shook hands, accepted promises of votes, and got on the train with the dignitaries. Mary stayed. She only wanted to say goodbye once.

The next stop for the "Union express," as the boys dubbed it, was Mannsville, where more men, pies, and another band got on. Speeches were declaimed, prayers offered, and girls and young women dispensed flowers, affection, and the communal sensuality of wild affirmation. It was like a camp meeting—duty and spirit and higher things simultaneously liberated into kissing, hugging and pledging. I spoke of the bravery of mothers and fathers, as well as the soldiers.

"If this is the army," Moreau told Merrick, "then bless it."

"Imagine what they'll do when we get back!"

In Rome, all the men and bands marched with more men and more bands down the main street. The first speaker mentioned the classical name of the city and invoked the Trojan War. He did this without mentioning the bickering of the commanders over a whore, the madness of Ajax, the adultery of Clytemnestra, or the mutilation of Hector. The parallels were inspiring, if selective.

The next speaker shook his big head and silver mutton chop whiskers. Such facial hair was not yet called "sideburns." The speaker spoke with bursting optimism. The Greek parallels became Roman models, which got mixed with Jesus Christ, the Crusades and the spirit of Oriskany and Saratoga. He spoke of the New Englanders who came to the Mohawk Valley "with a mighty tradition."

"They named cities after Greek and Roman places. Syracuse, Utica, Rome, Carthage, Ithaca! A renaissance in New York State founded on ancient learning and the ancient experiment of democracy! All equal before the law! Equal before work! Equal before God Almighty!

"Depart and do His work!"

The speaker, hurling whiskers and white forelock into a cool breeze, didn't mention other enthusiasms that swept New York, though their heat had been felt by many in the crowd. In the past half-century, no place in America had seen so much unbridled imagination and wild energy. Central New York was the "burned-over district" because of the blistering waves of evangelism that regularly poured over the country. It started in 1821, when Charles Grandison Finney, a lawyer in Adams, went to the woods, prayed, wasn't eaten by a bear, and received word directly from God. Break with Predestination! Each must establish a personal relationship with Me! Each saves or damns him- or herself! The news spread like fire and the message inflamed central New York.

"Burned over." Spiritualism was born in Hydesville, near Rochester, when two sisters, bored and cold during a long winter, heard rappings. The rappings turned into an industry—the Other World spoke and New York listened. The citizens listened to anything—lectures about bumps on the head, lectures about bumps in the night. Electricity. Mesmerism. Abolition. Wondrous cures and patent medicines, like those John D. Rockefeller's father sold out of a wagon. Religions and cults sprang up like corn. Some folk waited for the world to end, others practiced free love. Many believed if alcohol were banished, the lion would lie down with the lamb. For others, paradise was giving women the vote. A man named Miller said the world would end on a particular day in 1844. The world didn't oblige; Miller selected a new date and his following grew. Twenty-one-year-old Joseph Smith saw an angel in Palmyra who gave him *The Book of Mormon* on gold tablets, which, like a British cannon lost at the Battle of Big Sandy—a famous local story—disappeared in the mud. My father said if people didn't have chores, they'd all be taking off their clothes and communicating with the dead. Central New York went over the nineteenth century in a barrel.

Now it was war. All the passion, rational, spiritual, crazy, was coming together. It didn't matter how the speakers invoked God or American ideals. The country was moving. Men were going to war. More would follow. Everything was simplified and lives would be transformed. Men had found the Lord, helped runaway slaves, chatted with the dead, waited for the end of the world, but after Sumter and Lincoln's call for volunteers, all the energy and craziness marched under one banner. The moment of truth, the beginning and end of worlds, had come. What mattered was the moment. Whether men were fighting to free slaves, save the Union, or get out of town, they were going. The moment was militantly simplified. Moreau and Merrick and all the volunteers, all the speakers and all the crowds were following the energy—the dreams—of their fathers.

I spoke last. The mayor of Rome forgot the Assemblyman from Sandy Creek and summoned me as an afterthought. By then I was mad enough to spit, and was hardly noticed as I took the podium. Families were folding blankets, packing up picnic baskets, and un-uniformed soldiers made ragged lines to get on the trains. I looked at retreating, chattering people, put aside my speech, lowered my head, and recited the 23rd Psalm. People stopped. Eyes welled up. I spoke slowly. I wanted to upstage the mayor, but as I spoke, the psalmist's words matched what I felt, what we felt, named what we feared, and called for the strength we would need. Men bowed their heads. Women went to their knees. Voices joined mine. When I finished, I wasn't upstaging anybody. Tears were on my face too.

It was genius.

When I found Moreau by the train at Rome, I hugged him hard. I'd prepared parting words—thought they were needed—but when I held my son, the holding and squeezing and warmth and smell of Moreau were all that mattered. The embrace broke and Moreau stepped onto the train. I said, "God bless you."

We hugged again.

"Maybe we'll meet in church," Moreau said.

I didn't know why he said it.

6

Lorenzo and I got back to Sandy Creek late. We walked from the station under a cold moon and stopped at the mill. I opened the door and located a bottle of corn liquor. Lorenzo sat on a sack of corn meal and petted Rufus, the mill cat. Moonlight flooded through the open door. The stones were quiet. Water sluiced over the dam and we smelled the fine, strong smell of milled grain. I found tin cups and we drank to the boys.

Moreau

Hearing the Elephant

May 1861-September 1862

7

Father and I had hugged by the train at Rome. That was important. I didn't like what got said at the creek. I didn't like what had got said for months. I pretended to forgive. There was meanness in that. Father is a man who'll say anything to get what he wants. I'm a man who can be mean. We'd deal with it when the war was over.

The train left Rome—this time with no bands—for Geneva. Some of the boys slept with pie-filled bellies. Others talked. The recent female attention was an irresistible stimulus. I closed my eyes and remembered leaving Sandy Creek the first time. I left to talk to God and to not talk to Father. I left to become a preacher. I wanted to be a different kind of talker.

Father left once, but it didn't work. He didn't find a rich woman or friends in Washington City. He got a whipping, a good marriage, and Sandy Creek. I know how he felt. I didn't want the limits of a good life in a good town, a church full of relatives, and a gristmill. I used to think the difference between us was that I was afraid of the dark and he wasn't. Now I saw Father was afraid of other things and covered his fear—covered it better than any man I knew. I was afraid and couldn't cover my fear. I went to seminary because I had bad dreams and because I didn't want to be my father.

On the train I thought about William and John Salisbury who killed an Indian and got punishment worthy of Saul. William was a

Welshman and a Baptist who came to the new world to find land and baptize his children. It wasn't Eden, not by a damn sight. Some were Elect, others weren't. It wasn't God who decided, but hard men in Plymouth and Boston. William Salisbury wasn't Elect. The Serpent was here. English Cain slew Indian Abel. Men who came to live by God's word cheated their neighbors, killed Indians, hanged witches, profited by the slave trade.

When I was a child, dawn hours away, I used to see severed Salisbury heads at my window. They gibbered. Their tongues were cut out. Ants crawled in black mouths. "Where is God?" I blubbered to my parents. In our hearts, I was told.

I went to seminary to cleanse my heart. I couldn't put the world right, maybe I could put myself right. Maybe I could cleanse the notion I was cursed. "The voice of thy brother's blood crieth unto me from the ground." I tried prayer and poetry. I told myself the heads were symbols, a Sphinx. This helped, but who wants to be Oedipus? Oedipus didn't know he was talking to the devil.

I memorized Emerson's "The Sphinx:"

Who'll tell me my secret,
    The ages have kept?
I awaited the seer,
    While they slumbered and slept

Out of sleeping a waking
    Out of waking a sleep;
Life death overtaking
    Deep underneath deep?

Powerful. Tricky.

"Who'll tell me my secret?" What was my secret? That Salisburys were baptized in blood?

The poem asked good questions, but the answers were slippery. That's poetry, I suppose. Emerson *and* his Sphinx talk in riddles. Life death overtaking? That could be salvation, but the sage doesn't tell how to do it. Deep underneath deep? That's good. What's it mean? Damnation? Truth that sets free? Hell if I knew.

The train moved slowly and I kept looking at the button Helen gave me. It had a tintype of her face set in a black rim with a steel back. Her hair was parted in the middle and those eyes, those marvelous, knowing eyes, seemed to say so much. The button was the size of a five-dollar gold piece and I sewed it to my cuff so I wouldn't lose it and could look at it whenever I wanted. The button was wondrous.

I remembered how, after I returned from Seminary, Merrick said, "Talkin' like a preacher don't make you one. And for God's sake, don't walk like one." I *had* tried to talk like a preacher, with new words and smart arguments, and felt I could answer any question from this world—meaning father—with good grammar and Jesus Christ. I hoped I didn't walk like a preacher now. I don't know exactly what Merrick meant, but men hate hearing they walk funny.

I knew Seminary did not cleanse my heart. Seminary did not answer the heads. Would war? I milled that on the train. Was Gib the answer? Boy, that sounded good when I told Helen, but everything sounded good with Helen. I wasn't so sure on the train. I was sure I *was* angry at Father. All Father's talk and ambition came together as the Honorable Mason Salisbury, Assemblyman from northern Oswego County. The Honorable wanted his son in the Army of the United States, not the army of God. I resented the equation. Anger made it easier to leave.

I was so lonely for Helen on the train. I was never desperate to flirt, marry, or prove myself in the universal proving place, but always liked having women about. After Helen, women were all one woman, and the need for them and their mystery was all Helen. Helen Warriner, who knew her heart where God and man were concerned. I had my memory—the indelible day, she called it—the place in my heart. The girl left behind me. The song was played over and over at stations and on the train.

Can you fall in love in an afternoon? Yes, if you go to war. War will speed or end it, and it will speed or end you too.

The train moved quicker. Cinders and smoke blew in the window. Fellows talked and lit up cigars and speculated on how quick the fight would be. We chugged by greening fields and thick forest. I shut my eyes and thought of Helen. I praised and cussed going to war. Helen wouldn't have sought me out if I hadn't volunteered. Without war, no yesterday, that day of days, when we had everything and nothing to prove, and listened to each other, and held each other, and found such quick, deep understanding. Volunteering brought Helen. Good things come to good men.

I suppose.

Merrick slept, head against a sooty window. He was taller, heavier, had lighter hair. I knew he'd be the better soldier. Who was stronger hadn't yet been settled by countless wrestling matches "'tween sack-totin' city-slicker and honest farmer." Merrick was the better shot. Uncle Lorenzo had made sure his son could shoot. Merrick was the better fighter. I'd my share of fights, usually draws, but Merrick had a reputation. He didn't mind getting hurt. He liked to fight. I wanted him by my side.

In Geneva, amid more adulation, kisses and speeches about a short conflict with "men like this, at the ready," we marched to a steamer at a dock on Seneca Lake. The lake was beautiful in the late afternoon sun. Merrick and I stood by the railing and enjoyed the invisible moment when day slips into evening over water. Lake Seneca was cut from the soil by the same glacier as Lake Ontario. The glacier left five deep trenches that look like a hand reaching for New York's western tier, the Finger Lakes. The gorges, hills and mirror-like water reminded the settlers of Swiss lakes.

We were fed by local ladies. Later, after long marches and shivering nights, I would remember the food and generosity of home. The day was magic. Most of the boys had never been twenty miles from the place they were born. Never been away from family. Never felt like a hero. Merrick and I had seen Syracuse, Rochester, Watertown and the glittering Thousand Islands in a sunset, but not this beautiful lake… Or so many girls… Each company was made up of men who knew each other—cousins, neighbors, rivals, "pards." The "boys," we called ourselves. We would fight. For each other, if nothing else.

"Is this where the women declared independence?" asked Merrick, when we found a place on deck by the stern. Both of us were tired of crowds and prayers and pies and hoots and jokes. Afternoon turned into the beauty of evening. The lake lapped at the side of the steamer. I missed Helen and remembered how day faded and love grew, just twenty-four hours ago. The memory was as true as the shimmering light playing on the face of Seneca Lake.

"That was Seneca Falls," I said. "The world hasn't been the same since."

We laughed.

"Don't laugh," said Merrick, laughing harder. "First the Negroes, then the women. Who said that? The Douglass fellow?"

"What do the women want?" I said, still smiling.

"That question requires a tolerable clever answer."

We rested on our knapsacks that contained our bedrolls. We were prepared. Some fellows didn't bring anything to sleep on, as if they were going to a hotel. I unlaced my new boots, crossed my arms behind my head, and watched evening darken the lake.

"Our fathers once seen Washington City," said Merrick.

"What'll we see?" I said.

Merrick shrugged.

All day speakers told us the war would be quick and easy and provided good reason to think so. If asked, most of the men would agree and looked forward to a quick and glorious victory. Many weren't sure why they were going. To preserve the Union, of course, and prove we couldn't be licked, which men are always trying to prove. You could throw in freeing the slaves and punishing Simon Legree, but the price, the price of war where armies moved by railroad, weapons were factory-made, medicine was mostly amputation and the word antiseptic wasn't yet in *Webster's*—that price…that price…no man could calculate.

"Bet we don't see nothin' like New York," said Merrick.

"Maybe Richmond," I said.

"Be over before we get that far."

"I hope not."

"Doubt we get our heads put on stakes."

"You believe that story?" I said.

"Sure," said Merrick.

"That story scared me."

"Since I heard it," said Merrick. "I swore nobody'd ever get a jump on me."

"I thought they were watching me."

"Them heads ain't lookin' at nothin,' Ro."

Darkness came. Card games sprung up but we preferred each other's company. I was glad we were together. It was the only way to leave the North Country. I didn't say it out loud. I didn't have to. We drifted in and out of sleep. It was a cool lake night. A big moon rose and made a white path over the water. Then we kept awake and each told a story. A story for when neighbors can't listen and tongues wag. I mentioned Helen and her nerve in coming to the mill, my nervousness, not taking her seriously at first, the blossoming of sympathy as I understood her rebellion against her parents' religion. How much I got to appreciate her insight about things, people, life. Even the Battle of Sandy Creek.

"I could talk to Helen the rest of my life," I said, and wondered how much life that might be.

"It's love," said Merrick. "If you want to talk to her the rest of your life, that's love. Yes, ma'am. That's the way it's supposed to be."

The moon played hide and seek with a gnarled bank of clouds, men snored and rolled on deck. Merrick talked.

"In another town, way out in the fields, there's a house. Near Little Sandy. Found it looking for a dog."

"Find the dog?"

"Nope. Found a woman."

This, unfolding in deep night, far from home, was different from Merrick's usual hunting or fighting stories.

"A late-night story's got to be women or ghosts," I said.

"A woman lives there but don't nobody see her. One of them country women that don't go outside. Not so anyone sees anyway."

I knew such women. They flit behind curtains and don't come to the door. No one sees them for years at a stretch.

"She can't abide visitors," said Merrick.

"Maybe it's men she can't abide."

"Can't abide no one."

"Did only you see her? Like a dog seeing a ghost?"

"Ro, she don't live alone. Got a mother and sisters. Cows and chickens too. Somebody provides."

Yes, women provide. Even for ghosts. Town people get odd, but lonesome farm folk get weird strange. Such women aren't rare. Every time and place produces odd ones—witches to the Puritans, seers to the Indians, root doctors in the South. In the North Country they're just there. Spirits in lonely houses, but not to be confused with the newly dead. If a woman dies in childbirth or hangs herself in a terrible winter in a terrible marriage, she may haunt a graveyard or prowl about her house. This is different. These women are real.

"This weren't no ghost," said Merrick. "This was something nobody but me seen. I'm sure of it."

Two months before, Merrick surprised this white spirit in the flesh. She surprised him too—in the woods by a pasture near her house. Instead of screaming or running, the woman put her finger to her lips. They looked at each other for a full minute and Merrick returned the next day. She was there. After a week of staring, she came toward him. After another week, they touched. Silence was their magic. They looked. He held out his hand. She took it. They communicated by eye and glance and excruciating inch-by-inch exploration. Then words. But only a few. They kissed and explored and then it wasn't excruciating. She brought blankets and covered them. They made love.

"Like jumping off a rock. Nothing holds you back. Don't know her name. Don't want to."

"Sounds like a dream or fairy tale," I said. "Not that I don't believe it. It's just…I wished for such a thing. Many times, behind the sacks at the mill. I used to dream women would bring more than milling. It never happened."

"Dreams got a price," said Merrick. He listened to see if anyone moved and lowered his voice. "She's old."

"How old?"

"Not too old, a little old. You know."

I didn't, but said, "Yep."

"Old enough so you might not want to be seen with her."

"Ahh," I said. Fairy tales—wolves, hags, bargains.

"I love her, Ro."

"Then it makes no difference how old she is."

"I don't think that's so," said Merrick.

We listened to the breathing, rustling, and water around us. Everything was regular and safe. Merrick told more. They kept meeting. He kept looking for that dog. "Christ, if I ever found him, I'd have to kill him to keep going out." They warmed each other under blankets, talked, did things. Things Merrick had never done.

"We done things shame a farm animal. Things I wouldn't tell."

"Don't," I said. "Leave it unsaid."

"What's the point of being wild if you can't tell?"

"Is it over?"

"Yep."

I felt sad. I tried to imagine the woman in the woods. Was she old as Merrick's stepmother? I didn't ask. She was tender and passionate, but something was wrong. Was it never being able to say "I love you" in front of another living soul? Never introducing her to family? Never going in public?

One day, when the sun broke through the alders and oaks, she looked old. Old in a way that meant it was time for Merrick to go. How did he tell her he wasn't coming back?

I thanked God Helen came to the mill in the light of day. I was glad we only held each other. Thankful I took her promise, not her body. We did right. I touched the tintype.

Merrick spoke softly. He shaped memory, shaped the secret he carried to war. He was finding a place for what he found in the woods—for the person he was in the woods. Some carried a bible over their hearts. Merrick carried this. This thing that couldn't be in the world, shouldn't have been, but for a while, was. A gift received young. The wild, unknown person he could be. The wild, unknown person a woman could be.

"Did I do wrong?" said Merrick.

"Maybe you gave what she missed," I said. The wind rose and the deck moved.

"I'm glad for this war. What comes of seein' a ghost?"

8

Military training in '61 was drilling. How useless this was for battle wasn't learned till we got to battle. The generals never learned. We trained in Elmira. Twenty new, rough, wooden buildings, each housing eighty men, had been built a mile from the center of town. Drill was supposed to instill discipline. Useless activity was a big part of military training. The Regiment had many men from Oswego who had been in the Oswego Guard, and knew how to drill. The country boys had no idea and looked awful. "A goose could march better," said Merrick, who found it funny the men of G Company couldn't march, and not funny when Oswego men called us "Greenhorns."

Merrick and I didn't mention the loves that blossomed so quickly for me and mysteriously for him. I had the advantage of mail from Helen and thought about little else during hours of marching. I had sewn the tintype inside my uniform over my heart. Its smoothness was a constant reminder.

I had never seen Cousin's gentler side. He had a quiet side, to be sure, which can be a habit for men who grow up working alone in field or barn. I was surprised by the depth behind Merrick's fists and capacity for work. He found more than passion in the woods. He found sadness and got deeper. But Merrick's love was secret, so was the depth secret too? Is secret love really love, or just secret? I milled this while educating my feet to the rhythm of drill. I had a different love. A love for the world to see, if Helen waited, and I believed she would. Did Helen show another side of me? How many sides was the question! I thought I knew her completely because she made me feel complete. I hoped the campaign would be quick. I wanted to remember everything so I could share it with her.

If Merrick now had a gentle side, it took three days in Elmira for the ungentle side to show. After a hot, miserable drilling session, when the lines kept splitting over knowledge of left and right, the dismissed company finally returned to barracks too tired to do anything useful. Merrick, David Hamer, me, and handsome Lyman Houghton from Orwell, decided to see if we could stack our Springfield muskets so they'd stand. We were on a flat stretch of ground where the grass had been worn away by boots and wagon wheels. The late afternoon was warm, the sky dotted with thin, summery clouds. The green hills beyond the Chemung River made a nice backdrop beyond the town. The first few times we stacked the muskets, the guns clattered to the ground. We were wiping the unloaded muskets when a half dozen Oswego men strolled over from the barracks. There was a big fellow, a talker, and hangers-on—the usual breakdown of a crowd. They smirked and laughed at cracks the talker got off in a voice just loud enough so the Company G men couldn't hear the cause but couldn't miss the effect. The talker led the way and for some reason decided Merrick was the man to ride. Merrick still looked like a farmer, his sleeves too long, his blue trousers too short. The talker, who was Merrick's height but not as solid, said, "Hey, fella, which way's town?"

Merrick didn't say anything.

"Let me be specific." The talker was very impressed with the word specific. "Is it left or right?"

This brought quite a laugh from his audience. We country boys stood by our muskets. No one spoke. "Still thinkin' about that?" said the talker. The big man at his side had sandy brown hair, a nose that had been broken, and a scar over the left eye. Cuts, I figured, got in saloons, not at work.

The Company G men said nothing. Looking is country. Talk is city. The Oswego men would have done better watching Merrick's eyes instead of guffawing and elbowing each other.

"See here," said the talker. "This is my left," he held up his left hand, "and this is my right." He held up his other hand. "But since I'm standin' opposite, this is your right and this is your left, which is my left and your right and my right and your left." His pards, especially the fighter, couldn't contain their laughter and gave each other little shoves.

The second the fighter took his eye off Merrick, Merrick hit him as hard as he could in the jaw. David Hamer smashed the talker in the nose which broke in a splatter of blood and the other Oswego men backed away. Lyman Houghton and I went for them but they ran.

The big man tried to knee Merrick in the crotch, but got a leg as Merrick head-butted him and threw him to the ground. They rolled over. Merrick punched, the other gouged. Both grabbed and bled. Men came out of the barracks to watch. The gouger said later, "Some of them God damn farmers is plenty strong." City people assume a rube lacks the violence of the street; farmers can't believe someone who hasn't worked on a farm can stand pain. In this case both were wrong. Merrick was strong and took satisfaction in inflicting and receiving pain. The gouger, who probably would have used a knife if he hadn't just joined the Union Army, absorbed hits and kept fighting. He got on top of Merrick and swung wildly at Merrick's face, which he couldn't see as blood poured from a gash that opened the scar over his right eye. Merrick got splashed with his own and the gouger's blood, which also flowed from the big man's mouth and nose. Merrick caught a pummeling hand and bent back a finger, which sent the gouger off him with a howl. Merrick got on top and pounded the man's face and stomach. Then Merrick jumped up and started to deliver a savage kick, but didn't finish. David Hamer and Lyman Houghton grabbed him before he could change his mind. Merrick smiled, wiped his face and surprised the crowd by reaching down and helping the man up. Merrick shook his hand and said, "You're damn good."

David Hamer went up to the talker, who was trying to set his nose, and said, "That was a right."

9

The 24th was billeted outside Washington in a sea of tents that made another city surrounding the capital. Washington City was jammed with men in uniforms, clerks, women of ill-repute and black-coated gents cutting every sort of deal. The citizens feared invasion, welcomed Federal troops, got sick of drums and drunkenness, and waited for victory by either side to rid themselves of the blue horde. Southern sympathizers—and there were many, way too many—thought the Yankee rabble staggering in front of whorehouses, cooking in the basement of the Hall of Representatives, or climbing the unfinished dome of the Capital, would run when confronted with Reb valor. This wasn't all wrong. Many Federals were state militia, enlisted for ninety days, and trained to march in parades. The militia was the legacy of Lexington and Concord—the peckerheaded notion citizens and the right to bear arms can win a war. Southerners said we'd skedaddle.

Somewhere in this churning sea of whiskey, ambition, and greed was the six-foot-four-inch new President, whose election made seven states secede and whose face in photographs over the next four years would get lined and haggard, as if it would break in parts like the country itself. He was a practical, not a military man, and wanted a quick victory, though unlike the boldest in Congress, he didn't think the Confederate Army would disappear at the sound of the first Federal drum.

The 24th drilled and waited, heard rumors and tried to get used to the heat and humidity of a southern summer. Company G was not a ninety-day militia. We enlisted for two years, at eleven dollars a month, and unlike fellows volunteering later, got no cash bonus.

In June, now a corporal, I posed for a photograph with my new Enfield rifle at Matthew Brady's studio. Brady would get famous for war photography, though after the battle on July 22nd, he rarely left Washington. My photograph was an ambrotype—an image produced by light exposed over time to a colloidal solution on a glass plate. A million of these slightly brownish-red images would be made in the next four years.

Mine was typical.

A young man poses with his rifle. The soldier is new. The rifle is new. The uniform is clean. His face is full and despite a new beard, young. He looks serious, alert, ready. He can hold the pose long enough for the photograph. The parade ground taught this. Even so, behind him, looking like a third foot, is the base of an iron neck-stand to help those who have not endured drill remain still for the time needed to make an image. He stands on a linoleum floor which has a checkered pattern, like a kitchen floor. The cloth backdrop is dark. The soldier wears a .44 standard Army pistol, borrowed for the picture, a big US belt buckle, polished bright as the seven brass buttons down the front of his dark uniform. The kepi hat, cloth with slant top and short leather visor, provides some protection from rain, none from bullets, and is hot in summer. The photograph is used for a *cartes-de-visite*, a palm-sized image on cardboard, to be left, traded, cherished. Ambrotypes will be put in embossed leather cases, displayed, kissed, wept over. The portrait is the last record for many families. Unnatural as the pictures were, they're the only part of the war the bereaved saw. The rest they must imagine.

Mine shows a young man wary, proud, not overconfident.

Most of the men in these photographs, owing to the time they must sit or stand, look somber, lonely, isolated. No one can hold a smile, artificial or not, for the time needed for an image to settle on the emulsion on the glass plate. The men leave no fleeting glimpse of personality, no revelation, no joke or nervous unease. They are alone and anonymous. The portraits have a standard-issue quality. They stare at fate.

10

Camp Keys
Arlington
July 4, 1861

Dear Father,

Before we go into Washington City to see fireworks, I'll take some time to write. We are camped on the grounds of Robert E. Lee's mansion. It has a fine view of the Potomac and the city. I hope Mr. Lee never sets foot on this ground again, and he won't if the 24th has any say in the matter. His house has the biggest damn pillars outside a government building I've ever seen. It makes the Scripture place look like a dollhouse.

I understand you have been recruiting men for the Regiment. The boys and I thank you, and are in the process of raising money to help your effort.

I'm starting to get used to soldier life, but summer in Sandy Creek is nothing like this humid, heavy, mosquito-breeding heat. The streets of Washington are dusty and crowded, and the Virginia mud is hell to march in. Rain brings some relief, plus more mud, and a variety of things that fly.

We call ourselves boys but I see men born in this Regiment. It's not just feet that are hardening. Somewhere between routine and exhaustion, toughness creeps in. There was friction between the country and city fellows. This has been resolved, largely by your nephew. Let's just say both sides now have mutual respect. Captain Ferguson is a fine officer. You know he's a good man in Sandy Creek. He's a good man here. I don't know what it would be like to command men. It's more than giving speeches.

Lyman Houghton is the model for us all. Lyman never complains and there isn't anything he can't do, especially shoot. The Regiment has many fine marksmen. The Bass boys are excellent shots, but Lyman is the best in our Company. He's always doing something useful, or writing his girl at home. That activity, I can tell you, is very comforting. Helen writes faithfully. I hope you and Mother are taking good care of her.

Here's how some of the fellows are doing. Dan Buck complains about everything but I think he'll be all right in time. David Hamer and David Crocker want to fight and hope we see some Rebs soon. Tom Cox doesn't say much. I think he thinks about home a lot. Martin Dennison takes to military life, except for reveille. He wonders why we get up so early with no cows to milk. Everyone wonders who'll be dependable. The men I mention, even Dan, look like they'll be fine. We'll find out soon enough. Dan, by the by, might like to hear more from folks, and maybe some of our people could write him. We would all like to read *The Pulaski Democrat*, so if you could send a copy, we'd be most appreciative.

Merrick is downright restless. He's tired of the parade ground, and thinks it's time we found some Rebs. When we do, he's the man I want by me. Merrick's never shied away from a fight, and this will be no exception. He would never say this, but I know he's looking out for me. You know Merrick.

Merrick and I went to Alexandria last week, and saw the Marshall House where the Union Colonial Ellsworth was killed. It's vacated, and pretty well bullet-riddled. Union men don't take kindly to an officer killed for raising his country's flag. The place looks lonesome. The Union flag floats from a staff on the top, and will continue to do so, judging from the number of soldiers around. Merrick wished he had his rifle so he could add some holes to that sad hotel. Many more will die for that flag, I fear. The Ellsworth killing is this whole mess in miniature. Have you heard the story in Sandy Creek? The proprietor, a fellow named Jackson, decided to fly the Rebel flag on his property. Colonel Ellsworth took it down and raised the Union flag. Jackson shot Ellsworth with a shotgun, and was killed by one of Ellsworth's men. What did Jackson think would happen? These Southern fools are itching to commit suicide, and proud of it! But Ellsworth will be missed. He was a good officer.

I think the 24th could use more rifle practice. I know I could, but maybe ammunition needs to be conserved. got a new Enfield and had my picture taken with it. With bayonet fixed, it's as tall as I am. It's a fine weapon. I believe I could hit a man at 300 yards. I don't like to think about that, but I know when men shoot at us, we'll shoot back—no qualms.

Have you heard from Gib? He is most on my mind. I wish Gib could see me with my Enfield. I wonder what he's doing in Canada. Has he married? I'd like him to know I'm here.

Do you think we will have black Union troops? The boys often discuss this. Does Mr. Earl, who knows Secretary Seward, know what the Secretary thinks?

I have no doubt the ladies of Sandy Creek would be pleased to do something for us, but we are not in need of anything in the clothing line. If they wish to send anything, I think eatables would be more acceptable, although we have enough. Perhaps not too rich, please. We buy butter at $2 per lb, if you can imagine. We purchase sweet potatoes once in a while, and think we are kings.

Do you hear any word about Lincoln freeing the slaves? Some of us think we are fighting to end slavery, some assuredly do not. It's amazing how many blame Negroes for the war, but we all agree we are fighting for the Union. It would be better if Lincoln freed the slaves. It would give clarity.

Give my best to everyone. Don't forget cousins Sarah and Violet. Is Norman Scripture still courting Violet? And to Mother, of course.

Your son,

Moreau

11

On Sunday, July 22, 1861, Union and Confederate armies met near Manassas Junction. The 24th was held in reserve. We grumbled, hot for action, but not so hot for the thirteen-hour march over the "sacred soil of Virginia" in mosquito-filled summer heat. Company G's first taste of war was not war but rumors of war.

Sunday was long. Reports came by telegraph, handwritten note, then voice. The first were good. Union doing well: Confederate line breaking, prisoners taken. We looked at each other and nodded. Rightness of cause leads to victory. David Hamer lamented that we "missed the fight." All agreed a quick and decisive victory would end this damn Confederacy, so foolish to take on the United States.

Then rumors started. They arrived like the clouds of mosquitoes. No, the battle wasn't going well. Confederate reserves arrived at the crucial moment by railroad from Winchester. Ten thousand, maybe twenty. General Patterson was supposed to keep them bottled up. He didn't. No one did. The Federal line broke and the Army was retreating. No, counterattacking. No, running away. Jeff Davis himself led the last charge. It was a disaster. A rout. Defeat snatched from victory. No one was sure. Everyone was sure. Nobody knew anything.

As the day wore on, the news got worse. The Reb army crushed the Union Army. Men running, killed, wounded. There weren't enough ambulances. Officers ran. Rebs will overwhelm Washington.

They could walk in. The 24th was marching.

When? Three a.m.

Why? Someone must guard the route to the city.

Captain Ferguson told us to try to get some sleep. I tried but all I could do was sweat. I lay on my cot under the mosquito netting and stared into the dark. “We’re being thrown to the wolves, Merrick.”

Merrick, almost asleep, said, “That what we’re here for, ain’t it?”

“I suppose.”

“It don’t matter. Duty’s debatable, orders ain’t. Get some sleep, Ro.”

I lay in the damn heat. If this were the last night of my life, I wanted company. Talk. Words. It would make tomorrow easier. Profound words. Diverting words, anyway. Words? I was here because the time for words was over.

I volunteered. I didn’t have to be here.

Mill that.

I was here because I was sincere. Here for Helen. Here to die.

What else were soldiers supposed to do? It wasn’t all parades and pies and prayers and speeches or getting drunk and slapping backs and finding ladies. It was a game until now. Yes, a game. Drill, wait, play soldier. I milled that as mosquitoes hovered and Merrick snored.

Aw Jesus. I said I was sincere, not brave. Brave you’re born with, like tall or rich. Some have it, like Merrick or Uncle Lorenzo. And others, well, others are… sincere. Some, like father, are neither. This was a hell of a time to substitute one for the other. I thought about father and Uncle Lorenzo leaving the North Country and how it was their great adventure. That wasn’t war. That was a whipping, a scar. War for them was the Battle of Big Sandy. A tale, like that British cannon in the mud.

How could Merrick sleep? Philo Bass and Byron Eastman also slept. I figured we weren’t going into battle but defeat. The battle was over. The war too, maybe. We heard muddy defenders of the Union were already sitting in Washington bars. What would Helen think? Gib? Father? What did Corporal Salisbury think?

Corporal Salisbury thought: why fight when all is lost? But all wasn't lost. We weren't dead.

I got up and went outside. The air was heavy and damp. The night dark with clouds and no moon. Three men smoked by a fourth standing watch. It was the Davids, Hamer and Crocker, and tall Lyman Houghton. Tom Cox stood guard.

"Can't sleep," I said.

"I know," said Hamer. "Too much to think about."

"Thinkin' don't help," said Crocker.

"I'm scared," said Houghton.

I smiled in the dark. No one saw. "Lyman, you said that to make us feel better. You ain't afraid of nothin'."

"Don't it feel like rain?" said the tall man. "Rain'll slow everythin' down. The Reb army don't come if it pours."

After sharing a pipe with Dave Hamer, I went back to the tent and fell asleep. It started to rain about three o'clock and we got up to the command to "Fall in! Fall in!" I hadn't slept an hour.

We marched at four. New brogans got soaked and muddy as rain came in torrents. Fifty-pound packs stuffed with hard tack, dried pork and bits of bacon were heavier. The covers of canteens didn't have to be wetted to keep the contents cool; everything was wet. Bayonets were fixed. Were Rebs that close? We hadn't been issued bedrolls or tents. The 24th left in a hurry. No thought about when, how, or if we'd return. The regiment lined up in the rain, which came hard. Rain rolled off kepis and soaked skin, but held down the hoards of mosquitoes and gnats that would come when it stopped. I marched next to Merrick and was happy for it. I wished we'd had more practice with the Enfields. Merrick, still sleepy, was glad we weren't "strollin' on the parade ground." We looked at each other. We could march, drill, and shoot. Who'd be alive tomorrow?

The regiment hadn't gone a hundred yards before the city men started to gripe. "This is clodhopper weather." "God, don't you know it." The "clodhoppers" didn't look good doing it, but they could march all day and sleep anywhere. I was wet and miserable but happy the city men felt worse.

The minute we got out of camp, soldiers came the other way. They came in ragged groups, alone, in carts, on horseback. It was worse by dawn's light. Ambulances went by and the groans were terrible. Men passed who weren't hurt but had no weapons. No hat, no cross belt, no cartridge box or knapsack. Just crazy, frightened eyes. They shivered and yelled, "We're whipped!" or "We was betrayed!" Since no Confederates followed, it was difficult to tell who betrayed whom. A lanky fellow whose sleeves were ripped, limped, grimaced and said, "Niggers!" with every step.

A heavy-set corporal shook his head and answered in cadence, "Ain't worth it!"

"Niggers!"

"Ain't worth it!"

"Niggers!"

"Ain't worth it!"

Lyman Houghton shouted, "You two shut up or you'll get a real wound!"

The light got stronger in the gray morning rain, and we saw real wounds. Dark bandages soaked with blood, wet with rain, tied about heads, arms, thighs, legs. An arm with no hand. An ear gone, leaving a dark hole. Branches used for crutches. Mouths blackened with powder from biting cartridges to load rifles.

We marched half a day in the rain and took up a position on the woody top of a hill on the Warrenton Turnpike. If Rebs came, we'd be firing downhill. The road was crowded with troops, stragglers, and wounded in carts. The rain slackened, but Virginia mud is thick. The red clay slime was a foot deep in places. It was heavy glue, not like mud back home. Artillery pieces, ambulances, and carts got stuck. The 24th didn't hear or fire a shot but put our shoulders to every sort of slippery conveyance and got mud caked to our waists.

"This is bad," said Merrick, "and we ain't seen a Reb."

Soldiers on the pike asked for water. They told of the awful sound of the cannon. "Bullets ain't so bad till they're all around you." "Sweet Jesus, the last time the Rebs charged, they made an inhuman noise. Turn your spine to jelly." "The Rebs is fierce, dirty, savage. Got no fear at all." "You see one close, he don't look like much, but when they charge…when they fight." We shook our heads. The 24th hadn't seen any yet.

"Skedaddlers don't take prisoners," Merrick said.

Company G pulled together a makeshift breastwork of logs, branches and mud. It might stop bullets, but not artillery. At least we couldn't be seen from the road. We dug a trench with bayonets and lined it with branches but there was no getting dry. I stood by Hamer, Crocker, Cox and Houghton, which made me feel better. Even soaked and covered in mud, Lyman Houghton was the model, handsome, unafraid, uncomplaining, and the best shot in the company.

"If the Rebs is comin'," Lyman said, wiping his rifle, "they ain't in a hurry."

The regiment made a line on either side of the road. We felled trees, cut branches, gathered rock—anything for cover. Captain Ferguson, a Sandy Creeker, said, "Here we stay. There's nobody between us and Washington that ain't running. Dig in."

We appreciated Captain Ferguson. At Elmira, he admitted he didn't know "a diddly damn" about marching and apologized for the company's poor showing. When there was talk of disciplining Merrick, Captain Ferguson blamed himself and offered to resign his commission on the spot. We respected that. Merrick wasn't disciplined, nor did he fight again. The gouger became a barracks' brawler and spent a lot of time on guard duty.

We were thirsty and hot, but no one complained. Seeing a stream of frightened, wounded, beaten men, covered with dust, blood, powder—men who looked as little like soldiers as the grass and twigs we rested on resembled carpet and floor—sobered us. We wondered how long we could stay.

"Not long if a bunch of Rebs comes through," said Merrick.

As the afternoon and rout wore on, and no one saw or heard a Rebel, men began to stroll down the pike. Captain Ferguson let us go in groups. Merrick and I walked together in the deep ruts of the road. A dozen men slogged up the hill. They were glassy-eyed, dirty, and dragged along, looking at their boots. None were wounded. None had rifles. Some had lost their caps and had lost or thrown away their packs. Merrick said they looked like children who went to camp out, gave up, and went home. A short man accepted a drink and said, "Thanks and damn the Seceesh." Another took a drink and muttered, "Our officers run 'fore we got to the battle." It looked like they all ran, but we didn't say anything, and offered canteens.

A carriage caught up to the cluster of rifleless men. It was an expensive black barouche with a collapsible top that was down. The occupants squinted in the sun. The collapsible didn't help the driver, a Negro in a top hat, who was spattered with mud from head to toe. The top did preserve the black suit, if not the dignity of a portly, older man in the back seat. A pretty women in yellow held a large picnic hamper in her lap as if it were a baby, and looked as miserable as any woman I have ever seen. A man not much older than Merrick and me took off a brown coat, rolled up his sleeves, and looked sheepishly at the soldiers.

"Stop them, Cicero!" yelled the man in black.

The carriage pulled into the middle of the ratty, disorganized men who paid no attention.

"Stop! I tell you stop!"

Not one stopped or paid attention.

A shot rang out. The man in black stood and pointed a pistol, an Army .44. "Stop or I'll shoot!"

Several men stopped and looked at the carriage. The man's black hair hung in stringy clumps to his shoulders. If combed, it might have aped the coif of Thaddeus Stevens. He waved his arms like a preacher. I was surprised at his energy. The woman ran a petite hand through lovely brown hair. The Negro looked bored. The soldiers started walking.

"I am Congressman Cook of New Jersey! Halt! Stop! This is disgraceful!"

Merrick and I looked at the Congressman, the woman, the younger man, presumably an aide, as if they had stepped out of *The Arabian Nights*. The horses, carriage, Cicero and his top hat, were so out of place on this road, in this mud, with this Army, that if the earth swallowed them, I wouldn't have believed they were ever here.

"What are you cowards staring at?" shouted the Congressman and pointed his pistol.

"Point that at me and I'll blow your damned head off," said Merrick. He said it, didn't shout it. The sucking noise of men tramping in mud, the rattle of a mule-drawn, heavy-loaded cart of wounded approached slowly, background to Merrick's threat. Together, they were as dramatic as the Congressman's pistol shot. The Congressman looked startled, as if he'd been slapped. He looked at his pistol, the men in clean uniforms, the tramping, beaten men, the cart with groaning, bloody men, and said, "Hang it." He climbed out of the carriage, looked at Merrick and me, and said, "Who are you?"

"The Twenty-fourth New York Volunteers. Rear guard."

The Congressman put his pistol in his belt. He didn't know whether to be angry or friendly.

"It ain't wise to fire a gun around men who have guns," said Merrick. "'Less you tryin' to shoot somebody."

"By the Infernal, I won't stand for this!" said Cook.

"You'll stand for it if you want to get back to Washington before dark," said the woman curtly, as she, with Cicero's help, climbed down from the carriage. Her shoes sank in the mud and mud clung to the hem of her skirt. Her clothes were wrinkled, but dry.

"If you don't mind my asking," I said, resting on my gun—the bumpkin who knows the city folk need direction. "What are you doing here?"

"Trying to preserve some damned order," said the Congressman.

"Stop it," said the woman. "I've had enough of your order."

The young man, well-dressed and clean-shaven yesterday, joined them. I eyed him closely. At his age, he should have been a soldier and, from his blushing face, he knew it. With those clothes and full, pleasing face, this dandy would be a staff officer. A man to hand maps to men who make decisions. A stand-in to escort ladies and provide handkerchiefs when other men are killed.

"We came to see the battle," said the young man. "Yesterday was Sunday," he added, as if this explained gentlemen and ladies who would spend an afternoon watching men kill each other. "We thought...." He didn't finish.

"We thought it would be glorious," said the woman.

"And well it might have been," said the Congressman, "if men hadn't run. My God, the filthy Rebels may go all the way to the capital."

"We've seen terrible things," said the young man. "Terrible."

"Terrible behavior," said the Congressman.

"We thought," said the pretty woman, as if explanation were suddenly needed, "it would be like a tale of Walter Scott. A great adventure."

We didn't have anything to say to that.

12

Later that day Merrick and I ate hardtack under a large oak whose leafy branches shaded the rising Warrenton pike. The road wasn't so soupy now the afternoon sun had broken through. The crackers were hard as stone and tiny white worms squirmed inside. Some of the city men threw the hardtack away. I smiled. A miller has seen enough worms to know to "break it, rub it, forget it." Eating worms doesn't cause harm, unless you see them and get sick.

We stopped sharing food with the dregs of McDowell's army. They'd see Washington before we would. The 24th supplied water, hope, medical assistance if possible, but when would we get supplied or relieved? Enough knapsacks were tossed away on the march to Manassas so the fools could damn well pick them up if hungry.

Merrick and I had a lively discussion about the pretty woman with Congressman Cook, and whether or not Merrick might see her again.

"Not before that aide fella," I said. "See his excuse for shoulders? That man's never worked a day in his life."

"Women like 'em like that," Merrick said.

A ragged-looking civilian came up the hill. He walked, stumbled, looked at his feet, heaven. This man appeared more confused and lost, more hurt inside, than a wounded soldier. A soul in hell couldn't look so hopeless.

This civilian was unlike the others. He didn't have carriage or horse, and he looked worse than the Congressman had. He wore a long white coat that had the lightness and consistency of a smock. The coat was wrinkled, muddy and useless against any sort of weather. It hung to the ankle and he had a sword under it. The man could be any age except young. He had bushy reddish-brown hair, a triangular beard that came to a point three inches below the chin, and oblong wire-rimmed eye-glasses. The left lens was cracked.

"That sword couldn't protect him from a swarm of bees," Merrick said.

"Water?" I asked.

The civilian looked at me as if unfamiliar with human speech. "Water? Water? Water. Thank you." An Irishman. He accepted my canteen and slid down against the oak, as if the weight of the canteen dragged him to earth. The sword stuck out from the duster like an artificial limb. The Irishman closed his eyes and kept them shut. I thought he was asleep, but he removed his wrinkled white hat and took a drink. We looked him over. He wasn't wounded, just scratched and miserable.

"Lost," said the Irishman.

"You're not lost," I said. "You're on the road to Washington."

"Lost."

"The battle's lost," said Merrick.

"Can't be done," said the Irishman.

"Rest up," I said. "You'll see things different." I saw Merrick getting annoyed. "You'll be in Washington before we will. We're here till the Rebs come, or go home." I sat down.

"Can't be done."

"What, friend?"

"Can't get close. By the Lord Jesus, it was the chance of a lifetime. No man's photographed war. He who does is immortal." The Irishman looked at us. "You wasn't there?"

"No," said Merrick. "We're the Rear Guard."

"Pray the Rebels don't get here, lads. The noise. Smoke. Men running, screaming. You can't photograph it. It's too far till it's too close. You get killed. You get lost. You can't get an image."

"You want to photograph men killing each other?" Merrick said.

"I'd photograph anything, lad." He rubbed his eyes. "I lost my driver, my wagon, my camera, the plates. We drug two hundred glass plates over every root and branch between Washington and Bull Run Creek. Never broke a one. And I lost 'em all. I'd photograph hell if I could, man."

"You tried," said Merrick.

The Irishman acknowledged the remark with a bow. "We set up on a hill, like you men here. I got a special wagon. The camera points out one end, like a gun. Totally sealed from light. Strange-looking. Every man who saw it says, 'What is it? What is it?' It's truth, lads. The camera sees truth. It sees nothing else.

"I sat in the wagon on that hill. I wanted to photograph those devils when they charged. It's too fast. You can't get close, and by the Lord, you don't want to. The noise. Oh, God. The heat. Smoke in waves. I choked. Hades in the wagon. I got out to breathe and got separated in the smoke. I must've run, everybody ran. Then it was night. I was in some woods. I could've walked right into the Rebel army. The New York Zouaves, the firemen in French pants. There's an Irishman or two in that bunch. One of them gave me his sword. I walked all night." The civilian sat back and closed his eyes.

"Damn," said Merrick. "We're waiting for the Reb army and what comes along but a Congressman who wants other men to be brave, a swell, a pretty girl, and a Leprechaun who drags a camera thirty miles to find out bullets don't stand still."

Merrick took out a pipe, lit it, and put a cloud of smoke between us and the photographer.

13

Upton's Hill Va.
Oct 4th, 1861

Dear Mother,

This is the first time I have had a chance to write since we came out here, so I'll scribble a few lines. Your letters are a wonder and a comfort. They are better than the socks you send, and that's saying much. A good pr of stockings is a gift indeed. Stockings outdo a good sermon, and you know how much we all appreciate good preaching.

"For where your treasure is, there will your heart be also."—Matthew 6:21. My treasure is home. There's nothing like leaving a place to make you feel it. Now I can't wait to get back. I'm always thinking of you and Father and Helen and nothing makes me happier than thinking of you and Helen together—knitting, cooking, sending socks and eatables.

It's not just eatables, marching and socks for us. We sometimes hear a sermon or two. You spoke of hearing Mr. Bliss preach. He was here yesterday, and preached a short sermon to our Regiment. I like him better than our regular chaplain, but please don't tell anyone that. Not even Mr. Bliss, even for a compliment. Hearing Mr. Bliss' voice was a touch of home.

You spoke of our needing some shirts, and socks. I have plenty as yet, and I guess most of our boys have too. We have just received a new suit.

(Two shirts, two pr stockings, two pr drawers, one jacket, one pr pants, one cap, and one blanket.) So you see, we are pretty well provided for. The only complaint (about clothes) among the boys is that they have got more than they can carry. I have no doubt you would like to send us some such things, but you would please us better by sending something we would not have to carry.

I know you worry, but so far Providence has been on our side. We started from camp last Saturday just before dark. We had been out nearly all day (with our knapsacks and other things on) to be inspected by McDowell. We marched four or five miles, then turned into a field for the night. We had our overcoats with us to sleep on. They made us stack our guns, and we lay down near them. I got to sleep, but did not sleep long, for we have such heavy dews here that it is cold before morning. I woke up and found that I was decidedly cold. The other boys were in the same fix, so they went to work and made a good fire, and I improved it. The boys were lying around the fire in nearly every shape, and as soon as I got warm I followed their example and lay down with my feet to the fire, and my head on a stone. I had nearly got to sleep when we heard a volley of muskets. It was not long before all of us were behind our guns, but we did not get any orders so we did not move. Captain Ferguson insisted we wait for orders. Some of the men were hot to shoot. The Captain said since we couldn't see a blamed thing, we'd wait. During the night we heard three or four volleys, and in the morning learned that a California regiment, and one other regiment of our men, had taken each other for enemies, and fired upon each other. They killed eleven men, and wounded nearly thirty more, but since then we have had no serious skirmishes. Somebody's prayers were answered that night. Thank heaven for the Captain. There is a place for prayer and caution out here. We have both.

I miss Helen and I miss you. I miss fall in Sandy Creek and think of wind rippling the creek and cooling the lake. The popples turning. I'll miss walking by the creek before it freezes, and taking John Brown to Woodville and Belleville and down by the lake. I serve this great Cause, but dream of pies, breads, apples and cheeses, Helen and you. I know you will look after her.

It is a comfort.

May God give us strength.

Your son,

Moreau

14

At twilight of the day we met the photographer, mosquitoes and gnats furiously swarmed over the redoubt. It had been fortified with more branches and mud and deeper trenches. Merrick and I ate hardtack and made a fire and coffee, which tasted good. The traffic on the muddy pike dwindled. After "dinner," we walked down the road to share a pipe.

A big carriage came slowly toward the leafy hill through the twilight. It was pulled by a handsome, mud-spattered horse.

"Must be a blooded horse," I said. "Everything in the South is ranked by blood."

"These people oughta get ribbons, like pigs at the Sandy Creek Fair," said Merrick.

We laughed.

"Another fool who went out to see a Sunday battle and came back with a Monday war," Merrick said.

The carriage moved slowly in the humid, gnat- and mosquito-filled air. It was the first rich man's equipage we had seen not in a hurry.

"He ain't bein' chased by the Rebel Army."

"We could push him faster," said Merrick.

We watched the carriage come closer, slowly start up the gentle grade, taking the ruts straight on, not side-to-side, as if driver and horse thought they were on a flat surface. The ruts had hardened, like plaster mixed with horse hair, and the carriage bumped along. The driver looked straight ahead. He was an old Negro who tried to keep the mosquitoes away from his face with his free hand. It was a fine carriage balanced on big springs that took ruts well. On a deep, black-leather backseat a bare-headed gentleman, coat off, silk sleeves rolled to the elbow, fanned a sleeping soldier whose head was in his lap. The bareheaded gentleman's face was swollen with bites and looked almost as bad as a man with syphilis whose photograph had made the rounds of camp.

I looked at the soldier, who had lieutenant's bars, and thought he must be Godawful tired. Mosquitoes, hovering around the older man like a halo, landed and bit. He made no effort to keep them off, and suddenly I knew, soul to bowels, the soldier was dead and the man was his father.

As the carriage approached us, it bogged down and Merrick, me, Lyman Houghton and David Crocker jumped up to help push it over the ruts and up the hill. The gentleman tried to thank us but couldn't. I saw the carriage floor, the old man's trousers, and the leather seat were covered with dried blood. I looked away. It wasn't the blood. It was the flies—walking, buzzing, gathered like a tribe on the carriage floor. I felt sick, but the way the old man held the dead soldier and kept flies and mosquitoes from the dead face while others sucked his own blood was brave. If he could fan his son, I could push his carriage. Lyman Houghton said, "I'm sorry, sir," and David Crocker removed his cap.

"It's his boy," said the driver. "Wound in de leg. They cut it off and he die a shock. Po' boy." The Negro spoke so the man in back might not hear, though he didn't appear to be listening. "Po' boy. Went to fight for de Union."

Merrick, me, Houghton and Crocker pushed hard. We pushed for our fathers. It wasn't easy.

Midway up the hill, I stepped away and cried against a white oak.

Mosquitoes, wormy crackers, wounded men, a beaten army, even a beaten idea were trivial. I thought I could look at wounded men. Not this. Not a face stung with grief and insects. A father. I cried. Had the son gone for his father? Had his father cheered? Been proud? His father found grief. He found flies, blood, and mosquitoes. For a moment, I couldn't stop crying.

I wiped my face and joined the men with their shoulders against the carriage.

"You don't have to," said Lyman.

"I do."

"It's all right, Ro," said Merrick.

We got the carriage to the top of the rise, helped it by our fortifications, and guided it down the easy slope of the other side. We helped them home, whatever home is when a father brings back the body of his son.

Moreau

The Elephant

August 1861-September 1862

15

The 24th returned to camp, suffering insect bites and dysentery, and camped in tents with sweat-soaked bedrolls and ate regular, if unappetizing, meals on the grounds of Robert E. Lee's mansion in Arlington, Virginia. The location was a great satisfaction to Merrick and me. We admired the house with its Greek columns and big-swollen grandeur. This was what the wide-pillared houses in Sandy Creek aped.

"Horse shit," said Merrick. "Who the hell do these people think they are?"

"Why would someone with such a fine view of the Potomac go to war against his country?"

"So he can keep his Goddamned slaves," answered Merrick.

"Sad, isn't it?"

As reward for three tentless weeks on a hill, two brigades, each with five regiments, were called to parade on an August morning. We were to be reviewed by President Lincoln, Secretary of State Seward, who was from Auburn, New York, and General McClellan. McClellan was the hope of the Army, Lincoln the hope of the Union, and Seward the key "insider" in the Cabinet, and an ardent Abolitionist. Another opinion—"Them's all politicians"—was voiced by Merrick. Many were skeptical of the President. Lincoln was portrayed as a baboon in cartoons, and called worse by those who didn't like him, including McClellan, though we didn't know it. The General looked down on "our original gorilla," because Lincoln's mother was illegitimate, and Mr. Lincoln, though a lawyer, had received no regular education. The General was a doctor's son from Philadelphia and a West Pointer. Many who wore a mortarboard and whose grandparents were married, felt the same. The President's lack of respectability didn't bother me—no Salisbury ever graduated from a college. I say better a bastard than a slave. I knew from father, who knew from Oren Earl, our Assemblyman before father, that Seward thought himself the real power with an ignorant westerner in the White House, and had proposed war with England, France and Russia to take Canada, Mexico and South America, to replace the Confederacy. Thank God *he* wasn't President.

The regiment turned out with polished boots and clean rifles. Merrick wished he'd polished his "damn face," which was lumpy with insect bites, but "a far sight better than David Crocker's chigger-bitten bum." The two brigades lined up smartly. I looked at our men. Each had shoes and a rifle. None were starving, though some were pale from illness, and I wondered how we did so poorly at Bull Run. It had to be leadership and courage. Officers who ran, scared men who dropped weapons. The review was supposed to provide *esprit*.

Merrick smiled a rather-be-fightin' smile, but we stood smartly and watched close. I wanted to see Lincoln and McClellan, even Seward. These were the men Father wanted to be, dreamt to be—men who rise and lead. Many are called by the god of ambition, but there is only one President and one Commander of the Army. One Secretary of State too, but that was second prize.

The brigades stood in rows across the parade ground. It was a clear, warm morning, not yet hot. We stood at attention. There was spirit, readiness, courage—an army, even if only on the parade ground. Even Merrick, ever skeptical, stood straight, shoulders squared, and craned his neck as McClellan rode out on his powerful horse, Dan Webster. McClellan's staff, in gleaming uniforms on fine-groomed horses, rode behind.

The troops bristled with pride. Here was the man the President called to save the Federal Army, and the Federal Army needed saving. No one knew this better than the 24th. McClellan was handsome, raven-haired, secure in the saddle and in motion. A man of action, or so he looked that August morning. Merrick and me and every soldier felt the need for a man of action, a deliverer, a savior. The man on Dan Webster waved his hat to the troops. Little Mac was the "Young Napoleon," the man of the hour—of the century, if he saved the Republic. I cheered, but wished the man of the hour had another nickname. I knew about Napoleon.

Merrick cheered and I cheered. Then we saw the carriage carrying Lincoln and Seward. It stopped at the end of the column and the President stood and bowed to the troops. Dressed in black, wearing a stovepipe hat and standing in a carriage, Lincoln looked ten feet tall. He wasn't handsome. He didn't cross a parade ground on a horse waving a general's hat, letting his hair fly like a matinee player or a god sweeping down from heaven. Lincoln was different. The boys didn't cheer as loud. We watched.

The carriage went down each column so every man got a good look at the President and the Secretary of State, who was a foot smaller than Uncle Abe. If Seward was unhappy playing short fiddle, he didn't show it, but he lacked the dash of the General and grit of the President. I caught Lincoln's eye. It held something I hadn't seen in a man of power. All day I wondered what it was.

Later I knew. It was humility.

This man who worked so hard to be President—and I'd seen how hard men work at the deal-making, backslapping, back-stabbing mess called politics—was humble. Lincoln had marshaled an army two hundred thousand strong and would be the most powerful man on earth, if the army learned to fight. Yet he didn't come on a bloodhorse, trailing subordinates. He came in a carriage so every man might look at him, and he looked at each of us.

He looked at each one of us.

16

I went to Washington City after the review and it wasn't for an ambrotype. The bumps and bites went down, the infernal itching stopped, and hardness got me. I wondered if I weren't getting like Merrick. Seeing dead men, wounded men, skedaddling, beaten, pathetic men, and getting our asses bit by flying critters showed who was hardy, as we put it.

I constantly thought of Helen and touched the tintype. We wrote letters, tender letters, but now I'd been hungry, miserable, wet and scared, awful scared, I was willing to look at temptation. Until we marched out of Bailey's Crossroads, I had intended to remain pure. The war was supposed to have been short, but we were here for the winter. Come spring there'd be fighting. Real fighting, Merrick figured.

I promised Cousin to go to town with him. "Not for combat, but as a forward observer." He'd gone to Washington City and got cut over the right eye. Cousin needed a pard.

Before we left for town, I wrote father about Lincoln and McClellan.

I don't know what sort of President the westerner will be, but I know this: He's no play-actor.

The men love McClellan. Little Mac makes us feel part of a grand machine. He's a hard worker and looks and acts his part as if on stage. I suppose we are all on stage, Mr. Lincoln too, but no one struts his part like the general.

Seward doesn't look unhappy, but he wasn't the star. Not yesterday. I doubt he is the power behind the throne. Mr. Lincoln doesn't look like a man on a throne, or a man who doesn't know what's going on behind him. Do you think Seward will be President?

Your son,

Moreau

Merrick and I left at midday and didn't have to be back till reveille. We walked, admiring all the ships flying the American flag on the Potomac. The wide river, basking in a hot, silver, late-summer sun, was full of warships, barges, and commercial vessels. The warships boasted the heavy, bottle-shaped, naval guns.

"If Rebs invade Washington City," said Merrick, "they best do it at night. Otherwise, they get the bejesus blown out of 'em."

I nodded. On the Potomac and in the endless Federal camps one saw the strength of the Union. "How can we lose?"

"How, my ass," said Merrick.

If the summer river was magnificent with ships and guns and stars and stripes, the streets of Washington City were awful. Dust rose from carts and wagons. We passed dead horses, stinking in the heat and covered with flies. Green flies crawled and ate the eyes of a dead mare. Everything for sale, everything a cheat, horses beaten by drunken teamsters, abandoned when dead, whores yelling from windows—prices, insults, come-ons. Half-dressed, drunken women sang "Bonnie Blue Flag," the unofficial Confederate anthem.

We saw the half-finished Capitol dome. Orators likened it to the Union and the war—unfinished, a work-in-progress, foundation strong and design revolutionary. The iron skeleton reminded me of

Pandora's box. We walked on the other side of the street from the Washington Canal, a 150-foot-wide ditch filled with garbage and sewage. Its color, odor, and floating items were a stew of corruption.

I'd suffered constipation and dysentery, but the sight and stink of human waste and God knows what else was worse. I told Merrick the Washington Canal was the true picture of Washington City. We sauntered into thirteen blocks of dives, whores, gambling dens, pick-pockets. Vice, with its dangerous and intriguing face for men away from home. My hardiness began to evaporate.

"You need the cure for bad conscience," said Merrick.

"It ain't my conscience, it's my nose."

"Whisky'll take care 'a that."

"Does it cure the clap?"

"Look at this," said Merrick, and handed me a small package. "French letters."

I opened the tightly wrapped brown-paper package and found two condoms. "Lamb skin?"

"Intestine, Ro. The best money can buy."

"Where did you get these?"

"Ain't nothin' can't be bought in this city."

I looked at the opaque, slippery-looking items. "I don't have any use for them."

"It don't count if you use one of these."

"My ass," I said.

Before crossing into the thirteen blocks that would be known as "Hooker's Division" after General Hooker who, like Burnside, added a nonmilitary word to the language, Corporal and Private Salisbury got a lesson in rank. A barouche driven by a bored Negro carrying two pretty, well-dressed women slowed down to observe us.

"Don't waste your time, Belle. They ain't officers."

The carriage didn't stop, as if the Negro were afraid we might jump in. Up close the women weren't so pretty. Their yellow satin dresses and red beaver hats were soiled and worn. They were heavily made-up. And drunk.

"One of 'em is cute," said Belle, pointing a finger shiny with pinchbeck rings at me. "Young too."

"Young and cute don't pay," said the other.

"Wait a minute," Merrick told them.

"Go to Nigger Hill, you dumb private. Apollo, get us out of here."

Belle waved and the other spat in the dust of unpaved Pennsylvania Avenue.

I was flattered and disgusted. Merrick shook his head and said, "Stupid whores don't know what they're missin'."

"I'm afraid they do," I said. "Cash."

"Take a look," said Merrick, pointing at row upon row of low houses, shanties and alleys where soldiers stood smoking, passing bottles, rolling dice or being talked to by ratty-looking men not offering the word of God. Groups of hard-looking civilians prowled the dusty street, eyed soldiers, and kept their hands in the deep folds of long coats. Blue-coated men pissed in alleys. A sergeant pissed right in a rain barrel.

"I've never seen a place so gone to the devil," I said.

Merrick shoved me aside as a wagon full of barrels damn near hit me. The teamster yelled, "No offense, boys!" We dodged a Negro on a mule and then two sutler wagons, one driven by a woman. I blinked, shaded my eyes, and looked in disbelief at the hardest thirteen blocks in the country.

"What you think our fathers did here?" I said.

"Same as we're gonna do."

"They had a gun."

Merrick laughed. "Jesus, Ro." He pulled out a .38 caliber pepperbox pistol and handed it to me.

"Good God, where'd you get this?"

"Don't I always take care a you?"

I might have argued, but instead studied the strange-looking gun. It had a curved wooden handle, filigreed etching on the hammer, and a six-shot revolving barrel. It felt heavy in my hand. "This thing works?"

"By Gad, it better. Let's get off the street."

We stepped out of the sun, away from the smell of the canal and the fish markets, went up pitchy planks, and entered a dark, smoky, low-ceilinged room. A cloud of cheap tobacco smoke cut the close, acrid, sweaty stink of men. I coughed and tried to get used to the dark. Before my eyes adjusted, Merrick put a bottle in my hand. "To the Union!" He raised his and clanked mine.

"Drink."

Tears came. A dozen sounds assaulted my ears. The liquid was fire.

"Welcome to Hell," said a big man. The gouger. Merrick bought him a bottle and the big man elbowed his way to a table. There, he straightened up, toasted New York State, and fell on a stool that broke. The gouger slid to the floor, cussing. No one noticed. The din of toasts, gamblers' oaths, shouts and hoots stimulated by tanglefoot covered the noise.

"A good many men of the regiment are here," said Merrick.

"Not our finest hour," I said.

"We're less likely to be killed."

"Maybe." My brain clouded with tanglefoot.

"I want a bit of Venus after every battle," said Merrick. "And before too."

"I can't, Cousin."

"Suit yourself," said Merrick. "It's good luck. Like bettin' against death."

"We haven't been in a battle yet," I said.

"Been near one."

"True."

"Any time we don't sleep in a tent is a battle," said Merrick.

I saw rooms with curtains for doors. Men went in dressed and came out with unbuttoned shirts, missing coats, pockets turned inside out, even missing shoes.

"If you don't pay Venus, Mars will take you," said Merrick. "Come on!"

I shook my head and touched the tintype sewn over my heart.

Merrick winked and joined a line outside a burlap curtain. It was the longest, so he thought it offered the most valuable prize. He rolled dice with two men and improved his position. I drank—the tanglefoot went down easier—and kept my back to the wall. Merrick went in and I was without Merrick and Merrick's gun. I looked uneasily at the gouger, who was propped against the wall. He didn't appear likely to rise.

I watched the noisy, smoky room. A man dealing cards took his shirt off. Another followed suit. They sat at a rough wooden table, in rough pine chairs, in blue Federal trousers with white cloth suspenders and bare, sweaty chests. A pistol shot in a neighboring house brought a cheer from the men at the bar—a plank resting on two flour barrels. Soldiers three-deep slapped one another's back, challenged each other to shots of tanglefoot, and loudly cussed their officers and Stonewall Jackson, who got his nickname and fearsome reputation at Bull Run.

I hoped men from other regiments didn't learn our Major Barney's uncle, Dr. Lowry Barney, once convinced a Thomas Jackson to come to Henderson, New York to take Dr. Barney's famous cure for dyspepsia. For six weeks the quiet Virginian drank buttermilk, ate vegetables, and walked daily to Lake Ontario to drink the waters. He visited little Jackie Barney at Union Academy in Belleville. Unfortunately, Dr. Barney's cure took, and the man with poor digestion was now "Stonewall."

I wondered if a place with no music and a plank on barrels was a saloon or whorehouse. Did it matter? My hardiness didn't hold up well in the stink of sweat, cheap tobacco and cheaper whiskey. The drunker I got, the more I thought of Helen. The tingle of sin competed with memory and the aroma of men not wearing shirts. I wasn't hardy, just hardened.

A curtain moved. I saw a large black woman. Completely naked. I was disgusted. Was this the debt owed Gib? Was this the Union Army?

This was the scum of the earth waiting in line to fornicate. Most didn't know how to soldier, or even keep clean. They dug latrines between tents, hated "niggers," blamed blacks for the war. Many officers were incompetent, if not cowardly. The capital was awash in whores, thieves and louts. And here I was, one of them. Aw Jesus. Are all armies like this? Swearing, gambling, whoring mobs? Are all capitals like this? Were the Rebs worse?

I took another burning swig and thought of Gib, starved, scared, willing to suffer anything to get away from a country that wouldn't let him be a man. Thank God he wasn't here.

"Your turn, Ro!"

Merrick, David Hamer and David Crocker pulled me out of a chair and pushed me to an open door amidst howls and catcalls.

"Fifty cents say he do!"

"Fifty cents say he don't!"

"Ro!" "Ro!" "Ro!"

"For the honor of the Twenty-fourth New York!"

I was swept by something I couldn't control into something I didn't want. I was undressed, put on shoulders, slapped all over and hauled to a curtain. My cry, "I got a girl at home!" fetched howls of "Get some practice!" and "Be a man!" I struggled but my pants were at my ankles. My shirt was gone, money too.

The curtain got pulled down and a wedge of 24th men bulled through a drunken cluster of Pennsylvanians, who were shouting encouragement to a hairy, bare-assed man rutting on top of the enormous black woman.

"Billy's a man now!"

"Didn't I tell ya niggers was worth fightin' for?"

"Tie a board to his ass 'fore he fall in!"

The chorus of laughter, advice, chortles and a stuttering corporal saying, "F-f-f-f-fuck her!" in a spray of wild, red-faced enthusiasm turned into singing "The Yellow Rose of Texas:"

"The Yaller Rose of Texas

"Done the balls of Pennsylvanee!"

With a shout like Holy Spirit descending, the woman threw the Pennsylvanian off her. He landed on his pants at the foot of the bed and looked up drunken, dumb and furious.

"Nobody watch while I works!" yelled the woman. "You gots to pay for that!"

She was enormous. Her wet, pendulous breasts shook. Her whole body shook. She looked like a mountain and she was angry.

"Keep fuckin'!" Billy's shout was high-pitched, hysterical. He shook with rage, neglecting to cover his erect cock. He got up, looked at his mates who screeched with laughter, and socked the woman in the jaw.

She stood her ground, big hands on massive hips. I stood, trousers down, drawers up. The woman didn't flinch. Her bulging arm muscles looked like iron. The cords in her thick neck were hard rope. She had scars on her arms, the marks of a whip. She glared at Billy, me, all of us.

"You don't hit no better than you fuck!"

"Nigger whore!" yelled the Pennsylvanian, and threw another punch, but the woman moved and the punch missed. He lost balance and landed on the mattress.

"We just havin' fun, woman!"

"Think I'm havin' fun?" yelled the woman. "Ya men is stupid as ya look!"

Billy lunged at her, fists raised.

A scream cut through the heavy, close air. Blood squirted from a cut from Billy's ear to his neck. Splashed the wall, the floor, the bare mattress.

Merrick pushed me back toward the door. I stumbled and pulled up my pants. Men ran outside; others jammed around Billy. Two big men with clubs slugged their way into the room.

The woman shouted, "I free! I ain't yo' slave! I's a Christian woman!"

We shoved and pushed and got into the street. Cousin handed me my shirt and said, "We can lose this war."

17

The winter of '61-'62 was long. Lincoln wanted war. McClellan drilled, overestimated the size of the Confederate Army, and did nothing. Allan Pinkerton, the little detective who kept Lincoln alive by not underestimating assassination plots, didn't underestimate anything else either, and as chief source of intelligence, was less spyglass than magnifying glass. If the Union was the colossus we kept hearing about, the colossus was bedeviled by unscrupulous contractors, radical Republicans, Peace Democrats, shrill reporters, and the stalling, exaggerating McClellan.

The 24th remained on the grounds of Lee's Arlington mansion. Washington City filled-up with profiteers, prostitutes and embalmers. Talent of all sorts flowed in. The city's defense was Lincoln's business and Lincoln made sure it was defended by two hundred thousand men, heavy fortifications, and naval guns on the Potomac. Washington City was never attacked, even by the audacious Army of Northern Virginia.

We went into Virginia on scouting forays and skirmished with the Confederates. Sometimes a man was killed or wounded in the thick swamps or riverbeds. I thought I'd seen war. After all, I'd been shot at, carried wounded, seen friends die, and bedded down in enemy territory. Cousin didn't agree. He said a big one was coming.

"You can't win a war scoutin', and the Rebs don't show no sign of quittin'," he said.

I made forays into Washington City and battled my conscience.

Two weeks after the slashing incident, Merrick and I went to the thirteen blocks. We'd been in Virginia and Ollie Jenks had gotten killed. His father came from Sandy Creek and took the body so Ollie could be buried where "Ma can visit." Private Jenks had walked into the woods to piss and got shot in the head. We found him twitching with a hole behind his ear, blood splattered on an oak, and his pecker out. It wasn't sporting or brave, just bad, dumb luck. I'd just pissed on the other side of camp.

After Ollie, I went to the thirteen blocks, got tempted, and gave myself over to the flesh. Merrick said, "I guess you ain't a preacher," and I said, "Guess not." Merrick didn't say anything else, which I appreciated. I gave in to the devil of lust and the devil of fear. I was scared of dying. I kept seeing Ollie Jenks with a hole in his skull, pecker out, his body shuddering in the woods.

"Whoredom and wine and new wine take away the heart." Hosea 4:11.

Ollie's death was no excuse, but recklessness came into me. It was followed by Jesus-awful guilt. The dark eyes in the tintype seemed to know I would fall. They almost forgave. I repeated Jeremiah 23:14: "I have seen also in the prophets an horrible thing: they commit adultery and walk in lies." I knew sinners walked in lies. They walked nowhere else. I was no prophet, and I wasn't married, but I was never before a liar. Now I was. I made a vow and broke it. I always thought Jeremiah too loud on guilt, till I got guilty.

I tried the usual dodges. I was still a good person. I didn't tell a lie, didn't say I was drunk. Everybody does it, paying makes it different, away from home don't count. I chose sin. I walked in it.

"For nothing is secret." Luke 8:17.

I tried feeling extra guilty, as if guilt could burn away sin. I told myself I didn't love the woman, didn't abuse or cheat her, wore a French letter.

"Lord, I have sinned greatly in that I have done." 2 Samuel 24:10.

I prayed, but praying didn't feel right. Hell, the Lord already knew.

It happened again. I thought about what I did. Truly thought about it. I decided: I am no better than other men, no more sincere. Less mean maybe, but no better.

After failing to wash guilt away with more guilt, I tarnished the stain out of recognition. The moth went to the flame as often as possible. I was part of the army of sinners and publicans. I won't say I didn't enjoy it. I liked it best when the women laughed. If that compounds sin, hang it. Would I have been upset if Helen did the same?

Yes.

Did I tell her?

No.

Was I better than Dan Buck who said he wouldn't tell his wife because "I can handle the guilt, but she can't"?

Mother often said, "Thou Hypocrite" to father, and father would reply, "Hypocrisy is the human condition. Only one Man I know wasn't." Well, I thought I was better than most; at least I tried to be. Thou hypocrite. Jesus was speaking to me. To all men, I guess.

I had a qualm, a serious qualm. I took it up with me. Not Merrick. Not God. Should I think about Helen while doing my business in sweaty beds visited by other saviors of the Union? After hard debate, I decided yes, but if I told anyone, even Cousin, that would insult Helen. I always took my shirt off. When it went on, the tintype was against my heart. My lying heart.

Merrick found a house devoted solely to Venus. No gambling, fights or stabbings, at least when we were there. I got fond of a woman named Betsey. She had a child I brought candy for. I preferred Betsey to Venus anonymous, even if she was "open to the public," as Merrick said. Her room had a door, not a curtain. Betsey wasn't like Helen. She was big and foul-mouthed. She told me if little Abraham's father hadn't been killed at Bull Run, she might not even be a whore. Betsey was voluptuous. A big woman. She had legs like a plow horse.

She was muscular, lazy. Her eyes were dark as an animal's, but lost, looking for things not there. I told her about milling and she told me about the farm she grew up on in Pennsylvania. Betsy was my woman in the woods. Part dream, part forbidden, part sentimental. I needed her. I paid her.

I paid her, but I still pretended we were a family. I bought a purple rug for her room. I brought candy for Abe and the little cigars that Betsey liked. I found a picture of a mill and said it was the Salisbury mill. I pretended Betsey was my sweetheart. I wanted a place like home, even if it wasn't home. Betsey resisted, at first. "There are others," she said, and I said, "I know, but not when I'm here." I started only going to her. She told me little Abe liked the presents, though I never got to see him. I wanted her to stop with the other men, but she told me it was "her business" and none of mine. I got hot about that, but we got over it and I kept bringing whiskey, which she had more than a taste for, and bottles of cheap perfume Merrick got for his whores. One Saturday night I procured a quart of Kentucky whiskey. Betsey drenched herself in perfume and we got drunk, and had the wildest time. Not long after, she started to change. She got serious. I thought she was beginning to love me, and felt flattered.

One night Betsey asked, "Where you reckon you be a year from now?" She was dabbing her ears with something that smelled like vanilla. Her dull eyes searched my face.

I thought of Helen and how much I wanted to be in Sandy Creek, and how I shouldn't try to fool her. I spoke the truth. "Probably dead."

An unfamiliar expression crossed Betsey's face. She bit her thumb, a sign she was thinking. "Are you sure?"

"I'm a soldier. You need to be brave, too."

Betsy kept biting her thumb.

I thought about her, and then I thought about Helen. And felt guilty.

18

Camp Keyes
Arlington, Va
March 10, 1862

Dearest Helen,

The winter is long, and to say I miss you is to say I'm breathing. I wish I could march home and take you to our place by the creek. I hope your pledge to marry is still good. I know it is. If it weren't, a bullet would be preferable. I don't worry about you, dear Helen. Mother says you always wear a velvet pouch around your neck. She thinks it contains a ring. Is it the white stone from the creek? You may trust that your tin-type is always over my heart. I touch it so much—Merrick says I look like I'm always giving the Roman salute. Well, I'm saluting you.

I want to marry you the moment I get back. I don't know how long that will take. So far, we sit and wait and hope McClellan comes up with a good plan. All the boys think the beating we took at Bull Run last summer was a mistake. We will surely do better next time. It's good we think so, but I don't think the war will end with one battle. I don't think it will end with two. I think it will last a long time. So you must last a while without me.

Sometimes I wonder at how little time we've had together. Those hours by the creek or behind John Brown now seem like a story from Arabian Nights where everything is magical. Sometimes I think I know missing you more than I know you. I wonder what me you miss. You and

I have to trust what we don't know. We must believe in what we can't touch. We can only believe what we want and hope. I guess love is always like that, before life takes away the newness and magic and it gets tired. For us it is different. We are schooled by distance, disciplined with absence, instructed by time that drags like my feet on a long march. Our now is thinking and remembering and imagining. I'm always thinking about what you are doing (hoping it's writing me!), remembering your soft hands, imagining what we will do when we are together.

Sometimes I feel sorry for myself. When I can't sleep because of the cold dew when we are on picket, or tramping through the Virginia mud, hoping not to get shot by a Reb sniper, or just laying in a tent listening to rain pelt the canvas and thinking of the rain sweeping over the lake or making dots on the creek or tapping the windows on Rail Road Street, then I miss you so much, and I wonder if rain is falling on you too. I sometimes despair of seeing home or seeing home soon, but I think of you again, and Gib, and your Congregational belief that people must do right. I know you believe doing right is the true religion. Maybe the only religion.

I saw a man die in the woods. You know him. Ollie Jenks. He was killed standing in the woods. It's a terrible thing to see the blood of someone you've known your whole life, a neighbor, a friend. It's terrible and I know I will see more of it.

If it weren't for Gib, and you, the price might be too high. I might doubt what I believe, but I don't because of him, and you. That's why your love is important beyond all measure.

If I am killed, let only the good of me haunt you, and that not for too long. There is much that isn't good, but let that be forgotten. I have tried to do right. War makes us do things we never thought we would. I hope you can forgive me.

I don't think of the heads much. They are there, but they only watch. They don't talk.

I don't mean to sound so sorrowful, but I get so lonely missing you and Mother and Father (yes, Father too) and Sandy Creek. I want you to look after Mother as much as you can. She is so strong and sensible (has to be, living with Father!), but if something happens to me or Merrick, or any of us, she will be saddened in ways she won't show, and she will need you. I believe each of us sees God's face once or twice in our lives. People see God's face in grief. It's not an easy face. If Mother is grieving, you must help her. Otherwise she'll be lonely the rest of her life.

Think of me. I think of you.

You have all my love,

Ro

19

At Christmas Betsey disappeared. I had whittled little Abe a toy boat, and bought Betsey a bottle of French perfume, real French perfume. I was determined to find her. I went to see Madame Bird.

"She's gone, Corporal."

"I know that much."

"Let it rest, Corporal."

Something in Madame Bird's tone struck me wrong. "Why? Just give me a reason. You know I treated her good."

Madame sighed. "She's married now. Trying the decent life as best she can."

"Who?" I felt numb. Of course, Betsey was with other men. But one who would marry her?

"A man in the Patent Office." Madame Bird shrugged. "A wet fish, but at least he'll take care of her and …"

There was meaning in that 'and'. I heard it and it terrified me.

"She's got something good with her Patent Office man, all right? It's got nothing to do with you…"

"A man has a right to know," I said. "Is she...?"

"You're not going to let this go, are you?"

I met her gaze. Madame Bird was hard as a sutler, but I held it until she looked away.

"Betsey's with child."

My body went cold. "Mine?" I asked.

Madame Bird shrugged. "She said one night you didn't use a French letter."

I thought back to the night we'd gotten drunk. I could barely remember any of it.

"Betsey can't work now. This Patent Office man is her only chance. Don't spoil it for her."

"But…but if it's my child…."

Madame Bird glared at me. "This is her one chance to leave the business, to make a little bit of respectability. You're a preacher, show your kindness."

That hurt a lot, but I knew I wasn't going to do anything. I knew then in that shabby red hall I wouldn't tell, not even Merrick. This would be a secret. For me and Betsey. I didn't want Helen to know. Or Father. Or Mother. I wasn't going to ruin my life, and I wasn't proud of it.

Walking out of the whorehouse into a light rain, I was relieved. That didn't feel good either. Suddenly I realized what Betsey had been trying to tell me. It hurt that I didn't see that poor, dark-eyed woman who'd given me a few moments of real comfort was making a decision that would change her life. But what would I have done if she'd told me? I had no answer. I decided to walk all the way back to camp, trying to mill all I was feeling. I told myself I was helping Betsey by not giving away her secret, that I would hurt her chance of something better in her life by trying to find her. The rain fell harder. I walked quicker, knowing I was lucky—lucky I didn't have to deal with it, with the baby—and knowing I wasn't a good man. I knew I'd just learned something about sin, but didn't know exactly what. I knew I'd learn more if I lived long enough.

20

It was cold and snowy in January. Our war was with mud and a despondency that settled over Washington City like the winter fog. A private in the Second Infantry killed his sergeant and was hanged on the Commons between O and P Streets, by Vermont Avenue. Thousands gathered to see, but Merrick and I missed it. People talked about war with England. McClellan got typhoid, but recovered. Every day the telegraph informed the world: "All quiet on the Potomac."

Merrick wanted to get away from the others one cold Sunday afternoon. We headed for the river as snow flurries mixed with smoke from tents and shacks. We sloshed through heavy mud pulling our heavy coats round us and cursing our thin kepis. It was so cold, the dead horses in the streets didn't smell. A bootblack offered to wash, not polish, our brogans. The whores we saw stayed in doorways and didn't bother to yell.

We tramped through freezing mud to the river, sat on a rotted log, and watched Navy ships, barges, and a ferry working its way towards the other side. A sailor saluted us and we saluted back. The river had a skim of ice and didn't stink for once. Bottles, broken staves, and a dozen busted hay bales glided by between dark patches of ice. The water looked dead.

Merrick eyed me. "Haven't said much these last few weeks."

I shrugged. I hadn't felt like talking, and I still didn't.

"Is this about that woman?" he asked.

"Betsey."

"There's lots of Betseys in Hooker's Division, Ro."

"She made winter easier. Made all this waiting easier."

"The waiting's awful," said Merrick. "Makes you think too much."

"I've been thinking about a lot of things."

Merrick looked at me carefully. "You oughta think about home. You've got a woman in Sandy Creek. She's waiting for you."

"Well, we're all waiting." I watched the river for a while. Then I said, "Betsey got married."

"Good for her."

"I miss her. Her room almost felt like home."

"What could you give her?" said Merrick. "You wasn't going to marry her. She'll get a better life and you don't have to care for her."

"I always figured I'd have a family," I said. "Never figured I'd die first."

"I used to think if I had a son, I wouldn't make him work as hard as we did. But hell, after what we seen, I might make him work harder. Make him grow up strong."

Merrick had turned contemplative, and that was unusual. I wondered if he'd guessed what was going on. "Would you let him be a soldier?"

"Doubt it'd be up to me, Ro."

We watched some geese fly toward the unfinished Capitol. Would I let my child with Betsey be a soldier? It wouldn't be up to me. I'd never even know if he learned to read and write. I wouldn't know if he grew up strong and tall, or if he'd take after Uncle Lorenzo, short and sturdy like an ox, but good-looking. I'd never even know his name.

"Looking at this miserable river makes you think 'bout the crick, don't it?"

I nodded, but I was thinking if I had children with Helen, I wouldn't make them work too hard, or tell our boys they had to be a soldier or preacher or miller. I'd let them be what they wanted and hope they'd stay close to home. I told myself I'd have a wonderful home with Helen and children—and tried to believe it.

"The crick be froze-up now," said Merrick.

"I'd like to walk by it," I said. "One more time."

"Yeah," said Merrick. "One more time."

21

Spring '62 was sweet, then bitter. The Union began to win in the west. A general named Grant took two key forts and many prisoners. Nashville and New Orleans fell. Union gunboats took the rivers and destroyed the Confederate strongholds. Ports in the Carolinas were seized. A fearful battle was fought at a place called Shiloh and Grant won it, though it cost him. McClellan landed an army on the peninsula between the York and James Rivers—marching directly to Richmond was too much for the young Napoleon. We called him "Not Quite" because he wasn't ever quite ready to fight. The Peninsula went well at first. The Rebs fell back.

By April, we thought the war might just be the short, predetermined affair we'd heard about. I thought of home and worried about my sins and my secret. I knew I'd got off easy. Betsey was gone and Betsey had less reason than me to tell. Let Helen imagine what soldier's sins she might. A flesh-and-blood baby was another matter. I was worse than Dan Buck now.

Merrick noticed my moping and asked if it was still Betsey.

"It's everything, Cousin. Once home, I won't tell about whores, and if asked, I'll lie. I'm a liar and a hypocrite."

"Best practice for marriage I can think of," said Merrick.

The 24th thought we deserved victory. We lost men. We tramped around Virginia. We were ready for home, ready to keep secrets and tell lies. Maybe the war would be over soon. Maybe the advantages of the North would overcome the bravado of the South. Maybe the Seceesh would come to their senses. Merrick didn't think so. He said, "The Rebs can't be beaten without beatin' 'em."

The war changed in May. Stonewall Jackson fought five battles in the Shenandoah Valley. He marched men so mercilessly they called themselves "foot cavalry." Jackson defeated a Federal army twice the size of his. His dyspepsia cured, Stonewall had a stomach for war. Little Mac inched toward Richmond. Joe Johnston was wounded. His replacement was Robert E. Lee.

Bobby Lee routed the Federal Army in front of Richmond during the Battle of the Seven Days. McClellan, who had superior numbers, figured his army was surrounded, and skedaddled.

That summer the Rebs went on the offensive.

22

In August war came north. On the ninth, the slow-moving Union Army, led by Edwin Pope, met Stonewall Jackson and his army at Cedar Mountain in Virginia. Lincoln had replaced Little Mac, who was loved by the troops, despite his running from Richmond. Cedar Mountain led eventually to an invasion of the north.

The Rebs marched a thousand miles that summer. Lee had good generals—Jesus-loving, deadly Jackson; quick-moving Stuart and his cavalry; shrewd Longstreet; John Bell Hood and his Texans; and A.P. Hill, the man always there when he was needed. Bobby Lee and a poorly fed, poorly clothed, poorly shod army turned the tide in ninety days.

I knew from Father that the Rebs thought this was the second American Revolution, and the second had to be won like the first—by foreign intervention. All summer, James Mason, the Confederate minister in London, begged for diplomatic recognition. Slavery wasn't popular with the British workingman but Lincoln didn't free the slaves. Aristocrats and mill owners favored the Confederacy which, like a belle withholding her favors, embargoed cotton, pending recognition. By September, Britain was dangerously close to recognizing the Confederacy.

The 24th marched into Virginia with General Pope. Pope's army was trying to keep Stonewall Jackson from breaking out of the

Shenandoah Valley. It was a hard, thirsty march and we got dubbed the "Iron Brigade" for our stamina. We lost the name to the Wisconsins who fought beside us, but, in the North Country, the 24th remained the Iron Brigade.

We were in reserve at Cedar Mountain. We were supposed to keep the Rebs on the other side of the Rapidan River. While waiting by a field where Union dead had been recently buried, I started to write Helen, but before I had time to make a promise, we heard heavy cannon fire and the bristling crack of rifles.

"Move! Double quick! Rebs crossin' the river!" The order came sudden. And loud. "They broke through at Germania Ford! They'll surround us!"

I put away pencil and paper. We grabbed bedrolls and rifles, formed up, and in minutes, were moving. We marched all night. We had iron in our legs that night. The next day we got to the Rappahannock River and crossed on the bridge at Rappahannock Station. Three hundred Union men didn't get across in time and were taken prisoner. The 24th lost two. Orson Gale of Orwell got caught, but was paroled. The Rebs couldn't keep all the prisoners they took, so some were let go after taking an oath not to fight again. If you took the oath, and got caught again, they'd hang you.

For two days the armies shelled each other. The banks of the Rappahannock shook, but the 24th didn't lose any more men. We waited, hearing the elephant's rumbling stomach. Then we got orders to march. East. Back up the Warrenton Pike towards Manassas Junction, the site of last year's defeat, now the chief Union supply depot. It was a skedaddle.

"Jesus," said Merrick, the next morning. "When do we fight?"

The Iron Brigade marched north for two weeks and two days, recrossing the rolling hills of Virginia, and didn't stop till we came to Gainesville, Virginia, a few miles from Manassas. At five in the afternoon, sun still high, men tired, I set down my pack and thought

I'd be asleep in a minute in the shade of an artillery piece. We were exhausted.

"Form up! Form up!" yelled Captain Ferguson.

A hundred rods across a field were Confederate soldiers with artillery behind them. I saw them. Some didn't have shoes. Their trousers didn't match their coats.

We made a ragged line. I dropped my pack and reached for a cartridge. Dan Buck rammed a ball down his rifle, another on top of it, a third and fourth. He didn't notice.

The lines straightened. Men stared. No sound, no orders, just hot afternoon. Hot afternoon and the recognition men give before they become what men become in war.

A shell exploded. Dirt mushroomed.

"Good God!" yelled Merrick. "Our cannon's our only cover!" Words got lost in another explosion. Dirt flew.

"Lay down!" yelled Colonel Sullivan.

Without firing, I dropped to my belly. I tried to dig a hole to put my head in. I dug with my fingers. Merrick put his hands over his head. A cannon ball smashed into the near gun crew. An arm flew straight up. A corporal was torn in half. He sat where his legs had been. HIs legs were ten feet away. Dirt and smoke hurt my eyes. Shells went over and burst behind us. I tried to put my head in the ground. I peered between my fingers and saw a gunner try to hold his face together and a cannoneer with a red hole in his chest. Red mist fell. I smelled the acrid smell of powder. My ears rang.

Men pulled our cannon back. Others ran.

"Stand and prepare to fire!"

Who gave the order? Who could think? I wanted to run.

Merrick was on his feet, tearing a cartridge, jamming a ball. I got to my knees. Canister shrieked over us. I couldn't get a ball in my barrel.

"Fire!"

Rebs came. A wall of smoke lit by red flashes. I was on my feet. Noise behind us—horses, gun carriages.

Good God! Who's behind us? Rebs? Are we surrounded?

A black-haired officer jumped off a horse. He yelled, pointed, directed. Wheels rumbled. Horses neighed, snorted. Cannon was unlimbered, fired. It was the Wisconsins. How'd they set up their guns so quick?

I saw Confederate butternut a hundred paces away. Shells burst in their line! The white cloud streaked red. Black holes cut in it. The Reb line stopped, wavered. A Reb battery was blown to pieces. Rebs were tossed like dolls. Others dragged cannon back. The line broke. Rebs ran into the woods.

John Gibbon and the Wisconsins blew the Reb guns to splinters.

Delivered! My God, delivered! I kneeled, got a ball in the barrel, fired. I never thanked God or man the way I thanked those black-hatted westerners.

We knelt behind cover. The lines fired sporadically. After dark, we stayed down and the Rebs stayed down. No one went to the wounded left on the field. They cried for water, mother, God. My gratitude shriveled to a small knot in my chest. The wounded cried for hours. They cried into the dusk when the whip-poor-wills started their thin, clear call and an owl hooted like a solitary sentinel. Moans and birdcalls made strange music.

I smelled shit. Wounded men shit themselves. Men blown apart stink.

23

We marched out of Gainesville at eleven that night, heading for Manassas. I thanked God. The wounded still cried out as we headed toward Bull Run Creek. I knew some day I might lie between armies, groaning, crying, a soul in hell. We'd heard about men left for days, stripped by soldiers, then locals who came like jackals. Pockets turned inside out, boots taken, bloody photographs tossed on the ground. David Hamer heard a wounded man ate grass for five days for want of anything else, and died after being found by the Union Army. Lyman Houghton and Merrick wanted to die outright and not face the surgeons. Every man knew about field hospitals, tents at best, sometimes just planks on barrels, with piles of arms and legs in a pit if someone had time to dig one, or just piles. We'd heard about exhausted surgeons in smocks encrusted with blood and pus, wielding knives and saws. We knew about wounded men waiting for chloroform, screaming, whimpering, held down. Left in barns or outside on straw. Praying for someone to clean their stumps or give them water.

I'd been on the line now. I'd been shot at, and not by skirmishers, not foraying, not pissing on a tree. I'd heard Minié balls and grape and canister—the iron hail that makes red mist. Shells had gone over my head. At Gainesville, the Rebs had fired high. Gibbon and the Black Hats had arrived in time. How they had unlimbered their guns and fired was a miracle. How often do miracles come? I knew that nothing—nothing—I did affected whether I lived or died. It was chance. Pure chance. If the Rebs had fired lower, if Gibbon hadn't arrived, if his gunners weren't superhuman...

What did I prefer? Quick death, or agony in the surgeon's tent? I'd probably die in a storm of iron. I pinned my name inside my shirt after Gainesville.

We marched by a sliver of moon toward Bull Run Creek. My elbow touched Cousin in the dark. I asked myself whether God cared how you died. Did He care who you left behind? A mother, a father? A child you never saw? I got no more answer tramping in Virginia than on my knees in Cazenovia.

I started to shake. Cousin took my arm. We didn't talk until we paused to wash in a stream.

"I pissed myself," said Merrick.

"You?"

"I was scared," he said.

"But you stood and fired," I said.

"I can fight and be scared, Ro. So can you."

"That's called bravery, Merrick."

"Don't matter what you call it," he said. "It's what you gotta do."

"We not gonna get out of this alive," I said.

"No matter."

We marched for three days and the third was the hottest I remembered. We were south of the Warrenton Pike, near Groveton Junction, heading towards Bull Run Creek, a half-day away. I looked at oaks and chestnuts as if each tree, each leaf, was the most gorgeous thing. Solitary, intricate, beautiful. I wanted to stop, count points, feel ridges, touch branches. I wanted this forever.

We marched, drenched in sweat. I figured God had made trees and lost interest in men. Why weren't men like trees? Why didn't men take what they needed from rain and soil instead of stealing and fighting? Why didn't men stand for centuries, as trees did?

The oaks and chestnuts didn't move at all in the heavy August heat. I remembered the popples by Lake Ontario, how their leaves turned over silver when storms rolled in off the water, how their green and silver turned gold and danced in the autumn wind, and dropped, swirled, joined the earth. Trees—God's perfect creation.

We came to the edge of a field near Groveton. I wondered if I should write Helen and tell her to forget me. Would I live? The war was march, march, march all over Virginia, get whipped, go back to Washington, then find another place where men stand and fire at each other. It would get worse. We hadn't been in a charge. We hadn't been feet, inches, from bayonet wielding, Rebel-yell-yelling madmen. Should I tell Helen to forget me? If I wanted Helen to forget me, I wanted to die. Should I write Betsey and ask about the child? What was the use of that? If I lived, I lived for Helen. The child? I didn't even know if the child was alive. I wanted to stop, rest, fill my canteen, examine a leaf, take off my wet kepi. Feel if God was here.

If the child lived, it was a son. I don't how I knew, but I was sure.

At two o'clock, the day couldn't get any hotter. We came to a hill covered with trees that overlooked a road and a small creek. Captain Ferguson's map showed we were close to Stone Hospital. Not too close, thank God. I didn't want to hear moaning or weeping, or see men trying to comprehend life without arm or leg. We'd heard the casualties yesterday at Brawners' Farm were fearful. The 24th had been in the rear. The Wisconsins hadn't been so lucky. They'd got caught by artillery, then had scaled a hill topped by Rebs, waiting for them. Twice the Black Hats went up. I don't know how many men were lost, men who'd saved our lives.

Shots rang out deep in the woods.

"Lay down!" yelled Major Barney.

"Make yourself comfortable," said Cousin, which I did, at least as comfortable as a man on his stomach, hoping he doesn't get killed, can be comfortable. It felt good to rest.

We lay there three hours. I drank from my canteen, fired at will, listened to the roar of artillery beyond the trees. Our guns answered. The batteries couldn't reach each other, but made a steady rumble. If only war were limited to this alone. Lie on your stomach, watch trees, load, fire at will. Artillery dueling far away. If we could just lie in the woods the rest of the war. God, I hated open space. You marched or died in it. I lay and listened to the trees.

At five, a hot red sun hung over the afternoon and we got orders to march again. I picked up my pack. Back to the dance of armies probing, skirmishing, flirting, until they finally meet. And meet they would, by accident, design, or because someone with gold on his shoulder made a decision or mistake. We left our wooded hill and marched towards a creek. We were going to wash and drink our fill. We came over a rise.

Suddenly, nightmare.

A Reb line. They fired. Again. Men fell. I stood, unhurt.

Rebs behind a rail fence.

"Rally to the colors! The colors!" yelled Major Barney.

Merrick and I ran for the flag held by Albert Beeman. I went to one knee, pulled a cartridge—rip, ram, load. Tear packet, pour powder, drop bullet. Ram. Hammer at half-cock. Percussion cap on nipple. Full-cock. Fire.

Load. Fire. Load. Mind blank. Hands under control.

A ball ripped across Albert Beeman's face. Eyelids gone. Blood. Hands to eyes, no scream. The colors falling. Grabbed by Sergeant Bell. I stood, fired. Tear, bite, ram, fire. Three shots a minute, four if you don't ram, bang rifle on ground.

Men formed up by the colors. Sergeant Bell stood full-front. Hit. Corporal Martin grabbed the colors. "Come on men! Rally!" Hit. Corporal Cook took the colors. Hit.

I loaded and fired. We made two ragged lines. Some ran. Some couldn't either run or shoot. Merrick cussed. Sweat stung my eyes.

"Bass! Private Bass!" Captain Ferguson waved his sword. Shouted. End of the line, Philo Bass, dark hair, black eyes. Dead shot.

"Shoot that damn flag!" Ferguson pointed his sword at the fence. A Reb color bearer waved the blood red Seceesh flag.

Philo leveled, sighted, fired.

Flag-holder down.

Another Reb took the flag. Hit before Philo got a loaded rifle.

The flag didn't touch ground. New Reb. Men writhed on the ground. Our men. Doubled-up, screaming. The right side of our line rose. Captain Ferguson pointed his sword. "Charge! Flank them!" A cheer went up. Three Reb color bearers shot! Seize the fight!

Merrick, me, Hamer and Crocker ran for the Reb colors. My hands wet. Uniform sticky. Touched tintype. Socks drenched. I stumbled. Pain. Ankle. Not shot.

Men came at us. Blue. Running. Rout! Rout!

We ran. We ran back to the wooded hill we'd just lain on. Balls whizzed. I'd have run to Sandy Creek if I could.

I stumbled. Someone pulled my arm. Up.

"Stop! Stop!"

"Hell with it!" I yelled. "Hell with it!"

I fell. My rifle clattered against a tree.

"The guns!" yelled Merrick. "Come on!"

I picked up my rifle. Followed.

"Rebs gettin' our artillery!"

Merrick, me, Hamer, Crocker, and Lyman Houghton ran toward a knoll where three Union guns stood. A fourth was dragged by Rebs up a neighbor hill. We ran uphill. Slipped on loose stones. Grabbed roots, a small tree. Rebs were on the other side of the knoll. Muzzle flashes dotted the woods. Balls whizzed.

Yanks and Rebs ran for the guns. The Rebs grabbed a twelve-pounder. A hundred more poured down a neighbor hill. We grabbed the wheels of a twelve-pounder. Tried to pull it from its plant. Horses dead. Gunners dead.

I was hurled to the ground. Merrick thrown the other way!

The cannon fired. An artilleryman had pulled the lanyard. Half the Rebs on the hill went down in red mist. Another gun fired. Rebs staggered. Ran. They were twenty yards away when the guns fired. The hill was strewn with bodies and parts of bodies. I saw.

Three hours later, seventy 24th men pushed our cannon over rough ground in the dark. We were flushed with pride. I was exhausted, ankle aching, groin hurting, filthy, sore, friends dead, but Merrick and Lyman and Hamer and Crocker were okay. Darkness covered the arms and legs and heads on the hill. For the first time, I felt part of an army. I remembered the President. The President who came when we weren't an army, but a beaten, chigger-bitten mob. I wished he could see us now. Hoped he'd hear the 24th had saved its guns. Seventy Yorkers pulled and dragged, soon to wash in Bull Run Creek. Clean our faces of powder, sweat, fear. Wipe away death.

Victory.

We walked in the dark to find fires, brothers, sleep. I thought of Gib and Helen and father. This was their moment too. This was what the colors meant. How many died never knowing it? We walked parallel to Bull Run Creek. A dark line of men was by the water. Wisconsins bathing wounds? Men who ran rejoining the brave?

The Reb line opened fire. Half the 24th went down. It was like a firing squad. Men screamed, "I surrender! I surrender!" I ran. Merrick ran. Men ran in all directions.

Another volley. Some fell, others collided. The color bearer gave up the colors.

I didn't care.

I ran.

24

That night what was left of the 24th collected itself. I sat and cried. Cousin put a blanket over my head. No matter. Others cried. The war was like God, never satisfied.

I opened my shirt and put my hand on the tintype. I squeezed it to my heart, my love, my guilt. Cousin smoked his short-stemmed pipe with short, rapid puffs. He took his worry out on that pipe. Lyman Houghton bent over a crinkled letter from his girl. He never talked about her, but I once heard him said, "Blue, blue eyes." Philo Bass prayed. His hands were folded and his left eye twitched. Philo's eye twitched when he wasn't sighting a rifle. His brother Allen slept and groaned in his sleep. David Hamer arranged bullets. He put them in rows, then a circle. David Crocker massaged one hand, then the other. When he stopped, they shook. Dan Buck slept with both hands on his rifle. Martin Denison stared at nothing.

The next morning a roll of drums summoned us to fall out and march. The regiment was smaller. We closed ranks and marched. No one talked. No one looked at the man next to him. We looked ahead or at our feet. No one joked. I felt numb and wanted to feel numb. I didn't want to think. I wanted Cousin at my side. That's all I thought about. The next minute, next hour, next day would have to take care of itself.

The armies weren't courting now. Men found men. Nothing coy about it. Nobody leaves the dance.

Later we heard Pope thought he'd catch Jackson at Bull Run

where McDowell failed in '61. He planned to catch and destroy Bobby Lee's army. Pope would fight the way Little Mac hadn't on the Peninsula. He wouldn't fail for lack of nerve. The army would attack and attack and attack.

I marched all morning with Cousin, David Hamer, Crocker, Lyman, Philo and Allen Bass. They had luck and luck kept men alive. We marched, left, right, left, right; the cadence to canister and grape and Rebs who were all goddamn sharpshooters. Left, right. Left, right.

At midday we heard rifle fire in the woods to the right. On the left, cannon, more rifles. Somewhere ahead was the unfinished Manassas Gap Railroad bed. It would be a trench, maybe six feet deep and wide enough for railroad tracks. Yesterday General Reno's men had failed to drive the Rebs out of the position. When Rebs get a place, they fortify it. They'd had this one for two days.

I had no hardness. I looked at my feet and walked.

We came out of the woods. I saw clear ground and a snake fence where skirmishers fired at the occasional Reb, who fired over the lip of the railroad bed, then ducked under it for cover. I knew we'd be ordered over the fence to attack the sunken railroad. I tried not to think.

A cannon ball struck the ground, threw dirt, bounced, hissed furiously, cut a shallow trench, and rolled into the woods. Another spewed dirt, ploughed a trench, bounced like a bowling ball and rolled into the woods, crashing through the undergrowth. Two more. Ploughed. Bounced. I was fascinated. Bowling? Thank God they used solid shot.

A black dog jumped out of the woods and chased the balls. The dog had gone mad.

"Form up!" yelled Captain Ferguson. "Over the fence!"

We made a line in front of the woods. It was like a dream. I tried to blot out everything.

"We can do it," said Cousin. "If we stand together."

"That's Stonewall's men!" shouted Captain Ferguson.

"They ain't got no stone wall!" Sergeant Hollis joined the line.

"Remember the fallen!" shouted Lieutenant Corse.

"To the fence!" Lieutenant Balch raised his sword and advanced over clear ground.

The line followed. Shoulder to shoulder, bayonets flashing in the sun. Twenty yards to the sunken railroad. Rebs held fire. The fence wouldn't go down. "Damn Virginia snake!" yelled Merrick. The line bulged, wavered, men helped each other. We got over and reassembled.

"Charge!"

A cheer went up.

Attack. On line. Ground uneven. Earth dry. Day clear and hot. Uniform drenched. Didn't feel heat. Didn't feel sweat. Didn't feel anything. Just go! Go! Go! Heat exploding!

We cheered.

We got twenty feet.

The Reb line fired. Whizzing of Minié balls. Men went down all along our line. I stopped. Lieutenant Hollis, sword high, mouth open, got hit in the chest. Went down. Lieutenant Corse, saber high, hit in the forehead. His head jerked. Red, gray spray. He twitched like a headless chicken.

No line.

Men down, men screaming.

"Form up! Goddamn it! Form up!" Balch yelled. He waved his sword. The point gleamed.

"Attack before they reload!"

Cousin stood. Sighted. Fired. Cousin put his rifle down, picked up another by a body. He pulled a detached finger from the trigger guard. He aimed. Fired. Put the rifle down. Picked up another.

"Charge!"

We pulled together. New line. Easy targets.

Rebs rose behind a kneeling line. Fired.

Men fell. Crawled. Doubled over, jerked, slithered, rolled. Ground all wriggling bodies. Blue snakes. Some went mad. Jumped, howled, flung their arms in the air. One barked. Another ran on all fours.

My left shoulder exploded in pain. On the ground. Pulled up. Pulled back. Rebs fired at crawling men. Uniforms puckered. Fish in a barrel.

"Let me go, damn you!"Cousin held my good shoulder.

"Move! Move! They're killing us!"

Groups of two, three went forward. They walked to the sunken railroad. How such courage?

Lieutenant Balch reached the lip of the sunken railroad. His sword was over his head. A Reb jumped up and put a ball through the lieutenant's hip. Balch sat, dumbfounded, on the edge of the railroad bed. He pulled his pistol and fired at the Rebs who popped up. Philo Bass found a tree, a white tree, and fired at any Reb near the lieutenant. Philo loaded, aimed, fired. A ball ripped through his cartridge box. He reached for it. A ball shattered his arm at the shoulder. Private Damon, youngest in Company G, reached the bank. He fired, loaded, fired. A Reb jumped up. Damon bayoneted him. He bayoneted another. Red blade in butternut. Damon sat. Reloaded. A Reb jumped up. Shot Damon in the head.

Lyman kneeled at the edge of the sunken railroad. He fired down. Kneeled, fired, tore, loaded, fired. Trading life for seconds of glory. Two Rebs jumped up. Lyman shot one in the head. The other put his musket in Lyman's face. Lyman put his hands up. Disappeared over the bank.

How could they not kill not kill not kill not kill...

25

Cousin dragged me back to the shelter of the trees. My wound bled copiously but no bones were broken. I was embarrassed that I had screamed and embarrassed that it got me out of the fight. Merrick said, "Jesus, Ro, it saved our lives." That much was true. Wounded men crawling to the woods were shot. Men who reached the sunken railroad were killed or captured. They traded their lives for glory or fury or madness or whatever men find at the supreme moment. Life, all past, all future, for a minute of heroism. Was it choice? Destiny? Lyman Houghton wouldn't fail to do what had to be done. That was Lyman. He was born to it. Others? If Cousin hadn't taken me back to the woods, would he have sat at the sunken railroad, firing and loading, until he was killed?

That night, I lay on a blanket on a hill covered with wounded. Merrick was with me. Captain Ferguson gave permission. The captain had been hit in the arm but not bad. The Company's other officers, Balch, Hollis and Corse, were dead. Colonel Barney was dead. Company K had left his body behind the Reb lines.

Cousin sat on my blanket, checked my forehead, wet my bandages, and smoked his short pipe. We watched the acres fill with wounded. Cousin made sure I stayed far from the surgeons. The moaning and crying didn't stop, nor did the stream of wounded. Men lay on straw put down by nurses, mostly women. Over and over, men cried,

"Let me die! God, let me die!" as chloroform wore off and they woke, legless or armless, in this place of pain. We watched hundreds of points of light, candles carried by nurses or men looking for comrades, flicker in the night breeze. One tipped candle and thousands on straw, unable to move, would burn to death. I couldn't get that out of my mind. Neither could Merrick.

After midnight, I said, "Cousin, when you pulled me out, all I wanted was a wound bad enough to go home."

"You ain't that lucky, Ro."

"Didn't think about nobody but me," I said.

"Who you supposed to think about?" Merrick said.

"I just wanted to get out," I said.

"You stood, Ro. You stood."

I closed my eyes. "Easy next to you."

"I was scared," said Merrick, watching lights move. "Scared of losing an arm or leg. Scared of not seeing Pa and my stepma again."

"Don't think about that."

"I didn't till you got hurt," Merrick said.

"I used to think we'd win and go home. That ain't the way home."

"Home is a arm or leg," said Merrick.

Ambulances queued at the bottom of the hill. Lanterns hung at their sides. I tried not to think about the men waiting for surgeons.

"We used to wonder about being brave," said Merrick. "Never thought about having a arm or leg cut off. Never thought the surgeons'd be worse than the line. You was lucky, Ro."

"If our fathers saw this hillside, they wouldn't worry about bravery. They'd worry about us staying alive."

"Brave don't have much to do with it," said Merrick.

"Father wants me to be brave for him," I said. "He thinks he's a coward. It goes back to that time he was whipped."

"Brave," said Merrick, watching candles move like fireflies down the hill. "My father was brave with that slaver. When he had his shotgun. He don't know this. Uncle Mason says we pay the debt for slavery. He's right. He just don't know how big the debt is."

"He talks," I said. "We pay."

"That ain't his fault, Ro."

"I saw slavery's face. Gib showed it."

Merrick looked at the points of light. "Most of them lights is carried by women. Them women just come. They wasn't with regiments I know of. We got our surgeon and men nurses, but we ain't got enough. Where's the men to nurse the wounded?"

"Merrick, Father told me I was a coward. He said it so I'd volunteer. He thinks I came for him. I didn't, I came for other reasons. Mostly Gib. If I'm killed, I don't know how Father'll get over it."

"You'd a come anyway, Ro. Uncle knows that. There's no getting away from this war. You're no coward. You proved that yesterday."

"Do you worry about your Pa?" I said.

Merrick looked at the clouds in the night sky. "Four acres of wounded men. Three, four thousand more coming. I don't want him to see this. Let him believe in glory. Let him believe brave makes a difference."

"I think about Helen. About children we..."

"Just get hit every battle, so I can take you out."

I smiled. "I'll try."

"Maybe you'll take me out," said Merrick.

"You're invincible," I said. "It's courage."

"It's luck. Maybe it's 'cause there's nobody I want to see."

"Your Pa."

Merrick nodded. "Everybody worries about Ma and Pa." He looked at the clouds, then the lights on the hillside. "Don't worry about Mason, Ro. He's a good man. He took men to Canada. He ain't just talk. He took your friend Gib."

"When we're marching and thirsty and miserable, I think about Gib walking from Virginia. A man walks all that way to put his head in Lake Ontario and call it freedom. Jesus, Merrick, after what we seen, I'd be a slave before I'd do this again. I'm a coward." I was a coward for more than that. I thought about telling Merrick about Betsey, about the child growing inside her, but I didn't want to hear what he might say.

"Don't matter if you a coward," said Merrick. "You seen the elephant."

Seen the elephant. Been on the line. I'd seen the elephant. "Wish I hadn't."

"Sleep," Merrick said.

The next morning the Union Army started back to Washington. I was lightheaded and rode on an artillery caisson. Merrick walked beside me. He was one of eight men in Company G not wounded. No one talked. We were glad to get away from the hillside. We smelled men who shit themselves and we smelled the horrid odor of gangrene. We smelled death. The Army didn't have enough boxcars or ambulances. No one had foreseen this. The Union had lost at Bull Run again—five times the casualties. We left at dawn. Women still opened bales, spread hay, tended the wounded. Young women nurses were frowned upon. The Army wanted plain nurses the age of soldiers' mothers. Many, neither plain nor old, were here.

As the caisson moved out of the city of wounds, I saw a woman bend over a man with no legs. She dressed his stumps. Wounds must be dressed, but who could dress so many? The legless soldier gave the woman a look of pure gratitude, pure love. She wiped his face and gave him water. She stood as the caisson went by and I saw her in the pale light. Her black hair was parted in the middle, her cloak and skirt covered with dark stains. She must have been up all night and didn't stop tending, dressing, wiping. Her face was broad, unlike Helen's. I saw her only a few seconds, but her face touched me like Lincoln's. Humility. Strength. Here was a woman, one of dozens, who didn't have to be here, didn't have to see men blown apart, turned to meat, dying in the dew.

Who were they?

We heard later that a call had gone out in Washington City for volunteers to nurse the wounded from Bull Run. Government clerks—men, not women—went. They brought spirits to ease the suffering of the wounded. Most eased their own and bribed drivers to take them back to Washington.

26

Captain Ferguson rode up to the caisson. He pulled Merrick aside, gave him a bundle, spoke to the driver and rode off. The caisson slowed and pulled through a copse of oaks and beeches to a stream. The ragged line of the 24th kept going.

"Got to water the damn horse," the driver told the last of Company G. No one answered or joined us at the stream.

Merrick took the bundle, said, "Come on, Ro," and handed me a captured Confederate musket.

I followed, a bit unsteady, upstream, and up a knoll to a clump of birches.

"You're gonna make sergeant."

"What?"

Merrick took out a 24th battle flag. It was a new blue flag with a large NY and a bold 24. The colors. The sacred colors. Men rally to them. I did. Men die for them. The colors were the Regiment's soul.

Merrick threw the colors on the ground. He jumped, stomped, kicked and trampled the blue flag. Merrick wiped his face, took the Reb musket, aimed and shot the flag. "God damn."

"Well?" I said, resting against a tall birch, shoulder hurting.

"Didn't you see our colors given up at Gainesville? Given up without a damn fight?"

"Yes."

"Well, some fellas don't believe it happened, so the Captain says doctor 'em. Shoot 'em. Drag 'em. Muddy 'em. So when we get to Washington, nobody can say we lost 'em."

The 24th that came back over the Long Bridge was different from the 24th that left. We were fewer. Different. We trudged up Pennsylvania Avenue, observed by the usual bunch of whores, pimps and copperheads. Two women in a carriage—stout, tipsy, painted—tapped their driver on the shoulder and stopped. A redhead with uncombed hair started to sing "Bonnie Blue Flag," but saw Merrick and me, and a flicker of knowing silenced her. Hard acknowledged hard. The caisson moved by. "Bonnie Blue Flag" dissolved in the morning air.

Two drunken young men approached the carriage. One was clean and slick—too clean, too slick, his face a sallow approximation of health. How do embalmers manage to look embalmed? The other was rumpled, his black clerk's coat wrinkled and missing a button. He lifted a flask and saluted us, then saluted the ladies but the ladies didn't look. I recognized him. It was the man we saw with the Congressman after First Bull Run. He wasn't embarrassed about not being in uniform. No, this fellow had seen enough wounded to know what he was missing. He wasn't worth slapping.

Merrick and I went to whores every night. We spent every last Army-issued shinplaster. Secretary Stanton's paper currency was good in Hooker's Division.

"Blood money," Merrick said. "Our blood."

Hooker's Division was different. The pianos weren't as loud. Laughter was less high-pitched, though broken by an occasional scream of a bandaged man bumped before his tanglefoot kicked in. We knew we were going to die. Merrick said there was no deal, no arm or leg in exchange for your life, no pact with the devil, just bone breaking by Minié ball, vaporizing by canister, decapitation by iron. We gave names to the ordnance. Bullets were swifts and bumblebees. Artillery shells were bootlegs, tubs, camp kettles. We had a language for death. We were on speaking terms with it.

The whores were different. The first night a woman insisted on dressing my wound. She did it so carefully, tears came to my eyes. Lovemaking was different. I wasn't drunk. Sometimes I thought of Helen—a fleeting picture by a creek with flowers, dragonflies and waving summer hay. I had no qualms, no French letter. I dreamed about a place dead people meet, and knew there was no such place. Merrick and I were free. Death was as close as next week.

I fucked without the frantic abandon of spring. This wasn't cheating death. I didn't care about guilt. If somewhere in this city there was a child with my eyes, my hands, then God bless the child, for he was fatherless. I was gone. I held these women. I was saying goodbye. I didn't know their names. Halls smelled of vomit and urine, and beds had the odor of other men, but I didn't hold back, nor did I ask for anything in return. Some gave. Some had a heart to break. Ruth, a slender, plain, brown-haired woman, told me she hoped to marry me.

"You're gentle. Strong."

"I'm a dead man."

"You don't fuck like a dead man."

Cousin caught the eye of a Madame who took him to a back room to negotiate the price of a light-skinned woman. They didn't return until the next morning. What attracted Cousin? The woman had dyed-blond hair, smoked thin cigars and bullied her girls. She was frightening. I hoped he used his French letters. I thought of Betsey, her belly growing larger, and wondered if that Patent Office man was taking care of her. I thought of my child calling another man father.

Everything had changed.

27

September 10, 1862
Arlington Heights, Va

Dear Father,

I am grateful to Dan Buck for sending you news of me. There is no reason to worry. My shoulder is much recovered. I've seen a lot.

It doesn't matter why I'm here. I'm here.

Your son,

Moreau

28

After Second Bull Run, Lincoln gave command of the Army back to McClellan. Much of the army heard the news on the road from Bull Run. The reaction was electric. Men heard "Mac is back" and cheered wildly. Many loved his youthful looks, the way he rode Dan Webster, the way he loved us. They said we were in the right hands now. They said we'd been sabotaged by Pope, we just needed another chance, another general. The "Young Napoleon" rode out to meet the Army returning from Bull Run and was hailed as a deliverer. Merrick and I weren't so sure a deliverer was among us, but we saw how men reacted.

In a week, a very important week, McClellan reorganized the beaten Federal Army. Many in Washington thought McClellan delayed reinforcing Pope at Manassas out of spite, but if Lincoln thought so, Lincoln also knew the men loved Little Mac.

Second Bull Run had been terrible for the 24th. The report of dead and wounded sent to headquarters was returned for correction because no company could lose as many men as ours had. It went back unchanged. Merrick and I were somber.

We didn't know it, but luck befell McClellan. This luck wouldn't make sense in a made-up story where luck ought to seem destined and destiny not appear random. It was preposterous, unforeseeable, the kind called Providence or Hand of God, though I doubt pious Stonewall and saintly Bobby thought so.

On September 12, while crossing a field near Frederick, Maryland, a sergeant of the 27th Indiana found Lee's Special Order 191 wrapped around four cigars. Special Order 191 detailed Lee's plans. Those plans were now in Union hands. The "lost orders" were brought to McClellan, determined to be real, and acted on. McClellan learned Lee's army had been divided, where it was, and what it was going to do. Being McClellan, he announced this to a gathering of staff and civilians, so a Marylander got word to Lee, and being McClellan, he delayed a day before moving his army. But he moved.

He knew part of Lee's divided Army was at Boonsboro behind South Mountain in northern Maryland beyond Frederick and the Catoctin Mountains. We got orders to march.

The day before we left, we played baseball at camp. David Hamer yelled, "Play ball! New York game!" and two nines appeared on the parade ground. Cousin paced off thirty yards between the dirty shirts we used as bases, and I paced off a twelve-foot line the pitcher stood behind when throwing to the striker forty-five feet away, calling where he wanted his pitch. Home was a ripped sheet, and with the bases, made a diamond for the New York game, as opposed to a rectangle for the Massachusetts game. The field was bordered by white tents. Imaginary lines between stacked rifles separated fair from foul ground. Captain Ferguson secured a bat—a straight piece, quite swingable —and a ball, a real bounder. For the rest of the afternoon, the parade ground was our Elysian field. Time was determined by outs, then the sun, because we didn't keep score or count innings. It was home time, a game, ended only by Ma's call or nightfall.

"Let the miller pitch! Let Ro wheel 'em over!"

I stood at the Pitcher's Point. Company G played Company A, the winner to play Company B. Country versus city. The moment a cobbler named Jones slammed one to left that caromed off a stack of Enfields, and the cordwainer didn't stop till he got to third, the rooting was for action, not winning. I was crafty, kept my arm straight for the underhand delivery and snapped my wrist to vary speed. Since a striker needn't strike till he got one he liked, the pitcher usually made his pitches inviting, but different than expected. I wanted everyone to hit, so I laid them in with the consistency of a man at ninepins. Men whacked and ran. Fielders chased grounders and flies or scooped up bounders on one bounce for outs in foul territory.

The afternoon lengthened and I batted, played first, caught, or was summoned to the pitchers' mark as strikers favored my throws. We played hard but for fun. It was different from playing another regiment or laying money that New York men can whip Pennsylvanians. Everyone enjoyed striking and running.

29

I don't know what we would have thought if we'd known McClellan had Lee's plans. Little Mac wrote Lincoln that with the lost orders, he should whip Bobby Lee or go home. The General was right on both counts, but whipping Lee required moving quickly, and though Mc-Clellan whipped an army into shape quickly, he could do nothing else quickly. He waited a day and Lee's army doubled in size.

Dividing an army is dangerous, but Lee was outnumbered and out-supplied. He had to gamble. With Jackson attacking Harper's Fer-ry, and other troops a day's march away, two mountain passes stood between Lee and the bigger Union Army. Lee needed thirteen hours of daylight to reassemble his army.

The Union attack at Fox's Gap was thwarted. McClellan ordered First Corps, which included the 24th, to attack Turner's Gap.

The night before, Reb general D.H. Hill reconnoitered the posi-tion. He saw blue troops stretching as far as the eye could see. Hill said it filled him with loneliness. He saw 30,000 troops. He had 9,000. He saw the pass through South Mountain at Turner's Gap. He saw ra-vines, ledges, slender trees and fallen timber. An excellent defensive position.

It was a Confederate Thermopylae.

30

After a two-day march, I rested in a Windsor chair on the second floor of a farmhouse near Frederick. Outside, General "Fightin'" Joe Hooker was berating his staff. All were mounted. True to report, Fightin' Joe sat tall in the saddle and cussed. He cussed the 24th, 22nd, 30th, and New York 14th, the Zouaves. I tipped in the chair by an open window, my Enfield resting against the sash. I smoked a pipe. Merrick was in the next room on top of the farmer's wife, a big German woman past her prime in looks, but not in amorous energy. Her husband had joined the Union Army, she "couldn't manage der farm," so took to drink. On this "guten morgen," Frau Hess entertained a few of her husband's comrades-in-arms.

"Goddamn straggling brigade!" yelled Hooker to the officers, which included General Hatch of First Corps and Brigadier Abner Doubleday. "I'll have them arrested! Men will be shot! This is an army, not a convicts' saturnalia."

I hadn't seen Hooker close up. The man was clean-shaven and lively. Whether traveling with camp followers, winking at whores in the District, or demanding men fight, Hooker was lively, angry, salty, ready. I leaned back in the Windsor—it was like the broke-back at home—pulled on the pipe and blew a cloud of smoke out the window. Happy groans came from the next room.

The march from Washington into Maryland had been slack. Men

appeared for reveille, got in formation, started in columns, and walked off into the countryside. They picked apples, drank hard cider, kissed farm girls, napped in beds, did other things in bed, invited or not. Company G didn't rape. That was our deal, our superstition, like not believing in ghosts but being afraid of them. Of course, men who'd been in four battles and marched in and out of Virginia had their own definition of rape. For some of us, it was more than two men enjoying unasked-for favors.

Two days before, a dozen members of another company had encountered a haughty little woman in her Sunday best, standing in the doorway of her house. It wasn't a big place—two-storied, badly in need of paint, a sagging barn. The woman spat and, in a hard Southern accent said, "Yankee trash, be about your business." The only people on the place were an old slave and his daughter.

"Come with us, Uncle," a private said. "Take your freedom."

"That nigger answers to me," said the woman. "Julius, escort this trash from the property."

"Pardon, Ma'am," said a corporal, "but you're the trash. You own human beings."

"You're right, I own them. And this farm. You get yourselves off my property."

The woman, a small, sharp-nosed lady wearing a purple cloak, crossed her arms over her chest. It was a brave show. She stood proud, angry, in charge. This infuriated two men whose brothers had been killed at Chantilly. Without a word they grabbed the girl. She looked about thirteen, ratty pigtails, ragged flax dress, no shoes. They threw her down and tore her clothes off.

"Father! Missy Meredith!" The girl's terror cut through the air.

Her father leaped up, but was held back. A corporal hit him in the head with a rifle butt. The man fell to the ground and didn't move.

"He don't have to watch," said the corporal.

"She do," said a sergeant.

A circle formed. Four men held the girl down. The "lady of the house" was pulled into the circle. Trousers were unbuttoned. The girl screamed. Some men laughed, like they enjoyed the fright they caused, then a line started. Men undid their belts, cupped their hands over crotches, took off their kepis and fanned their faces like they had a job to do. Company G held back. We looked at the ground, at each other. The girl kept screaming and slamming her head into the ground. The sergeant grabbled her pigtails and held her head down. A piece of her dress was put in her mouth. She was punched in the head and stopped moving. A dozen men raped her. It didn't take long. I saw bobbing buttocks. Blood. Spit on the girl's face. After a while, her eyes rolled back in her head. She didn't move. Men got up saying, "Damn," or "God damn," or "I'm fuckin' for Uncle Sam," or "You could a had your freedom." They acted like this was a lesson or a job well done.

When it was finished, the lady spat in the face of the nearest man and got slapped, hard. A private ripped the top of her dress and said, "You're damn lucky we're gentlemen."

The Maryland woman, paying no attention to her small exposed breasts, removed her cloak and put it over the girl who lay naked in the dirt.

Men walked off, hitching up their pants.

We marched. I felt the need to vomit, but kept going. Under my breath, I said, "Forgive me, Gib."

I rocked in the Windsor and watched General Hooker cussing out his officers. Hooker had a pointy nose with a bump in the middle, a sharp nose and a sharp tongue. He wore a slouch hat with gold braid that gleamed in the sun. I picked up my rifle, cleaned it with rod and cloth, took a bullet out of my "forty dead men"—the cartridge-box—put it down the barrel, pinched a cap, placed it in the firing pan. I pulled on the pipe and stroked the barrel.

"These Goddamned men are under arrest! I'll court marshal every enlisted man and every officer! How can we have a damned army where men walk off?"

The officers looked away, patted their mounts, nodded agreement. This wasn't the first time they'd heard such talk, I was sure. No one moved to follow Hooker's orders, if indeed they were orders.

I polished my rifle—wiped the butt plate, sling ring and trigger guard, avoided the hammer, polished the barrel band, kept lint off the long-range sight, ran a finger over the blade sight as if it were a knife blade. I was relaxed. I felt good. If anyone—general, staff officer, enlisted man—came in the house, I'd shoot Hooker through the eye. No one was going to arrest my pards. No one was going to cuss me.

We were different, and if Hooker didn't know it, he'd be dead before he hit the ground. I wasn't angry. I wasn't hungry. I hadn't raped. I wasn't worried about being killed. I was just someone else. We all were—Merrick, Ferguson, Hamer, Cox. Lyman was gone. Nothing—not officer, general, conscience—scared me.

I pulled on the pipe.

31

The men who ate in orchards, raped, relaxed, floated in nasty, full-belly trances, were ready to fight. Hooker didn't know it, but we did. The grand ball was here. The armies had flirted, courted. Consummation was unavoidable. For those who hadn't seen it, the elephant was coming. The circus was on Union soil. Bobby Lee's gamble was working. Jackson took Harper's Ferry and its supplies, but Longstreet had to hold the passes at South Mountain. There were two: Crampton's Gap and Turner's Gap.

McClellan ordered an attack at Turner's.

At four in afternoon September 14, the 24th went into Turner's Gap. We called it Frog's Gap, or "Hell."

"Hell's down," I said.

"Up today," said Merrick.

Turner's Gap was a pass—a rocky incline thirty rods wide between the broken sides of the mountain. Scattered trees, boulders, rocks big and small, and vines over the rock face, led to the summit where clumps of trees and a small depression fronted a stone wall. It was worse terrain than any I'd seen. I'd stood face-to-face, line-to-line, and fired at men who fired back. I'd lain on my belly under canister, charged a sunken railroad, been shot at point blank, but I hadn't gone up a mountain with musket fire on three sides and artillery on top. The Rebs had the supreme defensive position. I said nothing.

Every man knew.

The bottom of the mountain was a mess. Union artillery fired uphill, Reb downhill. Rebs were in the pass—behind trees, rocks, bushes, behind breastworks of fallen timber. Smoke drifted up. Minié balls came down. The cannonade thundered off rock, echoed, and shook the entire mountain.

The 24th lined up. Penfield of Oswego, who hit a fly ball over Merrick's head a week, a lifetime ago, yelled, "Let's go!"

It was good to move. The pass was littered with bodies. The Rebs had charged and the 14th Pennsylvania had driven them off. I stepped over a mangled body. Don't look. Run. Go. Move. Flies rose in a cluster. I jumped over a headless corpse. Shells whistled in both directions. I took cover behind a rock hardly big enough for my head. Merrick got behind a bush. Balls and shells shrieked over. The Rebs were firing high. I slipped and scraped my cheek. Sharp twinge in my shoulder. I jumped up and went five paces to a bigger rock.

There was no line, just men scrambling. Climb, find cover, move again.

The 24th went up. No colors. Men for themselves. I didn't see Merrick. I lay on a rock—bullets careened off each side. I got to a pile of logs. Balls thudded. I lay and loaded. Twenty paces left, a Reb loaded a musket behind a bush. Rod up, down, slouch hat bobbing. I timed my shot to the rod. The hat flew. I saw no more.

A cluster of 24th men rose and scrambled up. I followed.

Below, Hooker and General Hatch watched. We heard later that Hatch had yelled, "See those Goddamned stragglers now!" He had said it with pride, then was hit in the head. Soldiers carried him back.

Wisconsin men and New York men climbed and fired and climbed. It was early evening and the Rebs still held. Puffs of white smoke were all over the mountain. Broken blue lines, men clustered behind boulders, solitaries going log to log, all began to slow.

General Reno saw men hesitate and rode up the hill. "Don't stop!

We must get the top!" He put his hat on his saber and waved it gallantly. What an example! Men got up from bush, log, stone. I wasn't happy, and looked back. A bullet hit Reno square in the head. Quick red halo, riderless horse. Reno was carried back.

The mountain was suddenly alive with blue-clad men yelling. Everyone up. Penfield led one group, Merrick another. "Reno! Reno!" Men shouted. Men moved. Badgers in black hats, Yorkers in blue kepi. I didn't feel my bruised shin, scraped chin, shoulder.

On the right Pennsylvanians went over the stone ledge from which Minié balls had come all day. They went into the brush firing, bayoneting.

Iron Brigade and Black Hats whooped. I went up the mountain, feeling crazy, like at the Sunken Railroad. I dodged, ducked, pulled myself up by grabbing bushes between crags, small trees. Men shouted, "Reno!" "To the top!" I shouted, "Reno!" Fear gone. Pain gone. I fell, cut my elbow. I kept going up. Men moved together and alone. Two went down near me. I didn't see who. Their bodies rolled down. One struck an outcropping of rock and was caught in a crevice. The other slammed into a pile of rock and brush, his neck horribly twisted. I went up, pulling and grabbing. The Rebs shot high. The bee swarm of Minié balls was mostly overhead. I gasped for breath. The mountain reeked of sulphur.

Men fell, but we kept moving. They'd have to kill us to stop us.

I reached a line of young trees and brush at the top of Turner's Gap. I saw the stone wall where the Rebs stood and fired. Red flashes streaked the twilight. White smoke hung over the wall, drifted through the trees, making a dirty curtain. Rebs fired. I found a tree, caught my breath, loaded, fired at a muzzle flash and splintered a birch. Our men began to reach the trees.

Company G took cover behind saplings. We pushed, tucked in our rear ends, peered around the trees. Suddenly, balls whizzing, men clinging to wood two inches thick, somebody laughed. Climb a mountain, see a general's head blown apart, make a frontal assault, watch friends fight over a skinny tree. Funny.

If that wasn't enough, Sewell Baldwin shoved Martin Dennison and Allen Rogers from a spindly tree, bent over, and was shot in the seat of his pants. Company G erupted. Merrick, me, all never laughed so hard. Nothing was ever so hilarious.

Then we charged.

32

“Forward.” Word passed among the trees. “Forward.”

We rose. Our line was solitaries, twos, threes. I saw Rebs rise from behind logs, rocks, trees. They rose in the dirty haze of early evening, and they ran. The laughter and yelling had been too much. We chased them.

I banged a shin, then a knee. I stopped advancing when a Reb officer rode out from behind the stone wall. He pointed his saber downward. Behind the wall, men with powder-black faces who’d been here all day fired point-blank into him.

We were furious! The battle was over! The officer ordered his men to surrender! The crazy sons of bitches wouldn’t stop!

Rebs reloaded and fired. They shot high.

We charged. Yorkers and Black Hats.

The Black Hats got there first. Part of the line went down. It reformed and went over. Merrick and Penfield and Captain O’Brien were on the wall. Clubbing, stabbing. Rifle butts up, furiously down. A bayonet went through a Reb’s eye.

I reached the wall as the Rebs broke and ran. I aimed, we aimed, rifles steadied on the wall, and fired. Rebs went down by the dozens. Men who’d fought all day to save Bobby Lee and had killed their Colonel died like rabbits.

I fired, reloaded, fired. I shot a man in the back. I fired at a running man and missed.

Reb reserves, held back all day, charged. They went in for a minute of daylight and died for it. Their charge was screams, wounded men, and corpses.

The next day was hot and we buried the dead. I counted five hundred Rebs by the stone wall. The bodies were beginning to smell. We'd seen dead men, but hadn't buried the men we'd killed. We hadn't won a battle either. Not the 24th. The rear guard at Chantilly had held, then retreated. This was our work. We saw it. The corpses were so new, we got to them before the locals. Some of the wounded had pulled their shirts up to see if they were gut-shot. If so, by morning, they'd be dead.

Merrick counted eleven wounds in Colonel Strong, 12th Virginia.

"Poor bastard," I said. "He was trying to save his men."

"Nope," said Merrick. "Just plain bastard. Look."

I looked. "Christ All Mighty!"

Merrick had pulled off the man's boot. It was hard, as the foot and ankle had swollen, but the boot came off. The name Colonel Frisby was written at the top of it. Colonel Frisby had been killed at Second Bull Run. Cusses and cries came from other parts of the field as men found Union shirts, boots, percussion cap boxes, belts.

"I'm not burying this son of a bitch," said Merrick. "I won't bury a thief."

Others crowded around. "Them bastards took our men's shirts and boots and left them to rot in the sun. They don't deserve nothin'. Let the crows have 'em."

"They were soldiers," said Captain Ferguson. "They deserve burial."

Men grumbled, admitted soldiers deserved burial, but wouldn't bury Colonel Strong.

"He rots here," said David Hamer.

"He rots in Hell," said Tom Cox.

I figured Rebs deserved burial, even if they stole. If I didn't have shoes, I'd steal. I went through a few pockets. Everyone did. I took tobacco, not photographs or *cartes-de-visite*. I stuck the tobacco in my nose.

"Wish them Washington bastards had to do this," said Merrick. "We kill 'em. Let the politicians bury 'em."

"The clerks who were supposed to nurse at Bull Run," I said. "I heard they got drunk and took the ambulances back to the city."

Merrick spat. "Men who don't fight, don't fight."

I walked off about noon. I'd seen enough and wanted to sit under a tree. I found a spindly birch and drank from my canteen. Then I saw the man looking at me. He was a Reb, he was young, he was dead. Ants crawled over his face and in his eyes. Not a mark on him. Just ants. He didn't look like the heads I saw in dreams, except for the ants. He wasn't a sphinx. He didn't have a question. I wasn't scared. It was all familiar.

I sat down and took out a scrap of paper and a stub of a pencil, and wrote Father a letter to be sent if I died. I pinned it inside my shirt. They'd find it on my corpse.

Then I wrote Helen.

Dearest,

Please understand, no matter what I see, what witness I bear, my heart shall not die. I am but deepened by sorrow. The man who says he loves you isn't the boy who held you by Sandy Creek.

I look at your picture as I write.

Love,

Ro

33

Two nights later, September 16th, was rainy, misty, and cold.

Men remember it differently. General John Gibbon remembered the night was solemn, dismal, silent. David Hamer remembered how close the lines were. I remember pickets firing sporadically. Occasional artillery echoed through the mist. McClellan could have attacked Tuesday and destroyed the part of Lee's Army camped at Sharpsburg, but McClellan was McClellan. He waited, finicking with details, laboring with anticipation, parading before subordinates, worrying about his men. The delay doubled Lee's Army as Jackson arrived and A.P. Hill started from Harper's Ferry.

No one forgets the next day. The 17th, the bloodiest day in American history. More men would die on a Wednesday in Maryland than in all the wars Americans had fought. Those remembering, commemorating, making meaning, sanctifying, know the stakes—British recognition of the Confederacy, peace Democrats agitating to settle with the South, and the Emancipation Proclamation—the document that gave the war the moral clarity of Lincoln himself. All this was only suspected, guessed at or wished for by those shivering and chewing coffee beans the night before. We had no fires. Our food was cold, sleep difficult.

I prayed.

Many Yorkers and Black Hats got stomachaches as we helped

ourselves to apples in the Miller and Poffenberger orchards. The Rebs had been eating green corn and apples for weeks. Ten thousand straggled. Those remaining had a variety of ailments. McClellan, with the help of overcautious, overestimating, overpaid Pinkerton agents, inflated Lee's number ten times, and decided a phantom army lay in reserve behind South Mountain.

Each army had moments of panic. A Zouave from New York City tripped over the regimental dog, fell into a stack of rifles and two regiments scrambled wildly, banging into each other, cussing and running amok until they discovered they weren't under attack.

In the West Woods, the other side of D.M. Miller's cornfield, a line of Rebel horses spooked. Sentries remembered it was quiet when something or Something—it was later described as a spirit—frightened the horses who broke their tethers and ran into the night. Major Sorrel and his men chased them till dawn.

The night was noises, blunders, palpable fear.

I sat with David Hamer—we were sergeants—and Merrick, who would have been a sergeant but for a reputation for recklessness, and David Crocker, Tom Cox, Dan Buck and Martin Dennison. Martin told again about Baldwin getting his ass shot in Turner's Gap.

"We got our laugh," said Merrick. "Tomorrow we get Rebs. Lots of 'em."

The men nodded.

"Both armies are big," I said. "It'll be a hell of a fight."

"We're ready this time," said Hamer. "We know how to fight."

"So do they," said Tom Cox.

"They learned quicker."

"They know what they fighting for," said David Crocker.

"And what's that?" said Sergeant Hamer.

"Show us we can't lick 'em," said Crocker.

"'Cause we invaded," said Dan Buck.

"They invaded us now," said Hamer.

"What the hell *are* we fightin' for?" asked Buck. "What're we dyin' for? Don't tell me niggers, 'cause I ain't and never was fightin' for niggers."

"We die for the Union," said a figure, stepping out of the deep shadow of the cold, wet night.

"Lyman!"

Tall Lyman Houghton stepped into the circle. We fell on him, hugged him, kissed him, felt his ribs. He was thinner. By daylight we saw the bruises on his face, but he was here. Alive and here.

"What happened to you?"

"Captured and paroled."

That meant Lyman had taken the oath not to fight again.

"Captured and paroled? What are you doin' here?"

"They'll hang you for comin' back!"

Houghton sat down and we sat in a circle—warm, forgetting night, drizzle, apprehension.

"They got to capture me first."

"They already done that," said Tom Cox.

"I thought you were shot in the face," I said. "You went down that Sunken Rail Road and killed a man. Why didn't they kill you?"

Lyman looked at each of us. "I don't know. Maybe they thought… I don't know."

Word spread through camp that Lyman was back, and the circle turned into a crowd. One of ours had come back from the dead. Nothing, nothing on earth, could have raised our spirits so. It figured, we said. Lyman Houghton, of all people, didn't leave his comrades.

Captain Ferguson joined the crowd. He hugged Lyman, gave him a cigar, listened to his story. He heard how Lyman had given an oath not to fight.

"Lyman," said the Captain, "if you're captured, they'll hang you."

We got quiet. We looked at each other. Looked at our feet. Escape, no matter how miraculous, was temporary. We knew it.

"Captain," said Lyman. "If I die, it's but one man. A few will grieve. If the Union dies, many will grieve."

"They'll hang you," said Martin Dennison.

"I am of little consequence."

The men got quiet, then cheered. Several flasks were passed. No talk of hanging.

Merrick touched my shoulder and pointed with his chin at a dark cluster of oaks. We walked away from men singing an unbearably slow "John Brown's Body." McClellan had banned the song as beneath the dignity of his army, but the words about the abolitionist's body rotting while his spirit marches on meant too much to men who routinely saw rotting bodies.

Merrick and I stood under dark, wet trees and Merrick said, "Ro, what did you learn in seminary?"

I looked into wet darkness. Merrick never asked such questions. It made me shiver. "Nothing we won't learn tomorrow."

"I figure you went about them heads. Ask forgiveness or some damn thing. Try to stop seeing 'em."

"I thought I could square it. Understand it."

"Lem Brown told me he saw God's face at Gainesville."

"He saw it all right," I said. "He got killed."

"Did you square it, Ro?"

"I called on the Lord," I said. "He didn't answer."

"Is He supposed to?" asked Merrick.

"'God is departed from me, and answereth no more, neither by prophet nor dreams.'"

Merrick smiled. "You got some preacher left."

Mist wet my cheeks. "The heads aren't squared. Asking forgiveness wasn't enough. Seminary wasn't enough."

"Ro, I think about your friend Gib sometimes. We got reason to be here."

"Reason to die?"

Merrick nodded.

I was glad he nodded. Awful glad. "Merrick, what did you learn with that woman in the woods?"

He leaned against the trunk of a thick oak. "I hope they bury me under a big tree."

"What did you learn?"

"Same you learned at Seminary."

"What?" I said.

"With or without Him, with or without her, we're alone."

"Is that what I learned?" I said. Could a man with a child ever really be alone? Did Father think that?

"Sounds like it," said Merrick.

"Like tomorrow?"

"After tomorrow," said Merrick, "them heads'll be gone."

34

We were up at 3:30. The rain slackened, then stopped. We heard the stray clatter of picket fire and exploratory artillery. I chewed coffee beans and salt pork and drank canteen water. It made a harsh, stirring swill. The bitter coffee-salt taste matched the damp.

Now we know McClellan had planned a three-pronged attack. If the attacks had been simultaneous, Lee's army would have been crushed.

If.

First Corps would hit along Hagerstown Pike, which passed the Miller farmhouse and a thirty-acre cornfield. Beyond the cornfield left were the East Woods, where pickets had fired all night. Beyond the cornfield right were the West Woods, full of Rebs. The three-quarters of a mile from East to West Woods was the left flank of Lee's army. It was defended by Jackson's Stonewall Division. Rebs were in the West Woods behind trees and limestone ledges. They were lying down on line behind the cornfield, hidden by a grass ridge. They were in the cornfield.

General Hooker rode out at dawn. Pink sky crept behind gray clouds, turned orange, made hard shades of blue. Hooker was on a milk-white charger. He was clean-shaven, as if barbered by the scythe of the Reaper. Many thought: Behold a pale horse. In the cornfield, bayonets gleamed in the early light. The corn was five feet high, the stalks yellow, leaves green-yellow white, ears ripe. Harvest time.

Merrick, me, all, tried to steel ourselves against the harvest coming. We'd seen killing, but no one, not Hooker, not Lee, not Jackson, not any man living or dead had ever seen anything like what was coming.

The night before, Hooker had told the men, "Tomorrow we fight the battle that will decide the fate of the Republic."

Tomorrow was here.

The 24th marched over a field of playing-card and naughty pictures, quick-buried or scattered under trees. Men didn't want "calling cards of Satan" on them if they died. "Fellas want to play a different hand at the Pearly Gates," said Merrick. Everyone laughed. David Hamer said, "As if God don't know." I laughed, but thought: *As thy soul liveth, there is but a step between me and death.* Cox and Dennison wrote their names on paper and pinned the paper inside their shirts.

Artillery boomed. It was unceasing. The earth trembled. We stood and waited, watching streaks of dawn—pink, red, orange, blue. Night meant safety. Armies didn't move. Every sound frightened, but no one died of fright. Morning was different.

The morning of Wednesday, September 17th was hot and clear. For seven thousand men, clarity itself. At first light, mist hung in the depressions of rolling fields. Brigades were hidden. Gunners couldn't see. At five, it was clearing. At six, gone.

The 24th had forty men. Our column was four across. We were behind Gibbon's men. The Black Hats made the first assault through D.R. Miller's cornfield. We stood as the air hissed and shrieked with shells. The noise was awful. The ground shook. To the right, on Nicodemus Hill, Rebs wheeled in artillery and fired at massing Union troops. Beyond the cornfield and a clover meadow was a white building and the main Reb batteries. The batteries were our objective. The white building was a Dunker Church, the pacifist German Baptist

Brethren who baptize by full immersion. The church had no steeple. We had to go through the cornfield and up the Hagerstown Pike. The Pike was a country dirt road. On our left rear, Union artillery fired into the West Woods and at the guns by the church. We waited behind the Poffenberger farm. We would march down a gentle hill, cross the yard, and go into the cornfield.

Full immersion.

35

We went into the cornfield at 6:31. A thousand Wisconsin and Indiana men went first. Colonel Phelps' Brigade had four hundred. The ten companies of the 24th had been reduced to four. Company G had eight men.

The air boiled with shot. Reb artillery fired from the Dunker Church. Federal artillery behind the Miller farm and Antietam Creek blasted the cornfield. I didn't see rows of men blown apart. I didn't see lines of butternut rise beyond the cornfield and fire into Union ranks. Didn't see Wisconsins, Indiana men, and New York Zouaves shout, load, fire at butternut, who fired back, across the Hagerstown Pike, ten yards away.

Thank God the 24th didn't go up the Pike. We took our chance in the corn. Cousin was on my right. David Crocker on my left. That's all I saw. Cousin and Crocker were all I saw.

We were angry. We were eight. On Union soil.

"Forward!" shouted Captain O'Brien.

We had two officers. Captain O'Brien and Lieutenant Penfield, promoted after South Mountain. The others were dead or disabled.

"Double-quick! Double-quick!"

We moved up a gentle slope. The corn was as tall as a man. Blue sky pushed out gray dawn.

The Pike was a quarter-mile of corn away.

Men came running at us. Twos. Threes. Blue. Bloody. Limping. Cussing. Two by me got hit. Simultaneous red halos splattered green-yellow stalks. I ducked and pushed bloody stalks away from my face.

"Forward!"

"Double-quick!"

Merrick was ahead. We came to an open swath littered with Reb bodies, parts of bodies, muskets, canteens, shredded haversacks. The dead lay in rows where they'd stood. I stepped in guts. Kicked an unattached leg. I went forward, bayonet fixed. Bodies thrashed. The ground was alive and trembling. The corn was bloody. We reached a line of kneeling Wisconsins. They fired at Rebs coming under a rolling cloud of smoke.

"Fill in! Fill in the line!"

On the Pike a dog stood over a dead man.

A Reb battle flag was tied to the rail fence. Two Federals raced for it. The officer got there first. Blood splashed the rails.

A ball passed my cheek. The air was thick and hot. I struggled to breath. My throat and chest hurt. My eyes burned. Ears pounded.

Rebs came through the smoke. They kicked and tripped over bodies. Balls whistled or thudded in men. I knelt. I tore, rammed, panned, fired. Merrick fired. Crocker fired. I was deaf and lay down. A corporal gave me a rifle with his left arm. His right was next to him. Two balls struck the corporal. I aimed over his stomach. My hands were bloody. I saw boots and bare feet under the smoke. I fired. The corporal convulsed. I crawled to another body and took another rifle. I steadied it on a dead man's back. The stock was bloody. I saw corn and Reb feet.

I was calm.

I pulled the trigger. It didn't fire.

I lay with my cheek on the ground behind a corpse, closed my eyes.

In God's hands.

I opened my eyes. Reb feet running. Men cheered. Men got up. I got up. Couldn't hear. Felt. My face was black, hands bloody, mouth full of grit and powder-taste, but I felt it. Power. I picked up another rifle.

"Right wheel! Right wheel!" Captain O'Brien led with his sword.

We were a ragged line, but a line. We wheeled to the Pike. Bodies were in the corn. Bodies were doubled-over on the fence. Reb bodies covered the ground from the Pike to the West Woods. Rebs ran for the woods. They limped. They crawled. We shot them.

A Reb officer, a general on a big horse, sword in the air, rode out. He shouted. "Stop! Stop it now! Stop!"

I saw his courage.

Captain O'Brien touched Lyman's arm and pointed his sword. Lyman shouldered his Enfield. Black-haired, powder-black, dead-shot Lyman Houghton aimed. Brave man at brave man.

Lyman fired.

Others fired.

The General tumbled off his horse.

That was the last I saw of Lyman Houghton.

"Forward! Up! Forward!"

Wisconsins and Yorkers walked over dead and writhing Rebs. They begged for water, for their mothers. We reached the rail fence and pushed off the dead. I loaded and fired. A limping Reb dropped. I loaded again. The rifle was hot, the barrel dirty. I fired.

"Forward!"

Crocker, me, Merrick, Cox, Dennison, Penfield. The line wavered. Balls came thick. A shell dug a furrow on our right. A haversack, a hand, and a leg jumped into the air. We were what was left of Company G. A shell cut a furrow on our left.

"Forward!" yelled Penfield.

One push! Destroy the guns! Turn the Reb flank!

Rebs came down the Pike. They came by the Dunker Church on the double-quick. Over road, over clover, over dead, over wounded. By crawling men and dead horses. Let out of Hell.

Crocker, Merrick, me, Cox, Dennison, Penfield.

A ball cut Martin Dennison's forehead. Lieutenant Penfield put his hand over the wound and pulled Martin back.

Crocker, Merrick, me, Cox.

Rebs left. Rebs center. A Reb dropped to one knee, aiming at me.

I saw him.

Ankle. Awful pain. Down.

Sky spinning.

Pulled up, hauled by something, someone.

"Let me down! Damn you!"

Three-legged beast. Rail fence? How? I was dragged out of the cornfield. Was it Merrick?

Couldn't see. Couldn't hear.

Mason
Fathers Bury Their Sons
September-October
1862

36

The telegraph brought news of battle, but the newspaper supplied the casualty list. Word traveled like electricity from the station up Railroad Street to Main. It flew like the Angel of Death and we hoped the Angel would pass us by. Three days after Second Bull Run, the Angel swept through Sandy Creek, Ellisburg, Boylston and Orwell. I, the Honorable Mason Salisbury, stood on my porch. It was a fine, clear September morning—ripe apples in full orchards, invigoratingly cool nights, the lake still warm for swimming. Little Wilbur Corse rode by bareback on a chestnut mare, tears streaming off his round, red cheeks. I thought of pity, the newborn babe astride the blast, as Shakespeare says. The word, the Angel, the almost telegraphic arrival of news passed our house. Someone, even little Wilbur, would have stopped if Moreau or Merrick were among the slain.

"It must be Henry," said Mary, joining me on the porch. "That poor child."

Up and down the street, cries ripped the crisp autumn morning.

I resisted a terrible thought. If Moreau or Merrick died, it would be easier to face other parents. Easier to be eloquent. Easier to stand for reelection.

I had asked for war. I had prayed for it. And now?

"Such a price," said Mary, joining me on the porch. She wouldn't cry now—later she would bury her head in her pillow and weep with grief for our neighbors, and relief it wasn't one of ours.

We went into the parlor because our neighbors' cries were unbearable. Mary and I didn't want to intrude. Later we'd make those dreadful, necessary calls. Men would look away, clasp a shoulder, remain wordless. Women would look each other in the eye, speak, hold, weep, and offer to stay over.

The war was here, now, in Sandy Creek. It wasn't pies and speeches. All of us were part of it.

Sunlight fell through the open curtains in bright ribbons on the Persian carpet. It was a beautiful day, a perfectly beautiful day. Every day we had no bad news was Eden. Every morning I stood by the American flag hanging proudly on the porch. We were proud. We weren't grieving. That September morn, Eden was lost. Eden wouldn't survive 1862.

By mid-afternoon, we still had no word of our boys. "I believe we've been spared, Mary." I sat in my cracked-leather chair.

Mary stood by the window, looking at the chestnut oaks and tall elms on Railroad Street, then closed the curtains. "I believe in the Cause, Mason, and I believe in you. But this is so hard for so many. How long will it go on?"

"Until it's finished."

"Until they all die?"

"Or the Union."

Mary took my hand. I rely on words. Mary on touch. Her way is better.

A knock at the door made us start. Mary did a turn like a startled deer. I was opening the door before I realized I was out of my chair. My brother Lorenzo and Oren Earl, Sandy Creek's most prominent citizen, came in.

"Mason," said Lorenzo, "one of our boys has been hurt. I don't know which or how bad."

My brother was powerful looking and broad-shouldered, though much weathered since we followed the Cheese twenty-seven years ago. His face had lines, especially around the eyes that bespoke, even at fifty, an abiding toughness.

Oren was taller, not weather-beaten, not strong-looking. He was clean-shaven, had a high forehead and receding hair, which gave an impression of intellect. Oren Earl was a banker, a former Assemblyman—his retirement had allowed me to stand—and married to our cousin, Jeanette. His eyes usually sparkled with a look between the childlike expression that childless men sometimes develop and the deep concern of a successful man who feels responsible for his family, church, and town. The Earls had no children and Oren was very much an uncle to those of the Salisburys. Today he was solemn.

"I heard of the casualty from Seward's office," said Oren. "I'm sorry."

The men removed their hats. Oren's was a fine beaver, Lorenzo's a slouch. My brother hugged Mary and said, "We must go for them."

I nodded.

Mary was crying silently. She didn't speak.

We sat in the parlor and Mary went for cider, escaping to the cellar. Escaping with her feelings. Her tears.

"And the battle?" I asked.

"The battle is well lost," said Oren.

"Some say our generals lost it again," said Lorenzo. "I don't know, but the Rebels haven't gotten to Washington."

"We've sent so many fine men," said Oren.

"And supplies and money and everything required," I said.

"There's defeatist talk in Washington," said Oren. "Peace Democrats. Men who want to compromise. Men who think the war is about property."

Mary came in silently with a tray of cider, freshly baked bread and biscuits. She might be terrified, but she would feed our guests. And show herself composed.

"I must go to Washington," said Oren. "I shall tell Seward, and anyone who will listen, there's no quit in the North Country."

Mary looked intently at Oren. She shook her head. Mary didn't speak, but couldn't control her head, which bobbed perhaps in agreement, perhaps in disbelief.

"I can help find the boys," said Oren.

"Thank you," whispered Mary.

"The Rebels are close to Washington," said Oren. "There's going to be a big fight. The war may be decided. Seward tells me Lincoln wants to issue an Emancipation Proclamation, but William counsels waiting for a victory. Much hangs in the balance. Perhaps the country itself."

"We shall go," I said. "Who'll look after the farm, Lorenzo?"

"I engaged two Canadians. They're good for a month or two."

"It's harvest time," said Mary.

"We will find the boys," said Lorenzo.

"If..." I stopped.

"If," said my brother. "We do that, too."

"You will find them," said Mary. "I know it." Her head stopped moving. Her eyes were steady. No tears, no trembling, no whisper. "You will find them and I shall take care of things here."

37

I packed my carpetbag. Mary came in and added articles I'd forgotten. She found a shaving brush, soap, cufflinks, a black cravat—things I never forget, but I was distracted. Mary rearranged the items and said, "This is your most important journey, Mason. When you went to Washington City with the Cheese, it was for yourself. Now you go for your son." I started to speak, but Mary put her finger to my lips. "Now I shall speak. I may not see you for a while." Mary kissed me on the cheek and mouth. She was warm, her hold firm, her hands strong.

She stepped back.

"I have heard your speeches, Mason. Some were very fine. I know your heart. You truly believe in the Cause. You believe men should be free. Much of what you said has come to pass. America is called to judgment for this terrible sin of slavery. The judgment has come, and at a terrible price. A price we imagined but, not until this day, truly knew. The price is our hearts.

"This is your most important battle. This is for your family. Our son. No Cause, or idea, or principle is stronger. This I know as I know the psalms."

Mary paused.

"You are a master of gesture and words, Mason. Now we are beyond gesture and breath and recrimination. I know your fears, Mason, your hard ambition, your scheming for Moreau to enlist. I forgive you. I love you. I trust you. Just find our son, and God preserve you. Go, Mason, with all my love and my confidence."

I put my arms around her.

Before dinner I overheard Mary and Helen in the kitchen. They were cooking together, as had become their habit. Mary kneaded bread dough. Helen cut apples for a pie whose crust had been rolled and rested on the counter by the soapstone sink. A beef stew simmered in a big iron pot. The room was warm with cooking, the women intent on work and talk.

Another day I might have barged in, but I stopped in the pantry.

"If you slice those apples so thick, that pie will never bake," Mary said.

Helen put down the knife. Her hands were shaking. "Mother, what if it's Moreau? What if he's badly hurt?"

Mary stopped kneading. "We must wait, child. We must be ready for him to come home."

Helen took the white heart-shaped stone from the velvet bag she wore around her neck, and rubbed it. "We wait and hope and pray... But..." Her voice trailed off.

"Mason will find them." Mary started kneading again. "When the men leave, we must stay close."

Tears filled Helen's eyes.

"You will be strong, Helen. I know it."

Mary stopped. It took a lot for her hands to be stilled. She wiped her floured hands on her apron and hugged Helen. "I was lucky, Helen. The man I love left Sandy Creek only once. He didn't find what he was looking for and came back. We've had a good life since. But Mason had to find what the world is like first. Moreau is like that too. Moreau and Mason seem very different, but they aren't. Each has had to find a cause. And Moreau, I pray, will come back, and know this is where he should be."

"Why do men leave?" Helen whispered.

The kitchen and pantry, the whole house, was filled with savory aromas. Bread dough rising. Two freshly baked pies on the counter, another to come. The stew added the scent of lamb, carrots, onions, peas, potatoes. The smell of home.

"It's their…" Mary stopped. "…genius," and smiled through her tears. "They don't know home until they return."

38

Our trip with the Cheese didn't prepare us for what we faced on this journey. The trains were jammed. Soldiers, cattle, lumber, crates of dresses, apples, wagon wheels, coffins, cannon limbers. The world was moving by railroad. The stations were busy, disorganized, crowded, and insane. Oren Earl was solicitous of wounded soldiers. Lorenzo less so. My brother thought if a man could ride a train sitting up, he couldn't be that badly hurt. I wanted to know where each man was from. I asked about the 24th New York. How many battles in a month's time? Three? Four? Five? It sounded like one continuous fight. Continuous and awful. I restrained skepticism when talking to officers attached to a general's staff. Many men's sons served without carrying a rifle. Lorenzo wouldn't talk to them.

Always I wondered: Which one? How bad?

We passed through New York City and soldiers on the train drank to McClellan's return and the Army's deliverance. The Sandy Creekers didn't drink. We watched the crowds at stations. Endless wagons, endless supplies were lifted into boxcars or put on flat cars by men Lorenzo thought could be fighting. Everywhere people and cargo moved. Chimneys belched smoke. The Hudson River and New York harbor were jammed with every sort of vessel. The urgency and bustle and confusion dwarfed what we saw in 1835, the time of the Cheese.

"Money is being made, brothers," said Oren Earl. "Fortunes. Win or lose."

We watched trains pass, teamsters crowd city streets, ambulances line up to receive stretchers—it hurt to see them—the crush of New York, the rumble of Philadelphia, soldiers guarding the tracks in Maryland. We watched in awe.

"The country grew up," I said.

"Like the boys," said Lorenzo.

Our sons were on our minds every minute. The closer we got to Washington, the more troops, the more frenzied the reports of Union disaster, the more I thought and prayed. Yes, I prayed. There are no prayers like the prayers of an unbeliever. Not for intensity. I got down on my knees. I didn't care who saw or how the click and bounce of the iron wheels on iron track hit my arthritic knees. Lorenzo put his hand on my shoulder and said, "Say one for me."

Forgive me, Moreau.

I'm usually talkative, especially with strangers; now, surrounded by them, I stopped. I was overcome with foreboding. A circle was closing. The circle went through Washington City. My first trip brought a mission and a voice—a mission and voice used ever since. This trip might fetch a dead or maimed son.

Trust me.

At seminary Moreau once dreamt he saw his head, my head, and Lorenzo's on stakes. I told him, "You use the story to make yourself important, like you used it to get your mother's attention. Then, it was her. Now it's everyone."

"Like you and the scar?" Moreau said.

"The story is your mirror," I said. "Don't mirrors exaggerate? Make us large?"

"Oh," he said, hurt. "Didn't you ever dream of those heads on stakes?"

"I don't use the sins of my ancestors to make me a saint," I said.

"Saint?" Moreau smiled. "You said they were American. American because they had a gun and used the gun."

Now Ro, as they called him, had gone to the Army and the Army was losing. Men were wounded. Dying. Thousands. One of ours. I was going to help if my son was wounded. I was going to apologize for thinking he wasn't brave enough to go on his own.

I love you.

Around my waist, under my clothes, was a belt containing a hundred and fifty dollars in gold pieces. In an inside pocket was a derringer. Lorenzo carried gold and a bigger pistol. We were lucky we could afford to go. If a man didn't, his son might not get proper care. He might not get his son's body. The boy would lie in Virginia or Maryland, in strange ground, under strange trees, strange grass—grass and trees his mother would never know. I had sent my son. If he were hurt, or worse, I would bring him back. That was the deal. My deal.

I kept thinking somewhere behind it, under it, hidden, was the old story. The heads. Oedipus' riddle. Shame and fate. I always said the heads didn't talk to me. Let the dead bury the dead. On the train they talked.

You—you—Mason Salisbury, are not done with blood.

I could not drive that from my mind.

Mary's words could not drive that from my mind.

Suppose I met Seward or Lincoln? Would I tell them the war must go on, no matter how many die? Yes. For whom would I be speaking? My wounded son or nephew? My career? The oft-displayed, oft-expounded scar? I watched the Maryland countryside and thought, I love you, Mary.

I thought of my speeches. All that talk of war and Abolition and Union, as if I were the soldier or the Deliverer of the Union. Now fathers, mothers, and political men talked of war, Abolition and Union as if they were holy mysteries sanctified by our sons' blood. Oh, fine talk! The train shook and soot came in the windows. I tried to sleep but remembered the men and women we hid in the mill. I remembered trips to Canada and the look in their dark eyes when they realized I meant what I said. *Trust me.* There's divinity in meaning what we say. As much as I need. It was different now. We were vulnerable. *Forgive me.* Sandy Creek was vulnerable. All of us. My talk and speeches and trips north seemed easy. Contained a bit of acting, hadn't they? A touch of the stage? Really, my scar was hardly visible.

I love you.

Lorenzo and I didn't talk much in Maryland. Lorenzo rode with a brakeman, a man with a limp from Watertown, and learned everything he could about the locomotive, cars, wheels, coupling, brakes, care of the tracks. I envied Lorenzo's hard, practical curiosity. I kept my hand on the derringer.

In Baltimore, we watched a wounded boy who couldn't have been more than sixteen carried off the train to a weeping mother and stoic father. Slaves loaded and unloaded the train. They grinned at passengers and soldiers. They were waiting. Why not? Everything was changing. No country could be so convulsed with cargo and rumor and wounded and not change.

Washington was frantic. Crowded, hot, dusty. Lincoln had abolished slavery in the District in February. Gangs of free blacks roamed the streets among the silk hats, soldiers, women, and teamsters. The streets were a tangle of wagons, hacks, ambulances, horses, and men, some in uniform, some not.

39

We got a back room at Willard's Hotel, paid the astronomical sum of five dollars, and were ushered through the crowded lobby of the Capitol's most famous hotel. Talk in the lobby hovered at the edge of panic or satisfaction about what rooms Lee and Stonewall might occupy tonight. Black-coated men smoked, talked, bargained, shook their heads. Money changed hands; papers were signed. The air was filled with smoke, the smell of whiskey and excitement.

Oren went to meet Seward. Lorenzo and I slept on an unmade dirty bed. We slept until late afternoon, removing only our coats and lying back to back. Around five, Lorenzo got up, yawned, stretched, and wondered if we could find something to eat before the Rebels occupied the hotel. At the desk we found a message from Oren saying he had no news but would keep trying. Fearing prices at the Willard dining room, we ventured into the crowded street and ate something called pork pie from a cart on Constitution Avenue.

We passed a dress shop with long black gowns and purple ribbons in the window. Next door was a harness shop, then a storefront full of hay. We watched a grizzled pig eat garbage in the dusty street. The pig reminded me of the black-coated men at the hotel. I smelled fish, sweat, rotting vegetables, and started to speak, but Lorenzo was staring at another window.

"Jesus."

In the window was a corpse in a new suit in a polished oak coffin propped up on sawhorses, so passersby could admire the work of Mack & Miller, Embalmers. A discreet, hand-lettered sign read:

Officers $50
Enlisted men $30
Coffins $4 to $7

"Damn," I said.

"Like buying a plough," said Lorenzo.

Where did this man come from? Who was he? Why was he displayed?

"They sell the corpse too?" Lorenzo spat.

I put my hand on Lorenzo's shoulder but Lorenzo didn't notice. He was lost in a hard stare. The coffin rested on newly made sawhorses; sap ran down a back leg. The best coffin, the best body, a well-swept floor, and a cheap, pine sawhorse. I was horrified by this exhibition of mortician's skills. Did Mack & Miller think they were cheating death, or just customers? Lorenzo stood bow-legged, bent at the waist, a farmer in the city, a plain man out of place. I thought he might smash the window.

"God damn," said Lorenzo. "Let's get a drink."

I was glad Mary couldn't see this.

40

The next day we heard fighting had broken out along Antietam Creek near Sharpsburg, north of Harper's Ferry. Oren still had no news, but procured a carriage. We were told it was impossible, but Oren got one. The most important man in Sandy Creek could operate in Washington City. Two other fathers, western Yorkers, a doctor and a lawyer, joined us. We left at noon as rumors swirled through the hot morning. The North Country men had heard enough speculation, lies and hope masquerading as news not to believe anything except rumors of fighting.

I left, despising Washington City. If the capitol was bad, what was the battlefield like?

I left in an open carriage, money cinched around my waist and carrying a pistol, overcome by a dread I called fate. Silently I repeated Hamlet's words: "If it be now, 'tis not to come. If it be not to come, it will be now; if it be not now, yet it will come." Those words, the rhythm, precision, the seeming paradox, were a comfort. The carriage bounced, stopped; the driver cursed and threw his hands in the air as the line of vehicles crawled, stopped, grew. Men were going for their sons. Women too.

Hamlet says, "The readiness is all."

What was readiness? Faith our sons weren't dead this very hour?

We got out of Washington City, and the space widened between vehicles. The line moved more quickly. The afternoon was hot, the sky high and beautiful. Lorenzo studied the countryside. Oren listened to the doctor, who chattered nervously. The lawyer, a skinny fellow with a sharp nose, read a small bible. I watched the sky and silently recited *Hamlet*. Numbness and panic were at the tips of my fingers, and inwardly I chanted, "There's a special providence in the fall of a sparrow."

Hamlet's own, ominous, beautiful epitaph. How does the Prince find providence? He's killed Polonius, unsealed the letter calling for his death, sent his school friends to an English executioner. He's lost control of his life, yet finds providence. Is providence knowing that nothing can be changed, that one must reconcile oneself to the world as it is? Hamlet returns to Denmark, no longer a grieving son, a disillusioned lover, a prince interrupted, but king of himself. He addresses death as an equal.

Hamlet had no son. No wife.

I had never felt such dread. Father, son, fate. I repeated it silently. Like a child's rhyme. Like a riddle. Age fifty-three, riding through the Maryland countryside, I understood. How does one address death?

One speaks the truth. Only the truth.

I looked at Lorenzo, who looked out the open carriage. I admired his calm. Lorenzo was waiting for a chance to assert himself. Oren listened to the doctor. I resented the chatter, but that was Oren's way. The tact and patience that got a room and carriage in Washington City. The road was crowded with men and vehicles coming the other way. We passed ambulatory wounded. Were they from Bull Run? South Mountain? Deserters straggling back to Washington City? Was a Salisbury among them? We saw two- and four-wheeled ambulances going in both directions. Carts and broken caissons. Spavined horses. Sullen teamsters. It was a preview. The world marches to battle, but limps away.

We saw fathers, mothers, uncles, sisters, brothers, wives heading for Antietam Creek. Readiness. Leave early. Take whiskey. Take money.

The lawyer looked up from his bible and said, "What's the difference between Hell and here?"

No answer.

"In Hell, only sinners are punished."

41

We traveled all night, stopping to rest and water the horses. Sometimes we were halted by other carriages with requests for directions or whiskey, or by a bad spot of road. As dawn broke, a teamster with a red beard asked aggressively for whiskey or "the wherewithal to buy it," and found Lorenzo's pistol in his face.

By sundown of this day, I was another man. I had paid a debt.

I have read Oliver Wendell Holmes, Sr.'s account of finding O.W., Jr. after Antietam. I don't think the "Autocrat of the Breakfast Table" lied, but I know he left things out, like how you feel when you see a corpse, skull split open and maggots eating the brain. Or flies crawling on the spilled intestines of a horse. Or a man whose last breaths were taken through a hole in his chest. The flies.

Holmes, Sr. is a doctor; maybe he wasn't shocked. Doctors know what not to say.

We didn't see the battlefield, but we smelled it. Putrefaction on the wind. Ambulances went by full of screaming men. Four-wheelers drawn by mules, two- wheelers by a single horse. Both kind bounced, and the wounded screamed as if tortured.

I saw horses and mules killed by artillery. I saw horses with maggot-covered brains. I saw a mule without a head, flies crawling down the ripped black throat. Nearby a gang of slaves dug a pit. Other slaves dragged a dead horse. Heads on stakes would be worse, I suppose.

Oren hailed a captain on horseback, who told us, "Today may be bigger than yesterday. What's left of the Army of Northern Virginia is sitting over there." He pointed. "On this side of the Potomac."

"Any news of the Twenty-fourth New York?"

"They went in early. The cornfield. Very fierce."

"Where are they now?" I asked .

"Waiting to attack, or Keedysville."

"Keedysville?"

"The wounded."

"Where's Keedysville?"

The captain pointed down the road. "Follow the ambulances." He rode off.

The road to Keedysville was filled with walking wounded, and men and women who weren't wounded. Their pockets were full. Some carried baskets. Some argued.

"Scavengers," said Oren.

"Don't stop," said Lorenzo. "I'll kill one of 'em."

At every group of soldiers, every officer on horseback, Oren, I, or Lorenzo asked, "Where's the Twenty-fourth New York? Colonel Phelps' men."

"Where's the Twenty-first New York?" asked the doctor.

"Where are the Second U.S. Sharp Shooters?" asked the lawyer.

The carriage barely moved, but we asked, Oren politely, The doctor shrilly, Lorenzo briskly. The lawyer asked when his nose wasn't in his bible. We were answered by enlisted men, stragglers, and stunned, pale officers who'd lost command of their men and themselves. Some were drunk. We heard:

"The Twenty-fourth no longer exists."

"Search yonder cornfield."

"Heaven, Hell or Keedysville."

"Keedysville."

"Go a damn mile down this damned road."

The sun burnt off the heavy Maryland dew and chill of night. We were in a line of carts, ambulances, two- and four-wheeled, government vehicles that didn't seem to have a purpose, men walking in either direction—stopping, sitting, asking for water. The mile was interminable.

The smell. It came on the wind.

Along the road were knapsacks, broken wheels, wreckage from caissons, crushed ammunition boxes. And men. Men sat under trees and looked indifferently at the parade. The smell didn't go away. The men didn't go away. We saw burned farmhouses and what looked like large anthills, but they weren't anthills. They were haystacks, some flattened and black, others alive, moving, covered with men. Wounded men. And the ground. The ground, too, was littered, strewn not with bales or sacks or caissons, but with men.

We had entered another world. Everything moved. Everything smelled. The fat doctor with little eyes and gold-rimmed glasses took out a cigar and broke it in two. He crushed a stub in his hand, then picked out scraps of tobacco and stuffed them in his nostrils. He offered tobacco to the others. Everyone took it but Lorenzo.

We let an ambulance pass.

"Keedysville?"

The driver nodded.

We followed.

I packed my nostrils and watched. Flies hung like mist behind the ambulance. Its doors were closed. A voice cried, "O Lord! Lord! Lord! Lord!" Blood seeped through the floorboards onto the dust of the road.

42

Keedysville was the City of Dis. Lawns, porches, fields were covered with wounded men. They lay everywhere. Some were attended, most not. The doctor held his head in his hands and wept, saying, “Forgive me. Forgive me. I go to my son.” Keedysville’s streets were jammed with civilians, soldiers, ambulances, carriages, carts, stragglers. All converged at the Baptist church.

The church was a hospital. The hospital was hell. War’s logic.

When the carriage could no longer move for the traffic, we got out. The doctor and the lawyer went into the church. The Sandy Creekers asked for the 24th. Something hardened in our step

We saw men—searching, wandering, wounded or nursing.

We saw women—nursing, carrying bandages, water, bowls.

We heard—screams, weeping, prayers, pleas for water, commands.

We smelled—blood, shit, vomit, sweat.

We saw blood—bloody men, bloody bandages, bloody stretchers, bloody limbs.

We saw bandages—shirts, sheets, tablecloths, bedspreads, napkins.

We saw litters, stretchers, crutches, carts. Such cargo. Men in wheelbarrows, lifted out of ambulances, laid on lawn where there was no lawn. And the dead. Brought out of the church, out of ambulances, off stretchers, laid in carts, stacked in wagons, taken away.

The surgeons' tents and tables were on the lawn of the Baptist church. The tables were doors or planks supported by flour barrels. I tried not to look. How do you look at a pile of arms and legs? A pile. Arms and legs. Like scraps. And blood. Pools. Puddles. Clotting.

Men on the ground waited. Some prayed. Some cried. Some talked gibberish. When their turn came, they were anesthetized with chloroform. They thrashed, shouted, were held down, passed out, were lifted to the tables. Limbs held, tourniquets tied, incisions made. Then the saw. Needles. Thread. Men missing an arm or leg were taken off the tables, put on the ground. Some woke screaming. Some woke in shock. Some cried. Some never woke.

"The Twenty-fourth New York Volunteers?" Oren asked again and again.

I couldn't speak. Lorenzo looked from side to side.

We tried not to step on men on blankets, litters, sheets. I stepped on a hand. The hand didn't move. The next man woke to a bandaged stump where a leg had been. He screamed.

"Better among the wounded than the dead," I whispered.

Everywhere, cries. "Water!" "Mother!" "Let me die!"

Everywhere, the smell of shit, the metallic smell of blood, the harsh odor of chloroform. We came to a table. You couldn't move without coming to a table. We stopped. A private not more than eighteen, face blackened by powder, distorted by pain, was lifted from litter to table. Three men in short sleeves held him. "More chloroform!" A man in a slouch hat held a metal cone lined with a white napkin a half-inch over the private's face. The private sat up and screamed, "The Angel! I see the Angel!" The man in the slouch and the two others held him down. The private's eyes were wild. Crazed. Animal. The private went rigid and fell back. His neck muscles spasmed, his head rolled. "Remove the cone! He can't breathe!" The cone was removed. The spasms stopped. After a few seconds, the cone was put over his nose and mouth again. The private was insensible.

A big man in an apron caked with blood, thick, clotted, brown, came forward. He was the surgeon. He wiped his hands on his apron, took a sponge from a bowl of bloody water and wiped off a long single-sided blade.

I had seen animals slaughtered. I had seen birth, with its welter of blood and cries and joy. This I could not watch. I looked away and saw a woman with dark black hair, parted in the middle, dabbing water from a soaked cloth on the lips of a man who'd had both legs amputated. A woman. My God. A woman.

"Double flap amputation," said the surgeon. He pushed up his rolled sleeves. White bicep showed above blood caked to the elbow. The surgeon had a thick black beard, broad shoulders and blood-shot eyes. His collar was bloodstained. He looked at me. I saw a man aging before my eyes.

The bandages on the private's right leg were removed. The leg was mangled. No kneecap, no foot. Bone stuck out of blackened skin. The thigh was yellow. I hate yellow. The faces of the wounded were yellow. The arms and legs under the tables were yellow. Yellow remains in my dreams.

"Tourniquet!" shouted the surgeon.

A bloodstained canvas strap with a buckle at one end and a buckle in the middle appeared. Two men wrapped it around the private's thigh.

The surgeon grabbed the anterior thigh two inches below the tourniquet. He lifted the skin with his left hand and wiped the amputation knife across his smock. It looked like a carving knife and glistened in the sun like fire. The surgeon pushed the point into the leg. He cut down. The knife sliced until it struck bone, stopped, went up, sliced again, and came out, having cut a neat flap. The surgeon wiped the blade on his smock, inserted it in the initial cut, cut down through muscle and fat, reached the bone, went under, and cut the posterior flap.

The man in the slouch and an assistant pulled back the flaps. I turned. Thought I'd be sick. Oren turned. Lorenzo watched.

The surgeon sliced the opening between flaps and bone. He cut yellowish, red tissue—muscle, fascia—what holds a leg together. The bone was visible. The surgeon put down the knife, picked up a suturing needle and threaded it, wetting the silk with saliva. He sewed sutures into the flaps. I looked at my feet. The surgeon put down the curved needle and picked up the capital saw. The blade was thick, the handle beveled with a diamond pattern for grip. The surgeon leaned over the table. The muscles in his forearm tensed. The man in the slouch hat and the assistant pulled back the flaps.

The sound. I almost screamed.

The surgeon bent to his work like a carpenter cutting a plank. The noise was smooth. Steady, quicker through the marrow, smooth again.

I wanted to run, but the operation wasn't over. The bone was severed, the bloody hinge of leg dropped off the table onto the pile.

The surgeon wiped the saw with the sponge, returned it to the amputation case and removed a hooked tenaculum, a slender instrument with a wooden handle. The point was curved like a fishhook, and the surgeon hooked the femoral artery, which looked like a big red worm. He pulled out a quarter inch. The man in the slouch tied the red worm with a silk ligature. They hooked and tied more arteries. The tourniquet was loosened and blood filled the tied-off arteries. The stump was beefy red. The tourniquet was retightened and the smaller veins were hooked and sewn. The surgeon examined the work, nodded, and said, "Arteries tied. Veins clotted. Rongeur, please."

A pair of forceps appeared and the surgeon removed spicules of bone from the stump. He trimmed the bone with a file. After wetting the thread again, he sewed the flaps of skin together with a curved needle.

"Good work," said the man in the slouch hat.

43

Which boy? How bad?

Was Moreau chloroformed? Sawed?

Was he dead?

This was the altar onto which I bound my son.

Forgive me.

Moving away from the table, I stepped in vomit. Stepped on a bandage covered with excrement. Saw a pile of arms and legs, and turned away because they moved.

God's price for slavery. How could it be less? How could it be more?

Lorenzo held me up.

"Them doctors ain't doctors," he said. "Just butchers who learnt on hogs."

"We are judged," I whispered.

"It ain't medicine."

Lorenzo was angry at the surgeons. Angry at the men who held down the arms and legs. Furious at the piles of limbs.

"They put them on boards," I said softly. "Saw, sew, and lay them on the ground." I said this as if I'd just described the universe. I squeezed my brother's arm. We looked at each other. Not our boys. Not this. Never.

Oren put his hand on my shoulder. "They must amputate to stop infection. Otherwise men die."

"They die anyway," said Lorenzo.

"It's all they can do," said Oren.

"Judgment," I said.

"We must find the boys," said Lorenzo.

We went from tent to tent, stepped over litters, avoided the tables, avoided men on the ground. Oren was pale. I shook. Lorenzo touched the pistol under his vest.

"They're not here," I said.

Oren grabbed the sleeve of a sergeant carrying a bowl of bloody water and bloody sponges.

"Yorker?"

"Ninety-fifth New York."

"Where's the Twenty-fourth?"

"In the cornfield."

"Cornfield?" I said.

"The cornfield," said the sergeant. "The Twenty-fourth went early. No one left. Not standing. Not men nor corn."

"Cornfield," said Lorenzo.

"You could walk over after and not touch the earth," the sergeant said.

"Cornfield," I said.

"Bullets cut every stalk. They fought five hours."

"Have you heard of Sandy Creekers?" I said.

"No."

"Salisburys?" said Lorenzo.

The sergeant shook his head.

"Where are the Twenty-fourth wounded?" said Oren.

"In the church."

I knew we had to go in the church. We had looked in the yard. We had looked at everything, even an amputation. I didn't want to go in the church.

The church was dark and the darkness moaned. Planks had been placed over pews, and litters and stretchers put on the planks. How could a house of pain be God's house? I saw the altar. The church was like the church at home. Rough beams, plain pews, whitewash in and out. A place people who work the earth come to God.

God wasn't here.

I leaned against a wall and said, "Deliver us from evil."

Men cried. Men screamed. Some just boys. A fat man without legs below the knees shrieked for morphine. I smelled urine and vomit and that other smell. Gangrene. And a metallic smell under the other smells. The metallic smell got in my throat. A few nurses, male and female, went up and down the pews, dispensing water, wiping faces, comforting.

So few. Here in the house of pain.

"There!" Lorenzo pointed, his face white.

"My God!" I whispered.

By the side door. Only a father or mother could have recognized them. Felt their presence. They lay on stretchers over pews. Next to each other. Moreau and Merrick had been in pain, shock, pain again, at first unbearable, then shut down by the body, then stinging back, for twenty-eight hours. Their faces had been touched with a wet cloth, but streaks of black powder ran around their mouths and down their chins. Both were bathed in sweat. Moreau's right ankle was bandaged. Merrick's right leg was covered. His fists were white.

It wasn't one Salisbury. It was both.

We went to them.

"You came," said Moreau.

Tears were on my face. "I came."

"Said I'd see you in church." Moreau took my hand. "Helen? Mother? Gib?"

"Helen's fine. Mother too. I know nothing of Gib."

Moreau closed his eyes.

Merrick looked disbelievingly at Lorenzo. The boy was so wracked with pain, he must have thought he was hallucinating. Lorenzo touched his hand and said, "I'm here."

"Don't let them cut," said Merrick.

Lorenzo took his hand. "I won't."

44

Lorenzo and I and a bloodstained man with rolled-up sleeves carried Ro and Merrick to the Regimental surgeon. It was noon. The sun was bright. I saw the open box and glistening blades. The surgeon was stocky, with big shoulders, a bald head. Blood was spattered on his temples, on the fringe of hair by his ears and stylish whiskers. The surgeon wasn't drunk. If he had been, Lorenzo would have hit him with the butt of his pistol. I was ready to plead, Lorenzo to explode. We stood close. Oren Earl shook hands with the surgeon. They knew each other.

Outside a church, my son on a stretcher, part of me died. Stopped believing in words. I vowed not to give another speech. I would not stand for reelection. A deal with God, absent or not.

Let him live. Punish me. It is my fault.

The stretcher bearer wiped blood off the planks with a sponge he rinsed in a bowl. Lorenzo and I lifted Moreau off his stretcher and put him on the wet planks. The surgeon acknowledged us with a nod, and removed the bandage from Moreau's ankle. Moreau winced. The surgeon wiped the black, blood-encrusted wound with the sponge he used to wipe the planks. Sweat ran down Moreau's face. I squeezed his hand. Lorenzo watched, hand on vest. The surgeon probed the wound with his index finger. Moreau gave a small cry, then managed a smile.

"I must amputate," said the surgeon.

"Are bones broken?" It was my voice. I surprised myself.

"No, but this wound will become infected."

"Can it be kept clean?" I asked.

"Yes," said the surgeon. "If a piece of cloth is passed through it every day for a year. Assuming he lives."

"You are sure no bones are broken?" asked Oren.

"Yes."

"Then he could live and clean his wound?" said Oren.

"He has one chance in ten." The surgeon nodded wearily to Oren. "Let's see the other boy."

Lorenzo and I lifted Moreau off the planks and put him on his stretcher. "Father, letter," he murmured, delirious. He pawed at his chest. I saw a flash of white. A crumpled envelope with my name on it was pinned under his shirt. I put it in my pocket, and Moreau slumped back on the stretcher.

The assistants picked Merrick up and put him on the planks.

Merrick's eyes were half open. His mouth soundlessly shaped the word no. Lorenzo stroked Merrick's hair, slick with sweat. The surgeon removed the bandages. I looked, then knelt by Moreau's stretcher and squeezed Moreau's hand. Merrick's knee had swelled into a large black ball. Streaks of dirt and dried blood ran down his leg. The surgeon looked at Lorenzo.

"Bullet probe," said the surgeon.

An assistant reached into the wooden box and removed a Nélaton probe. It was a foot long. It had an ivory handle, a thin shaft and a porcelain ball at the tip of the shaft.

"Turn the patient."

The assistant rolled Merrick onto his side. Merrick's eyes went back in his head.

The surgeon inserted the probe in the wound. A hard, professional look crossed his face. He twisted the handle, then deftly removed the probe. A black mark was visible on the porcelain ball. The surgeon showed the mark to Lorenzo.

"The ball is embedded in the bone. The leg must come off."

"One chance in ten?" said Lorenzo.

The surgeon shook his head. "If I don't amputate, this boy will be die in ten days."

"We'll take our chances," said Lorenzo.

Oren put his hand on Lorenzo's shoulder. "Are you sure?"

"I'm sure," said Lorenzo.

The surgeon pulled himself up to full height. The sun glinted off his spectacles. His smock, forearms and trousers were caked with blood. He wiped his hands on his smock and said, "One boy will survive if he has a constitution of iron. This boy will be dead in ten days."

Neither of us spoke.

"Mr. Earl, these men are gambling with their sons' lives."

Lorenzo pulled back his vest and showed the pistol. "Mister, you're gambling with yours."

45

What would I have done, had the surgeon insisted? I didn't know. What Lorenzo did, I knew. The surgeon didn't argue. Oren sided with us. A minute later it made no difference. We had our sons and the surgeon was cutting on another wounded man.

"Get the boys out of here," said Lorenzo.

With the help of a carter whose cart had lost a wheel, we carried our sons to a shady spot under a tree, vacated by men taken to the tables. I sat by Moreau, who said, "The letter. The letter."

"I found no letter," I said. I looked at Moreau's face and wiped his brow. I didn't want him worrying about a letter.

Lorenzo went to the surgeon's tent and returned with water, bandages and morphine syrup. I didn't ask what he paid. Oren went to find McClellan's Chief Surgeon. It took two hours. He found Dr. Letterman eating lunch. They talked about the medical situation and Oren got a note securing places in an ambulance and beds at the General Hospital in Frederick City.

On the ride to Frederick, I saw, in the most brutal way, the advantage of rank. Our boys rode in a four-wheeled ambulance with two wounded colonels because their fathers and a powerful man came for them. I thought of men whose fathers couldn't come.

Rank was life or death.

The ambulance worked its way out of Keedysville, then through the open hospital of the surrounding country. We saw operating tables, haystacks, lawns covered with wounded men. Doctors, if they were doctors, not "active men"—the stream of butchers, loggers, maniacs who appeared after battles to operate—were busy. Dr. Letterman told Oren that even if amputations were done correctly, "active men" didn't stay to dress or tend the wounded. Amputees lay in barns, houses, haystacks, lawns with no one to care for them.

"Piss on it," said Lorenzo.

Oren shook his head.

I didn't speak and I didn't shut my eyes. Watching a country of untended men made me as angry as at the stable where I received my scar. It mattered nothing who was brave, who a coward, who sacrificed himself. The privileged—officers, the connected, the men whose fathers came—got to hospital, got water, got the chance to survive. I swore again to give no speeches.

Washington City was a sewer. The day after battle, an abattoir. Truth didn't march. It hid. Bravery? Men were butchered on the field and butchered after. Character? Survival was position. Rank. Money.

Maryland stank.

All the way to the nostrils of absent God.

We passed a cart of dead men. A stoic Negro drove the stinking cargo—flies, yellow faces, mangled legs turning black in the sun, bloated stomachs, bulging eyes.

I touched Moreau's face and prayed.

Would Mary forgive me if she saw this?

46

The ambulance stopped at a farmhouse. The lead horse had picked up a stone and the driver wanted to remove it. "Take but a minute." The lawn was covered with wounded. A surgeon and his tent were by the barn, which was white, like the McTavish barn back home in Woodville. Faded Masonic crests were emblazoned over doors that stood open. A stout woman came out. Lorenzo and I checked our sons and went to her. Her blue dress was bloodstained.

"Are you doctors?" she asked.

"No," I said.

"He ain't either." The woman pointed at a big man in a straw hat, brim smudged with blood, bending over a chloroformed corporal. "'Active man' he calls hisself."

"We're here for only a few minutes," said Oren. "What can we do?"

"Give water."

The woman directed us to a pump, buckets and ladles. We each filled a bucket and went in. The barn was dark. The smell was immediate. Rotting flesh. Dead flesh. Manure under scattered straw. My eyes adjusted and I saw rows of men lying on the straw. They lay in rows like harvested wheat. Lorenzo and I each started down a row. Men were covered with lice. I dipped my fingers in the bucket and put water on their lips. I used the dipper when more was requested. They were grateful beyond measure. Eyes. Yellow. Pleading. Desperate to get a message home. I heard moaning and crying. Cursing. Praying. I saw infected stumps. Maggots, worms of the grave, ate the living. My gorge rose.

The driver yelled, “We gotta go!”

As we left, a legless corporal grabbed my foot and said, “Mother.” It took all the man’s strength. “Tell her…” He couldn’t finish. When his grip fell away, I walked quickly so no one else could grab me. Outside, the sun was blinding.

47

The General Hospital in Frederick was crowded, but our boys received good care, some dispensed by Lorenzo and me, some from nurses, male and female, some from regular visits from doctors. It was a terrible struggle for Sergeant and Private Salisbury. Moreau fought infection. I watched a piece of cloth pulled through my son's ankle to clean his wound. It was horrible, but the ankle had not become infected. Merrick ran terrible fevers. Lorenzo left his side only to eat and didn't eat often. The knee remained a big, black ball. Amputation was out of the question. Merrick wouldn't survive it now. If my brother had qualms, he kept them to himself. Lorenzo spent long hours by Merrick's bedside, and if he prayed, he prayed to strange gods.

I nursed Moreau. He frequently asked if I had found the letter pinned inside his shirt, which was to be read only if he died. Each time, I said I found no letter and you aren't going to die.

I watched Lorenzo and Merrick. There was something ungentle about them. It wasn't hurtful or crude. I think Merrick wanted to die hard. That way it was bearable. Die fighting.

I had reason to hope, as long as Moreau's wound wasn't infected and the fevers weren't too high. Moreau liked having his hand held and face wiped. He fought to stay in this world.

Merrick did not. Where was Merrick? What red hills or green

fields had Merrick found? I heard snatches of delirium. Merrick talked to his mother, dead now fifteen years, as if she were there, and maybe she was, in the boy's fever-wracked mind

The surgeon had been right, my brother wrong. Lorenzo had gambled and was losing Merrick. What good were words? What good was anything? The surgeon said Moreau needed a constitution of iron. Everyone in Sandy Creek knew Merrick was stronger. Harder. Indestructible.

Until the cornfield. Even now, men mean only one place, one time, when they say, "the cornfield." They say it with awe, if they say it at all.

Lorenzo changed by the day. He didn't get older, but stranger, though lines in his brow got deeper and his beard more grizzled. Maybe Lorenzo visited the world Merrick had found, a world of delirium filled with snatches of the past, glimpses of things unseen by the rest of us. Merrick repeated, mumbled, incanted words—field, woods, dog, green. I think he babbled about heads on stakes. Maybe the boy was tormented by the old story, maybe I misheard. Wherever Merrick was, Lorenzo understood. Lorenzo didn't curse death. Death didn't make him angry, which surprised me. At first he acted like it was a fight, and Merrick didn't lose fights. Lorenzo staked his son's life on toughness. If Merrick could breathe, he could lick anything. I sat in a ward of wounded soldiers visited by wives, sisters, mothers, fathers, little brothers who smelled of lavender water and soap, by a bed with fresh linen and a son who received fresh bandages, and watched my brother watch his son die. I tried to think of it as a prizefight. Merrick battling, jabbing, keeping Death at arm's length, but the fight tiring him. If Merrick could go fifty rounds, as he did once with a carpenter from Orwell, his opponent could go a hundred. No matter how hard Merrick battled, how bravely he stood, the opponent drew him away.

Then father and son knew it was time to stop. Not quit—they'd never quit—but change tactics, retreat, stop whipping the nag. I watched. I tried to understand.

Lorenzo and Merrick didn't talk to God or Jesus. Father and son shared some other mystery. What approaches when a man dies? What does his father see? Merrick's words didn't fit—green, fields, she, heads, green she-fields. A disappearing puzzle. I heard talk of a black, dancing dog and comrades and rogues and water. Fields. Woods. Merrick was hunting.

He whispered, "Dog. Crick. Dog."

48

For five days Moreau lay in agony, tossing, sweating through the night, talking senselessly. Until now, I hadn't believed Moreau could die. There hadn't been time to confront his death. I hadn't sat with the knowledge of death, but now, in the hospital, holding my son's hand, getting water, talking to doctors, helping nurses, seeing his wound dressed, made me think.

I saw men die. I heard their death rattles, and prayers intoned over their corpses. I saw their bodies taken away, their beds stripped and remade and filled with other wounded men. I watched my brother stare at his dying son.

Ghosts were everywhere.

The nurses were good, medicine the best that could be had. I waited while Moreau tossed in the dark, and hoped his spirit would come back from the place it goes when the body has been broken. I waited, hoped, and prayed for his fever to go down. His letter was in my pocket. I agonized about opening it. I wondered what my son wanted his last words to be. I feared them.

Merrick lay nearby, responding only to his pain and Lorenzo's hand. The room was big and close, two rows of beds, crowded with wounded and dying. Men moaned at night. Visitors tried not to cry. Heavy curtains kept out light. The quilts on Moreau's and Merrick's beds were stained with their blood.

The letter burned in my pocket. What had Moreau been thinking, going into the battle that might be his last? Had he paid his debt to Gib and the heads? Had only comrades mattered? Did he call me coward?

I stroked his face and remembered Mary rocking his cradle, taking him by the hand to church, the child doing chores, ice skating, chasing Rufus, the mill cat. I remembered hunting by the Creek, the boy asking me about God, asking his mother about Christ, the young man arguing. I saw him change from a thin, dutiful child to a questioning seminarian to a man going to war, and now—broken flesh.

Not knowing his last thoughts was unbearable.

Did he blame me as much as I blamed myself? I told myself I had lied to Moreau about the letter to keep him from worry. I lied because I wanted to know what it said.

At night, I listened to Moreau moan in his sleep. I squeezed the letter, torn between fervid curiosity and guilt. I fought myself.

I lost. It took five days.

49

South Mountain

Md

Sept 15, 1862

Dear Father,

If you read this, you will know I have seen God's face. I don't know if you will find me, or this letter. The battlefield takes so much.

I killed two men yesterday. At least two. The Rebs fight hard. They don't seem human. We probably don't to them. Once fighting has begun, no one is.

I don't talk to God anymore, so I'll talk to you. There's a secret I've been carrying, too heavy to carry to the grave. A woman in Washington City had my child. She married a clerk in the Patent Office. He probably thinks the child is his. I haven't tried to find her. What kind of father could I be now? I think about my child often. For some reason, I think Betsey had a son. It fills me with shame. I cannot bear to think how Helen would feel if she found out. I tell you because I want you to know the Salisbury line will continue without me, though not in Sandy Creek. And if a woman and child ever come looking for me, please be kind.

My death wasn't your fault. A man must do right.

I know you will look after Helen and Mother.

Your son,

Moreau Salisbury

50

Moreau's letter was what I believe religious people call an epiphany. He wanted me to know his secret. He thought telling me would help. I milled that. Moreau wanted me to know. This wasn't a promise, a hope, or a prayer. It was an act. I was the person my son told *in extremis*. I was his father. Flawed as I am.

I was never so moved.

That there was a child out of wedlock was no great shock. I had seen enough of Washington City to imagine what transpired there. It also seemed the problem had taken care of itself. We were all lucky for that. Moreau was hurt and sad and guilty. Of course. He was a fine person. That he was not as fine as he had thought was another of life's inevitable disappointments. The kind of disappointment most overcome. One more easily overcome in private conscience than in the glare of public opinion.

My son trusted me. Was this forgiveness? Love? I wouldn't tell Mary the secret. I wouldn't tell Moreau I knew. That would be love too.

For the first time since leaving Sandy Creek, my spirits rose.

51

Five days after the battle, Lincoln issued the Emancipation Proclamation. More was to come.

Mary arrived at the B & O station in Frederick City the next day. I walked from the private home where Moreau and Merrick had been moved to either recover or die. I didn't want to leave Moreau, but Lorenzo was with the boys. I waited in the crowd at the station, watching the rustling elm and maple leaves across the tracks. For a minute I didn't think about the war. What is finer than wind in leaves? A ripe, warm, fall Maryland day—autumn roses, blue hydrangeas, purple asters, yellow black-eyed susan, red cardinal flowers—mocked or comforted those coming to this city of the dead and wounded. It was good to be out of a house of mortality. How quickly does a home become a hospital. Who can domesticate pain or daily break bread with the King of Terrors? In Sandy Creek, our homes were not yet hospitals. Sorrow had not seen broken flesh. Leaves would fall, new frost kill weeds and decorate fields, and the harvest come in.

People lined the tracks and gathered and talked, or, like me, stared at flowers, whispering trees, or down the tracks. Frederick City was busy. Every train brought those who came to comfort and those who needed comfort. And supplies. Wagons waited. Drivers smoked, spat, ready for another load of bandages, morphine and chloroform, and all the sharp accouterments of the medical profession needed in a city staggered by blood. Slaves waited too, not freed by the Proclamation, but heartened by it. You saw it in their faces.

Coffins came. Coffins went. Many still lay unburied in Sharpsburg.

I thought of people coming to help, and took comfort, but I needed Mary, and Mary was needed here. I didn't look at people. I wasn't yet used to suffering faces.

The train came in, hissing and grinding to a stop. People were hanging out its windows. Some yelled for news, others pointed. Some looked lost. Most looked apprehensive. Mary spotted me immediately. I was in front of the stone station tower, waving my hat. Mary almost flew off the train. She pulled up her long skirts, stepped down, and forded the crowd of parents, slaves, soldiers, and porters getting off or rushing to the cars. We pushed toward each other, surrounded by happy greetings, cries of anguish. Tears. A stout lady followed by a Negro yelled, "Am I too late?" and got only a sigh from a stout man. It was a press of the desperate—shouts, sobs, tears, and tears held back.I seized Mary. We held each other as if clutching Moreau's life. For a moment we were one breathing animal, unable to move or let go.

Mary squeezed my hands. "Will Moreau be all right?"

"Yes." I held her. I looked in her eyes. I kissed her.

"I feel strength in you, Mason. Hope."

"You are my hope, Mary."

"You are mine," she said.

"Moreau will be all right," I said. "I'm sure of it."

Mary was here. Two of us now to look death in the face. We were lucky and Moreau was lucky. Many were alone with the angel.

Moreau and Merrick were in a long blue room. Mary crossed the threshold like a creature in flight. She looked at Moreau, kissed him, hugged him carefully, and stroked his hair. Her tears wet his beard. I almost couldn't watch.

Finally she said, "This one will be all right, praise God."

"I shall be, Mother." Moreau's voice was hoarse. Full of pain. And infinitely grateful.

Mary went to Merrick, who got a strange look on his face, then returned to that other place. His other place. Mary said nothing. Merrick's fevered eyes and the smell of his leg unnerved her, but after a hurried glance at me, she hugged Lorenzo, who acknowledged her with a nod and a shrug, as if what might be said were better unsaid. Lorenzo thanked her and took Merrick's hand.

Mary returned to Moreau. They looked and looked. Disbelief and thankfulness in one, sympathy and confidence in the other. It made that crowded, warm room bearable.

She stayed the night with Moreau. In the morning she watched how the cloth was threaded through his ankle and worked back and forth, and she saw his pain when the morphine wore off.

"I will do it when we leave," she said.

When we were alone, Mary laid her head against my shoulder. She was exhausted. She closed her eyes and said, "Now my battle starts." Her clothing was wrinkled. The hem of her dress was smudged with soot; bread crumbs stuck to her lap. I smelled her perspiration.

"You look tired," she said, opening her eyes. "Your hair is whiter." She smiled.

"Perhaps," I said.

She touched my mouth and cheeks. "Your trip was harder than mine."

"You look splendid," I said softly.

She closed her eyes and some of the worry left her face. Her hair was tied in a bun. Her gentle face was lined with fatigue. Pronounced wrinkles showed below her clear eyes and dark furrows creased her pale cheeks. Would we ever look like the proud couple of two weeks ago?

No matter. She was here.

"We have hope," Mary said, opening her eyes. "And the Lord. That is all we need."

"I have seen things I cannot tell," I said. "I cannot imagine what our son has seen. You will see things too. You will hear."

"You needn't tell," said Mary. "I saw his wound. I need know nothing more."

"There is something I must say. I sent my son to do what I could not, and I can barely look at what is wrought. I believe in the Cause, I believe in the men, but I cannot ask another man or mother or father to send a boy to the field. I will not give another speech. I will not stand for election. This is all the courage I have."

Mary stroked my hair. "You needn't sacrifice your career."

"I'm done with politics. Done with talk. It's what I owe. What I owe all of them."

"You must forgive yourself, Mason. Even if the worst comes. We are here and this is all we can do."

"Amen," I said.

"Everything has changed, Mason."

"No, Mary. You haven't."

52

The next night Mary saw a phantom—not a ghost; ghosts are for mourners, not nurses. Mary saw a man with a large hat and large beard. She saw him, very late, coming out of the room of a dying man. The man looked at Mary. He was soft. Soft eyes, soft hands. Kind, but stealthy. He made her uneasy. Mary feared a thief, but the man wasn't stealing. He seemed used to this reaction. bowed slightly and gave her a book, saying, "This will help."

Mary didn't read the book. I did. I don't know if it's proper to call it poetry, but the man was right. It helped. After speeches and sermons, arguments and hot political words, this was different.

> You shall no longer take things at second or third hand....nor look
> through the eyes of the dead.... nor feed on spectres in
> books,
> You shall not look through my eyes either, nor take things from me,
> You shall listen to all and filter them from yourself.

53

On a day in October, three weeks after the battle, Merrick was in less pain, but cold. He knew where he was and who was around him. He was happy to see Mary and held up his hand to Moreau. He said, "Comrade," and lay back. Lorenzo stayed by Merrick's side. No one intruded. Lorenzo stroked his son's hair, wiped his son's face and held his hand. That night, while Moreau slept, Merrick died.

Lorenzo stayed by the bed. I went into the night and cried.

The next morning, Lorenzo put a hand on my shoulder and said, "He's going home."

Lorenzo bought a wagon, an oak casket, and a pair of white mules. I don't know who embalmed Merrick. I helped my brother put the casket in the wagon. I hugged him and felt an inconsolable strangeness. Each of us had gambled. It turned out right for only one of us.

Lorenzo shaved his beard and drove away. I wasn't sure I would ever see him again. Had there been fighting, I believe he would have driven into it. But there wasn't, so Lorenzo, wagon, white mules and casket started down the crowded road. A company of Zouaves took off their caps.

Mason

Maryland to Christmas

October-December

1862

54

By the end of October, three weeks after Merrick's death, Antietam had been declared a victory. That was the talk in Frederick City and the northern papers. Militarily the battle was a draw. The chance to destroy Lee's army was squandered, as McClellan did not pursue it into Virginia. I heard from a captain that McClellan had the "slows." Lee was allowed to rest a whole day before recrossing the Potomac. The captain didn't like it. His men didn't like it. Lincoln didn't like it. The general sat in Maryland proclaiming himself savior of the Union and one of the great men of history. The President visited, stewed, and asked McClellan if he didn't mind lending him the Army since the general didn't seem to have any use for it.

In November, Lincoln fired McClellan. The general had played his last great role. Certain officers urged McClellan to stage a *coup-d'état*, but instead Little Mac bowed out gracefully. The cautious, vain, little man who had whipped an army into shape but could not fight, was at his best saying goodbye.

A week after Lincoln removed McClellan, we took Moreau home. We traveled by ambulance to Baltimore, where we stayed in a private residence while Moreau gathered strength, then by rail to the North Country. It was too soon. The trip was hard, but we wanted our son home. We wanted him in the room off the parlor where nothing moved in the dark, no one moaned, screamed, wept, or died. Home, we thought, was the place to heal.

Trains rocked. The waiting between trains was awful. Morphine helped. Sometimes we thought Moreau was lost, already in the place that had taken Merrick. Moreau's skin was yellowish, his nose sharper. I was gambling with his life again. But not only for him. We wanted Moreau away from the dying. We all needed home.

When we reached Philadelphia, his fever rose. We gave him morphine and wiped his face. Mary prayed. We held his hand through the night and feared we should have stayed in Frederick City.

Everywhere people were kind, helpful, and respectful. Here was a soldier and his parents. Here the Union. Here America. So many gone. So many to go. No end, Mary said. No end in sight.

At New York, Moreau was switched to a passenger car of the Hudson River Railroad for the trip to Albany. He was feverish, soaked with sweat. The car had been outfitted for stretchers. They were stacked three high, like bunks, fitted neatly on scaffolding. I didn't see one loosen or fall. They were well built and we secured a lower berth. Mary and I took turns standing or sitting on the floor to be at his side. Other parents did the same with their own sons. We wiped Moreau's flushed face, held his hand when he tossed on his cot. I told him he would live. I told him I loved him. Sometimes he didn't hear.

Moreau had what we could buy for him, quinine and morphine. I thanked absent God for Mary. She had cared for both boys, now one. She cared for me. Men make the world. Women hold it together.

As the Hudson RR car rocked towards home, Moreau fought for his life. It was a hard, hard fight. A fight with pain and infection. A fight to see how much a body could stand. It was hell, especially as we waited at crossings, for couplings, to change cars in Philadelphia, New York City, Albany, Rome. The world moved, but not on time.

Mary prayed. She knelt, her lips moving, on worn-out railroad carpet, scuffed planks, dusty baggage. Moreau was in God's hands, but her own never stopped. If Moreau died, it would be God's will. God wasn't cruel or absent for Mary. Moreau was alive and Mary was caring for him. That's all she asked. Without God, she believed, he'd be dead already.

I worried about Lorenzo. He would drive that wagon home or die. It was his choice. Lorenzo had Merrick and solitude. Lorenzo said he'd bring the boys home. I shook my head.

When the train chuffed by West Point, Moreau opened his eyes. His pain was eased by morphine and he said, "I will see Helen soon."

"She's waiting for you," I said.

"I got her letters."

"She's changed. Older. Not such a girl."

"I've changed." Moreau closed his eyes.

"We're all changed," I said. "But you, Merrick, all of you, did what had to be done."

"For now." Moreau sighed.

"Lee struck north to get British recognition. Oren heard from Seward. The Rebels can't win without British recognition."

"Less we quit." He looked away.

"They'll be no quit after your victory."

"Our victory," Moreau said quietly, and closed his eyes.

"If you'd lost, if Lee had got to Harrisburg or Philadelphia, there'd be noise to quit. That won't happen now. Seward says the Emancipation Proclamation is the end for British recognition of the Confederacy."

"Emancipation," Moreau said. "I wonder if Gib heard?"

I wondered too.

Moreau slept as we chugged by the broad, sparkling Hudson River.

The Proclamation had come out of that awful battle. How many times had I said Emancipation was worth dying for, if anything was? How often had I urged men to die for it? It was here and men were dying. I had helped sow the wind and my son and brother's son had reaped the whirlwind. I felt like one of Job's comforters.

I saw war.

Not battle, not the seconds of blood-splattered insanity, unreal and deadly, but the other part. The other ninety-nine percent of it. Supply trains, sutlers' wagons, railroad stations, jammed cities, dealmakers, Washington City. I saw it. I smelled it. What is talk compared to the real thing? The real thing is maimed men. The real thing is surgeons, men on the ground, on boards, dying, dead. It's ambulance drivers, medical wagons, and stretcher bearers. The real thing is a son beyond help, beyond all but pain. It isn't in newspapers or speeches. Most people don't see or know.

The real thing is women and men who nurse the wounded, stay with the bereaved and don't allow the dying to die alone. The real thing is endurance.

55

When the New York, Oswego & Watertown train left Utica, Moreau talked about Helen. His glazed, dark eyes burned with happiness. He was animated. He was better—though only temporarily, I feared. The memory of Helen, a phantasmagoria of need, romance, and love, floated in his feverish eyes and the hoarse timbre of his low voice. I saw what he carried, invented, had to have. Then his strength ebbed, pain returned, and we gave him morphine. He rested fitfully.

Miss Warriner and my son had turned each others' heads. Mary and I once had doubts about how serious an afternoon and a blanket might be, unless it brought a baby, which it did not. I believe Mary wished it had, especially after little Wilbur Corse rode down Railroad Street, tears streaming, crying for his brother, dead at Second Bull Run.

While Moreau was gone—fifteen long months—Helen called often. She brought corn, tomatoes, honey and pies. She brought pies and then made them with Mary. She brought a gentle nature and ready wit. We got to know the young woman and the young woman got to know us. In a way, Helen knew us better than she knew Moreau. Mary called Helen the Intended, then Faithful Intended, without irony. Mary approved of Helen.

For Helen, knowing Mary helped and knowing Mary hurt. In Mary, Helen saw fear and the determination not to show it. Together, the two gathered lint for bandages, sewed blankets, darned socks, discussed every syllable of Moreau's letters. Helen came to know the enormity of Mary's worry. Helen saw the depth and seriousness of worrying about a man away at war. It wasn't what Mary said, much of which could have graced Mr. Currier and Ives' cards, but her glances at nothing, an occasional sob in the pantry, the way Mary pronounced his name.

Ro's letters said his memory of Helen sustained him and Helen believed it. Ro's memory was her core, hers must be his. A man or a woman needs faith. *Is faith the filter the poet spoke of? The Lord for Mary? A wounded man for Helen? A son for me?* Why not in the most important person in your life? Helen believed Ro held onto his soul by loving her. She understood from his letters—what they said and what they didn't—that war takes more than an arm or a leg. It takes souls. Wears them down. Wears them away. War made men weary because it was worse than what they tell, worse than what they can tell. Worse in ways Helen couldn't understand. The men were exhausted, trying to keep their souls. What did Ro have but memories? What memory is stronger than love? Helen believed she was the keeper of his soul. I hoped she was.

Then Lorenzo, Oren and I went to Washington. Mary and Helen worried in a new way. This was a crisis. This was beyond words in the papers, the telegraph, or prayers in church. One generation was going for another. It felt like judgment, even for a Congregationalist with her clear conscience and good works. Lorenzo said he'd bring the boys back. Helen knew they only came back dead or wounded. Men all over the North Country were going for their sons.

Then word came Ro and Merrick were wounded. It came from me. This was no rumor. Both in jeopardy. Come quickly. Helen wanted to come, but Mary was against it. Helen had to stay for Lucius and her blind brother, Wallace. "I will telegraph," Mary said. "You shall meet us."

Now Moreau and Helen would meet again. Expectations and battered flesh.

After our terrible journey, we arrived in Sandy Creek on a cold November night. Mary telegraphed, requesting no crowd, but asked for Helen and our cousins Violet and Sara to meet us at the station. MacGregor, the Scotsman who watched the mill, would bring the wagon. Mary asked please, please, no crowds. She said Moreau wasn't well.

Mary was exhausted. She wouldn't stop or complain or get sick until Moreau was well, but she needed home. The inexhaustible can be exhausted.

Helen told me about the night we returned. Her father Lucius drove the Warriner buggy to the station to meet us. Lucius had a stone-cutting business and the war brought profit as it brought others grief. Whenever Helen challenged this, Lucius smiled and admitted it was easier to accept the profitable. Lucius was sharp. He adapted. Like his ancestor who played the fife in the Revolution.

That night father and daughter drove up South Main Street. They said nothing. Helen wished the town grander. She wondered how it would look to Ro, and how *she* would look to Ro. The velvet pouch was around her neck. Then she thought: Oh, God, these things don't matter. Helen didn't want to think about what mattered. *Would Moreau live?*

Lucius turned onto Railroad Street and passed the Salisbury neo-classical "domicile" with its attic dormer and Tuscan columns. Lights blazed. Sara and Violet, now Mrs. Norman Scripture, had left for the station after tidying, straightening and cleaning the whole place in preparation for Moreau's arrival. A hired girl watched the lamps.

The Warriner buggy joined a line of buggies, many more than expected, heading for the station under the leafless branches of elms and maples. A sudden, cold wind rose and whipped dead leaves, grit and twigs into a frantic canopy. The horse balked and Lucius pulled hard on the reins. Branches danced. Leaves spun and whirled. Shutters banged and lanterns swung against the sides of buggies. Helen thought of playing cards tossed in the air. It scared her. She clutched the velvet pouch. Railroad Street was a gigantic, whirling wreath. Houses deserted, stars gone, the night mad. Then it stopped.

Many, many times had Helen imagined this home-coming. Once a week she hitched the horse to the buggy and rode to the spot by the creek where she turned from girl to woman, flirt to lover, gossip to confidante. Helen had listened to a man, understood a man, and felt like a woman. Had the war ended quickly, she could have embraced her dream—the dream created hourly in her imagination—part truth, part imagination, all enchantment, as her eighteen-year-old mind created a warrior and knight out of her soldier.

The young woman meeting the train had left her youth in our parlor and kitchen. She left it in the letters that might have been sent to a dead man. She left it in awe of the world's cruelty.

The train pulled in, cinders flying. Helen thought of sinners fleeing hell, but kept the notion to herself. She touched her face, worrying about how she looked, and scolded herself. The engine stopped beyond the station and people crowded the tracks, waving to the train windows. Despite Mary's request for few spectators, there were many Salisburys, all wearing their best. Uncles, cousins, aunts, neighbors. They cheered and danced as cinders shot through the dark. Salisburys waved in the wind-shaken light of station lamps and uneven yellow light from the cars. Some raised and lowered lanterns. Benjamin Franklin Salisbury waved a flag. Reuben Salisbury took off his hat. Deacon Enos Salisbury said a prayer. Cousins waved handkerchiefs, boys raced beside the train, men raised flasks, women cried, and babies squealed. A sign said, "Your Home Ro."

I got off first, then Mary. Two men in uniform brought off the stretcher bearing Moreau.

"Stand back, friends," I said.

Helen thought we looked thinner. Our eyes were too bright. Our cheeks pale and drawn. Hair unwashed. My beard ungodly white. Mary's face was alert, pinched and worn. Helen thought we looked like we'd been in the underworld. If that's what we looked like, what would Ro look like?

The crowd separated for Helen, Sara and Violet. Amiable, detached Lucius wept in spite of himself. I forgave a lot for that. The crowd quieted. Helen rushed to the stretcher and put her hand to Moreau's cheek. He looked up, smiled and closed his eyes. His face so pale, beard so ragged, eyes sunk in pain, was angelic with relief.

"Let us pass, friends," I said. "We're all right."

Ro's cousins stroked his hair. He didn't look all right.

I recognized Helen's expression. Bravery crossing a face not used to being brave. It was beautiful.

"Speech, Mason! Speech!" cried the Salisburys.

I didn't give a speech.

56

In the days that followed, Moreau's life hung in a balance of fever, hope, advance and retreat. We took turns at night, sitting with him. I didn't pray. I didn't think Moreau would die. He was home, away from the bullets and the noise and the surgeons—away from battle and the battles to come. I couldn't bear the thought that Moreau might die. I knew whose fault that would be. No filter for that.

Helen visited daily, frequently spending days at a time at our house. She held Ro's hand and felt his strength begin to return. Helen changed his clothes, washed him and whispered to him. She whispered when he was awake, asleep, or delirious.

He needed her. He needed us. Didn't he?

"Live," Helen whispered. "Please live."

Ro heard, and fought.

"For Mason. For Mary. For me." That was Helen's prayer, if prayer is, as she believed, the deepest appeal to the deepest power. Helen didn't abandon or blame God; she did what was humanly possible. All she asked was for Ro to come home with arms, legs and a face, and maybe they weren't so important. She asked for a chance to make him well. She would render unto God what was God's later.

Moreau rocked with fever. When he didn't sleep, we didn't. When he called, we answered. He sweated; we washed. Every day was filled with concern, bandages, and morphine.

But he was home.

There was the matter of his ankle. It had to be cleaned every day, and this was done as the surgeon in Keedysville said. A piece of cloth was run through it. At first Dr. Bulkley did it. Mary provided silk, which she cleaned daily, boiled and ironed it, as if she couldn't bare the sight of his blood on it. After a week, Mary took over cleaning the wound. I watched her unwrap the ankle, sponge the wound with a warm, damp cloth, attach a strip of clean silk to a darning needle, and put the needle through his ankle. Moreau would groan or turn, never cry. Mary would remove the needle and pull two feet of silk through the wound, back and forth, until she was sure it was clean. The wound had to be kept from closing on the surface. This kept it from becoming infected. It had to close from inside and stay clean. The process would take a year, if Moreau lived.

I couldn't do it. I tried. I jabbed my son with the needle and couldn't hold it steady. The wound bled and Moreau twisted away. I stopped. My hand shook. After failing, I couldn't watch. This was cowardice. Unfiltered. *Look at what he did. Look at what you can't do.* I had seen many wounds in Maryland, but could not tend one in Sandy Creek.

From then on, his mother did it.

The sick room was off the parlor. The room was kept as clean as the wound. Between Mary, Helen and Sara, Moreau couldn't have been cared for better by a band of angels. I held his hand. I told him I loved him. I told him I admired and respected him, but I could not clean his wound, and we did not speak of it. His eyes spoke. We did not.

The cleaning of the wound was done in the morning, if Moreau could stand it then. It was done in the afternoon, if he felt stronger. Never at night. Mary did it after I left the house. She wouldn't let Helen do it. She said Helen did enough. Helen's job was to be wonderful, to give Moreau the certainty and confidence a man needed to be a man.

57

On Christmas Day, a month and a half after returning home, Moreau opened his eyes and said, “Helen.” The fever was gone. His hair was no longer slick with sweat. Color had returned to his face. His eyes were clear. The pallor of the other world had receded. He looked at his mother and said, “Merry Christmas.” We celebrated with glasses of Madeira. Mary kissed me and said, “You may rest easier, Mason.”

I was toasting President Lincoln, and telling myself: Saved! Not guilty!—and would have finished the bottle when word came that Lorenzo was on the Salt Road. Our neighbor, Norman Scripture, said my brother, two white mules, the wagon with a flag-draped casket and a tombstone dusted with snow, had been seen an hour ago. The short-stocked shotgun was across his lap. He didn’t respond to greeting.

Mary and I took the sleigh. It was cold. Snow was five feet in the fields and higher by the side of the road. The town tried to be gay for Christmas with red and green ribbons, American flags, and big wreaths on the front doors. Through the bubbles and swirls of imperfect glass, we saw candles in tiny sconces balanced on the branches of freshly cut fir trees. The German custom had arrived in Sandy Creek. People found magic in bringing a green tree into a house to celebrate Christ’s birth and rebirth.

58

News of Lorenzo reached his farm before he did. Catherine, his wife of fifteen years, wasn't comforted by the word that her husband was close to home. She hadn't heard from Lorenzo since he left Frederick City. Catherine said she stood in her kitchen and watched the wagon, two mules, and a man who looked old as grief approach the house. He got closer and she saw the ancient family gun across his lap, a snow-covered flag over a coffin, and a stone, also snow-covered, that made the wagon list left. He wasn't wearing a hat or gloves.

Lorenzo drove to the stable, got down and walked like a man whose feet hadn't recently touched ground. Jean and Dany, the hired men, came out of the stable. Catherine came out, a red and white apron her only protection against the driving snow, and stood, hands clasped, head bowed, as the men acknowledged each other. The men straightened the flag, took the casket out of the wagon, and carried it into the stable. They placed it on two sawhorses under a rusty lantern hanging from a beam.

Lorenzo waved Jean and Dany away and went to Catherine. He carried the shotgun in his left arm. "Thank you for running the farm," he said, and went in the stable and closed the doors. He did not touch her.

Catherine let snow pelt her face, then turned and went in the house. His eyes looked dead to her. She stood at the kitchen window and watched a red-tailed hawk circle high over the white fields and thought the bird, like Lorenzo, had no place to go.

This is what I believed happened.

In the solitude of the stable, Lorenzo put the shotgun, stock down, against a leg of a sawhorse. He brushed snow off the flag, lifted a corner, and touched the casket. He looked at the lantern. A rooster pecked at feed in the trampled straw. Four horses shook their heads and neighed. Forty cows paid no attention. Sparrows roosting for the winter crowded the rafters.

Lorenzo knelt. “Poor boy,” he said. “You’re home.”

He picked up the shotgun and ran his hands over the barrels, knocking off a crust of ice. He pulled back each hammer with his thumb. The noise brought a cry from the rooster. Lorenzo put the gun in his mouth. His aching body relaxed. He took comfort in the icy metal. Lorenzo had a covenant. He would drive Merrick home and kill himself. Lorenzo would drive so all might see. He would not wear a hat.

Merrick’s mother lay in Stevens Cemetery, the little burying ground on the Orwell Road. Merrick would lie there too. He wouldn’t be alone.

Before leaving Frederick City, Lorenzo had gone to Captain Ferguson. In a letter home, Merrick told Lorenzo he’d given the shotgun to the Captain before Antietam. Lorenzo found Ferguson in a private home, recovering from wounds received at South Mountain. The Captain shook Lorenzo’s hand and said, “He told me to give it back to you.”

“Thank you.”

“He said you’d come for it.”

“I come for him,” said Lorenzo.

“He said so.”

Merrick wanted Lorenzo to have the gun. He must have thought it would protect his father, if not himself. Lorenzo thought that on the way home. What good would the ancient weapon have been in the cornfield? What good, when all were equal before death?

Lorenzo had always told Merrick, "Don't be scared. Be prepared."

Lorenzo drove through rain, past ripe orchards, kept away from cities, accepted only feed for the mules, water for himself. People understood. In the town of Lancaster, Pennsylvania, a man came out with an American flag and said, "If you would, please," and draped the flag over the casket. "My boy was killed outside Richmond. We didn't get him back. Been savin' this." So Lorenzo took the flag. No slavers, no brother, just casket, covenant and flag. The gun meant, "I will come. I will follow. Anywhere."

The night he died, Merrick said, "It ain't your fault. You done what I asked. You didn't let them cut."

"I chose wrong," Lorenzo said.

"If I'd a had the gun, that surgeon'd be dead."

Lorenzo stroked his son's hair.

"I seen men die of shock after amp'tation. Let me die here with you."

"You're a brave man," Lorenzo said.

"I wanted to be like you," said Merrick.

The night brought higher fever, moaning, and talk of a woman. The end was near. The delirium broke before dawn and again Merrick said, "I wanted to be like you."

"I wasn't a soldier," said Lorenzo.

"You was always a soldier."

Lorenzo, for the only time anyone had ever seen, wept.

In the stable, the freezing metal of the gun stuck to Lorenzo's lips, tongue, the roof of his mouth.

"I'm coming," he whispered.

The gun had a last enemy. Grief.

Lorenzo's finger stuck to the double triggers. He opened his mouth and pulled his tongue off the barrel. Skin came off. Tongue and lips stung.

Covenant.

Lorenzo pulled the triggers.

59

On our way to Lorenzo's farm, Mary and I drove past familiar fields, familiar even under snow. The runners of the sleigh hummed as they glided over the packed and rolled Salt Road. *What would I say to my brother?* After a lifetime of brother talk, what could I say on this hard Christmas day? Who could have imagined Keedysville?

John Brown's back swayed in the clear, cold, Christmas afternoon. Mary huddled against me. Lorenzo's life had changed. The supreme moment hadn't involved courage, fighting or talk. Only luck. Readiness wasn't all. No solace in this divinity. No comfort in this end. What filter could my brother have?

Could I help him? Wind stung my face.

"Mary, I didn't let the surgeon amputate because I couldn't bear to watch. My cowardice saved Moreau's leg."

"Does it matter?"

I prodded John Brown, whose breath rose in short puffs. "It might to Lorenzo."

"I don't think so, Mason."

I looked at the frozen fields. "Everything dies, rests, grows again," I said. "Except children. The Lord does not give them back."

Mary sat hard by me, hood pulled neatly around her tired face. I felt her warmth. I was glad she was with me.

"Our son lived," I said. "It wasn't fair."

"That was not up to us," said Mary.

I squeezed her. It was luck. That was all.

The woods were thick and dark. The town once put a bounty of fifty cents on wolves. Once there were bears. Once no one lived between the lake and Tug Hill in winter. Only wolves, bears, foxes, mice tunneling under snow. Only animals that survive winter, storms that pile snow twenty feet high, and winds howling at zero. Was Ro ready for winter? Would Lorenzo ever leave?

"Moreau has left the valley of the shadow," said Mary. "I believe Merrick sent him back."

"He came back for you," I said. "And Helen."

"And you, Mason."

Was that true?

The sleigh hummed, hissed and bumped over the Salt Road. Snow melted on our faces and dusted the tracks and ruts in the rolled highway. Trees cracked with the cold, a quick, harsh sound. Winter breaks everything.

"The boys returned today," I said trembling, as we approached Lorenzo's farm.

"Will Lorenzo shoot himself?"

Mary's openness shocked me. I had feared it since Lorenzo left Frederick City. "Not until Merrick is buried."

"Talk to him, Mason."

John Brown kept a steady pace and we drove in silence. The neighbors said Lorenzo was carrying the family gun on his lap. How did Lorenzo get that damn thing? I'd thought it lost in Maryland. Jesus, it might explode if fired. The gun wasn't a weapon, but a talisman. I shuddered.

"It wasn't Lorenzo's fault," I said. "He just chose wrong."

"It wasn't yours," said Mary. "It was in God's hands."

I shook my head no. No. God was not to blame. God wasn't there. We made our choices. They were hard, but they were ours. I could not face my brother and talk about God. I brushed snow from my beard.

"It could have been different, Mary. All of it. Lorenzo could have killed the man who whipped me. Moreau might have stayed at Seminary. Merrick might have lived."

Wind chafed my face. My eyes teared.

"Just talk to him," said Mary.

We saw smoke rise from the chimney of Lorenzo's house. The wagon was in front of the stable. The wind picked up, scattering particles of snow. The red stable doors were open. The wagon was empty save for the tombstone. Snow stuck on the embossed letters MERRICK SALISBURY that curved across the top of the stone, and on the numerals 1837-1862. I couldn't read the rest. I put my hand on Mary's shoulder, then got out of the buggy.

Lorenzo walked out of the stable. His boots left prints in new snow. I saw an old man. *Where is the gun?* Lorenzo's hair was whiter than the snow sprinkled on his beard and coat. His face was a mask of the face I knew. The lines around his eyes might have been cut with a trowel. *Where is the gun?* The beard was thick, untrimmed, spackled with ice. The eyes were blank. His lips were chapped and bleeding. *Where is the damn gun?* Lorenzo stopped two paces in front of me.

"He's in the stable," said Lorenzo.

"I'm sorry," I said.

Lorenzo didn't move.

"Christmas," I said.

"Is it?"

We stared.

I looked in the stable. The casket, draped with a snow-matted flag, rested on sawhorses. The lantern moved in the wind. Had Lorenzo slept in the wagon? Had he never left Merrick? The short-barreled shotgun in the straw. A rooster pecked at it. I had to get that gun.

"Damn thing jammed," Lorenzo said. He turned away. "I'll bury him in the spring."

It was an old man's voice. Not weak. Old.

"Do I have your word?" I said. Lorenzo knew exactly what I meant.

"Yes."

Snow blew horizontally between us. Cold, brilliant, sparkling. I watched my brother's footprints blow away. The red-tailed hawk made a high, wide circle. I looked in Lorenzo's eyes. Empty as wind. My brother. I hugged him but he didn't seem to notice. He was seeing with the eyes of the dead.

Mason

Helen in Winter

January-February

1863

60

In the weeks after Christmas, when Helen wasn't helping, she was staring at Ro's face. Fever finally gone, he was between agony and bliss. He looked at her and perused her face as Ophelia says Hamlet perused hers, as though he would draw it. Ro stroked her hands; Helen stroked his. Their eyes met and played and danced. He drank morphine and slept, and Helen watched. She had drawn that face in her mind many times. Ro looked terrible—scraggly beard, pale yellow face, ribs showing—but that was changing. What hells had he been loosed from? We could only guess. But now he was getting color and gaining weight. Ro would be what Helen wanted and Helen wanted a soldier, a poet, a lover. She wanted intimacy. She had been faithful. She couldn't have been more faithful had Ro been at her side those fifteen months. She loved him. Anyone could see that. And he loved her. His letters said so; now his eyes did. It was a miracle of faith, hers and his. Hamlet says, "You shall know I am set naked on your kingdom." Their kingdom was before them. So we thought. So we tried to think.

Helen watched and stroked him. She loved a certain expression of disbelief that flickered around his eyes. He had been in Hell, now he was here and they were together. Ro had paid the price. That's what I wanted to believe. The price for being a Salisbury. And for being my son. Whether for heads on stakes, me, Gib, his conscience, his pards, it didn't matter now. He was safe. Let wind howl, snow pelt, and creek freeze, Moreau was safe. I wouldn't tell his secret. *Let everything be as it was.*

On New Year's Day while Moreau slept, Helen found me in the parlor. Mary had retired upstairs. Helen joined me on the sofa in front of a roaring fire, declined a glass of port, and asked, "Must sons always ransom a father's love?" Moreau was out of danger now, and Helen, apparently, was free to speak her mind.

"Yes," I said. "I suppose they do."

"Always?"

"I suppose," I said.

"It's eternal?" A hint of Warriner irony.

"Eternal as memory," I said.

"'I have some rights of memory in this kingdom,'" she said.

"Yes," I said, impressed that she had quoted Fortinbras, last witness to the slaughter in Elsinore. "Yes, Miss Warriner, you have rights."

"Has Ro paid the debt for the heads?" she said quickly.

"How can I say?" I said.

"You sent him to war."

"It wasn't for that."

"No," she said. "It was for being a Salisbury. For being your son."

"I could tell you it was the Lord's will, the price for slavery, or the pound of flesh I took for my ambition. They are all true."

I expected, and deserved, a quarrel. She had reason. But she surprised me.

"We all sent him," she said, quietly. "It was right, wasn't it, Mr. Salisbury?"

"It was right," I said. *It must be. It had to be.*

"I felt so righteous," said Helen, slowly. "So proud."

The fire lowered and rose, illuminating her handsome profile. She looked at me and looked away.

"He's a better man than I am," I said.

We didn't speak for a while.

"I wanted him to go before I even knew him," she said. "I wanted a soldier. It was long ago."

So Helen carried guilt too. Helen saw deep under deep, and felt deep under deep. I could see why my son loved her.

"Moreau went for many reasons," I said. "You came to the mill for many reasons."

"I worry," she said simply. "I want everything to be perfect."

"Amen," I said, wondering if anything could be the same.

We were quiet again.

"You get what you want, Mr. Salisbury."

"So do you, Miss Warriner. And I'm glad for it."

61

January got harder. Moreau was physically better, though in pain. Now he battled sadness. I don't know how else to put it. Helen had been right to worry. Deep in the night we heard screams. He suffered restless sleep and bad dreams. He was irritable. We knew he would live and we were thankful, but he had sorrow and anger. Was it the child? His dead comrades? Guilt about being alive when Merrick was dead? Anger at me? His anger was triggered by mundane, unintentional acts. A spilled glass. The smell of mutton. The question, "How are you?" was a provocation. Lord knows he was entitled to his moods, but we wondered, Why now and why us? I knew his secret, but didn't understand his agony. It couldn't be just that. He had Helen and Mother and me. He was home.

Helen sat by the bed in the room off the parlor and felt, palpably felt, the truth that sets men free, but her man wasn't free. In January She began to worry that the debt hadn't been paid, and that raised the question of what debt or debts, and how they might be paid. I feared our Intended began to suspect that love has its limits.

There was talk President Lincoln might declare the old Pilgrim holiday of Thanksgiving a national holiday, but he didn't. Few thought the country had much to be thankful for. We kept our thankfulness at home out of respect for grieving families. Many [had] lost sons and never recovered their bodies. Men disappeared into the war. We were grateful, but privately. Mary slept through the night, and sometimes during the day. Her health was breaking. She had given everything. Helen bathed her soldier now, but she did not string. Mary forbade it. She was trying to keep Helen innocent of bloody needles and bloody silk. Mary wanted someone to remain innocent. We needed an innocent.

Mary saw the change in Moreau and said, "God brought us this far. He will bring us farther." Her voice, if not her faith, was at the point of exhaustion. If she meant, "I can do no more," I didn't contradict her. Mary gave all she could give, and if that wasn't enough, God help us.

Helen was troubled and hurt. Why was Moreau angry and distant? Was it her? What wasn't she doing? What hadn't she done? Did he doubt her love? She would never, never, doubt his, so this must be her fault. Moreau deserved to be happy. She deserved to be happy. They had earned it, and she was doing everything she could, but... Sorrow. Troubled nights. Vacant days. Irritation.

Moreau slept, day in, day out.

He said it wasn't Helen.

What then?

Me?

He wouldn't say.

There were fine moments. Helen enjoyed washing him. When had heating water ever been such heaven? Helen touched him and what she hadn't touched, she'd seen. The expression "big man" brought a smile to her lips. Mary told me. Helen had a sly smile that seemed to say, I don't have to be good now. In February, that smile disappeared.

Had they done something they shouldn't have? No one on earth would say they shouldn't, but was that troubling them? Had something of the flesh come between them? I couldn't say.

It was best when Moreau was asleep. Awake was difficult. He was frequently in pain. Mary still forbade Helen to see the wound cleaned. Helen was glad she didn't have to watch. She said she could do it, but watching would be difficult. Moreau drank morphine, so the stringing didn't hurt. Mary did it, and afterward he slept.

One morning I watched Mary arrange Ro's hair as he slept.

"Children," she said, "are beautiful when they sleep."

It was lovely, watching her watch him. Moreau would always be her child. She had worried, nursed, prayed, seen Merrick die, cared for me, and now, lost, hurt, and angry, Moreau was hers again. A fine thing. The only thing. His mother could bear all.

"They fuss and fuss when they're awake," Mary said. "Our reward is their sleep."

Helen smiled. "Father says anyone who's raised a two-year-old understands devils and angels."

"Devils and angels," Mary said, her smile bright. "That's God's truth." Mary patted my shoulder on her way out. I hoped she was going to sleep, as she often didn't at night.

"Father says the devil is not paid with smiles," Helen said. "Do you believe in the devil?"

"No."

"I don't believe in Hell," Helen said. "If such a place exists, it's empty. Jesus didn't come so people might be thrown into fire. Men make Hell. Men must get out of it."

"My brother's there now," I said.

"The terrible battles," Helen said. "The wounds. That's hell enough." Her voice trembled. "If we love God, and keep Jesus' words, we needn't fear."

"Thy will be done," I said.

Helen stroked her sleeping soldier, and smiled a smile that might bribe the angels.

It wasn't angels that needed to be bribed.

62

Mary and I didn't visit Lorenzo in January or February. Catherine said he didn't want visitors. I thought he didn't want to see me. Lorenzo was fighting and Lorenzo fought alone. We would wait. The ground was too frozen to bury Merrick. The casket remained in the barn. Whatever peace my brother would make, he would make with Merrick.

"Lorenzo will be all right," Catherine said.

Then one brutally cold February day, word came from Catherine that we must come. She didn't have to say why. I wanted to believe my brother was indestructible, but I'd thought that about Merrick.

We hitched John Brown to the sleigh and drove into a cold, snowy afternoon.

Wind whipped snow off the drifts and raised glistening clouds in the fields. I made John Brown go faster. It was a long hour.

Catherine ran out to meet us, apron flying in the wind. She had been watching from the kitchen.

"He's in the barn. He won't come out. He's got that damn gun."

The barn door stood open. Snow blew sideways in a colder wind, crossing lake, fields, town, and woods.

Mary got out of the sleigh. She muttered, "I'm coming. Damn it, I'm coming." I had never heard her swear before.

I followed her into the barn. Lorenzo knelt in front of the casket.

The short-stocked shotgun leaned against the casket, which sat on two sawhorses. Cows shivered. A horse whinnied. Chickens hopped and a sparrow flew into the barn. The day was freezing, the light dying.

Mary went to Lorenzo—all the tears she couldn't cry over Moreau came to her eyes. "Stop this, Lorenzo! You have a wife! A brother!" She sat next to Lorenzo and put her arms around him.

Lorenzo didn't move. He didn't look at her.

She tried again. "We loved Merrick. We all did. But you have to go on living. All of us together. Are you listening, Lorenzo?"

Lorenzo didn't move.

"I was there when he was born and I was there when he died. Damn it, Lorenzo, we love you!"

She was angry. My angel wife. With the suddenness of a rope snapping, She slapped Lorenzo. He closed his eyes.

A strange, full minute passed. The wind hurled gusts of snow into the barn.

Another minute. Mary cried silently. My brother didn't move.

I picked up the shotgun, unloaded it, walked to the barn door, and swung it against the jamb. I swung again and again. Wings rustled in the rafters and a dozen, then a hundred, then a thousand sparrows fluttered and flew out of the stable in a dark, chattering cloud. The gun broke. I dropped the stock and said, "It's over."

Lorenzo pushed Mary away and came at me. I thought he'd kill me. My brother—the stronger, meaner man. Instead he stopped and looked me in the eye for the first time since Merrick died. Then he laid his head on my shoulder and wept.

63

One night, Mary heard Moreau's screams through the February wind. She was up first. I lit a lamp and followed her down the stairs.

"My gun! Where's my gun!" Moreau sat, grabbing at darkness. Helen, who'd been dozing in a chair, tried to put her arms around him. "Rebs!" He pushed her, flailing his arms, hitting her with dull thuds. I stood in the doorway with the lamp, not sure whom to help or how.

Mary put her arms around Moreau. "It's Mother."

"Sentry! My gun!"

"Mother. Mother."

He shook all over. I gave Helen the lamp and held Moreau's arms. He couldn't wake. I held tight. It was a struggle. Like holding a drowning man. I felt sweat, ribs, fists. I felt terror. Felt the war.

Moreau fought to wake. Mary touched his face, saying, "Mother. Mother." Over and over. Her voice or touch or smell slowly woke him. Calmed him. He was sweating, shaking. He said, "I'm sorry," and fell back.

The dead were rising.

Mary wiped his brow and sweat-slicked face and hair. She held him. Moreau stopped shaking and said, "I'm all right, Mother. Please go to bed. Let me be."

She kissed his forehead and said, "I shall go. Mason can stay in the parlor."

"Thank you, Mother."

Mary went out and up the steps. They had a sort of agreement. She knew when to withdraw.

"I'll be in the parlor," I said. Moreau nodded. He did that for Mary. At least I thought he did. I sat on the sofa and trimmed the lamp to a tiny, clear light. The wind rattled the windows and rustled the curtains.

After a few minutes, Helen said, "You hit me quite hard." She said it in a firm, caring voice. I expected a caring response.

"I told you not to stay," he said. "I don't sleep well."

"I want to be near you."

"What good's that?"

"I love you," Helen said.

"Whores took better care of me."

I felt her shock. I don't know what hurt her more, the fact of whores or that her soldier threw it in her face.

"There aren't any whores here." Her voice trembled. "Only your family." Helen glanced at the parlor.

Moreau laid back, his strength gone. She tried to kiss him. He pushed her away. "You don't know love."

"I may not," said Helen, "but I love you."

"You're ignorant. Foolish. You don't know how."

"Show me," she said.

"Can't."

"Why, Ro? I love you."

"Love don't help. We know that."

"What would?"

"A whore."

Helen shuddered, perhaps imagining what she hadn't imagined before. Confronting a man she'd never seen before.

"Take what you want," she said in a whisper. "I give it."

"I don't want it."

The lamp went out. I don't know if they saw or cared. I loved my son, but I cared for Helen. A daughter, a comfort to Mary—and they were clawing at each other.

"I know the devil," said Moreau. "When he comes, you're alone, no matter who loves you."

"No," said Helen. "You're never alone. Jesus is here. He's here now in this sad room."

"If He's here, He don't give a shit."

"Moreau, the Lord doesn't come to you. You must go to Him."

"I went," he said. "Didn't like what I found."

"You answered the devil, Ro. You fought to free men."

"No man is free."

"That's saying no man has a soul," said Helen.

"Mine's gone."

Moreau. My son. Did he believe even less than I did?

Helen faltered. "What about Gib, Ro? What would he say?"

"Gib ain't here."

"Wars end, Moreau. Even this one."

"Only the dead have seen the end of war, Helen. Where's the damn yellow bottle? I want to sleep."

Her voice finally broke. "And your letters? Those beautiful letters?"

Moreau turned away from her, his voice muffled by the pillow. "It's different now. Don't you know that? Let me sleep."

64

Winter wore on and Moreau was sinking, going away, as he got stronger. He would not talk about what was wrong. My son had a pact with silence that reminded me of my brother. Not-telling was important and he had much not to tell. More, I'm sure, than I knew. Not-telling was not showing pain and Moreau wouldn't show pain. Maybe it was a way to hurt us, like he'd been hurt. Maybe it was guilt. The women couldn't imagine why Moreau would hurt them. I wondered if my son couldn't forgive himself, as well as me.

Maybe he can't forgive the war?

Was it the child?

Something he did?

Something between him and Helen? Something in the dark?

Moreau would not give in. To us, to pain, to anything, except silence. He was giving in to that. He was fighting—fighting us. And himself in some brutal, proud way we didn't understand. We were proud of him. Was that what he hated? We tried to understand. Did he hate that?

Moreau did the cleaning now. We asked what we should do. All of us gave him love and respect, but Moreau was going where love and respect couldn't follow. Maybe he was already there. I'd seen this before. He knew it hurt us. Mary bore this as she bore all Moreau's troubles, with strength, prayer, and love. Mary believed love would cure him and worried only that she didn't have the strength to give it. Helen couldn't believe Ro could love her so much, and then stop. I had thought Moreau needed someone far from the country of mother, but now he needed no one—unless it was someone to hurt. What country did he need now? A country, it seemed, neither his mother, nor Helen, nor I, could enter.

One night, as the wind beat against the house and snow raced by the icy windows, I said, "What's wrong, Moreau? Is it the stringing?"

"No." His eyes flashed. "I enjoy stringing."

"I'm sorry I can't do it," I said.

"No matter."

"What does matter, Moreau?"

"Nothin'," he said quietly.

"Your mother? Helen? Gib? Something else?"

He looked into the dark.

"You're cruel to Helen," I said. "Does it make you feel better?"

"Makes me feel worse."

"Why do you do it?" I asked quietly.

"Want to feel worse."

"Be cruel to me," I said. "Don't be cruel to the women."

"Winter will pass," he said.

"Winter?"

"The winter of our discontent." He smiled.

"Are you all right, Moreau?"

He looked at me. "I'll think about what you said. Let me sleep."

The next day, I tried again, sitting at his bedside. "I think you made a deal. I didn't let them cut, so you don't complain about stringing. You don't complain about anything. Even me."

"I thank you for not letting them cut," he said formally.

The day's stringing was done. Moreau drank from the yellow bottle. The irritation, goading, the sense we owed something we couldn't pay, was gone. He wouldn't have to string for another twenty-one hours.

"Do you want me to clean your wound?" I asked.

"Hell no."

"Do you hate me for sending you to war?" I asked.

"Ain't about you."

We were quiet. I didn't believe him. "The stringing gets you."

"It don't," he said quickly.

"Something's got you."

"It ain't that."

"I sent you to war," I said. "I cannot take that back. I cannot take back what it did to you. I wanted you to go for my ambition. My career. I wanted you to fight for me. It was cowardice. And wrong. That's why I won't stand for reelection."

"It isn't you. Not then. Not now."

"I didn't understand the part of you that went to seminary," I said. "I never understood the part that dreamed of the heads or talked to God. Or went to war. The best parts." I took his hand. I tried to make him listen. "Let the doctor string you. Talk about what bothers you. Let me string."

He turned away. He wouldn't listen.

The days went deep into February, got colder, and we were frightened. Moreau treated Helen better, at least overtly. He said stringing in the morphine-deadened mornings made him happier than the rest of the day. I didn't believe it. I think words could not bridge the distance between what Ro had seen and what he felt about what he'd seen. Maybe he was thinking about his child. Maybe he had other secrets.

What scared me was not that he wouldn't tell, but that he thought it wouldn't matter if he did. None of us pretended to know how he felt and that was right. I knew that was right. We all did right, but...

Moreau drifted in and out of but. I kept thinking he hated the mornings. I asked. He said no. He said it from the other side of the world.

Numbness. Pain. Fits of anger. Moreau suffered. Every day he pierced and strung in awful, solitary dawns. He did it in the stable. He limped eight paces on a crutch from kitchen to stable through the killing cold. He did this every morning, but would not, did not, ask for help. I admired his courage and his courage scared me.

On a day when ice coated the windows in the room off the parlor, I asked if he talked to God in the mornings.

"Why would God talk to me?" he said.

"Maybe you talk and He listens."

Moreau shrugged.

"Don't you thank God you survived?" I said.

"No."

I thought about mentioning the child, but only as a last resort. I was sure that was part of it, but I thought my son used the child to punish himself. Why did he punish himself? It was mixed up with those awful battles, of course, but I believed Moreau thought he should be able to make peace with the war, with himself and with us, but couldn't. I knew he didn't trust me, and my mentioning the child might end what little trust there was. My telling his mother would be unforgivable. Telling Helen might drive her away. Telling Moreau might bring absolute silence. I was glad he hadn't mentioned the child when he quarreled with Helen. He hadn't said the meanest thing he could. He hadn't destroyed Helen's love.

Yet.

We didn't know his ritual. We didn't know Moreau held a .44 to his head in the mornings. He didn't intend to use it. He was pretty sure of that. He was absolutely sure about not showing pain. That's what he was living for. Not-showing. Not-telling. And morphine. Moreau didn't question not-showing any more than he questioned cleaning the wound. It was a duty and a deal. Like the child and the .44 under the straw in the stable, it was secret. Rituals needed to be secret. Ro liked the feel of the cold .44. He wasn't waiting for spring when ice would break and the creek run to the lake. He wasn't waiting for a sign. He was waiting for the .44.

Something pulled at him. Pulled like the heads in his dreams. I dreamed them one night. He dreamed them many nights. The heads were outside his window. He was back there. Back where Mother couldn't help, Father didn't matter, and Helen was invisible. The heads watched.

Mary knew Moreau didn't sleep the hour before dawn. She knew he tossed in bed, waiting for the stable. Morphine eased the pain of stringing, but if he drank too much, he lost coordination. Then Mother would have to do it. Mary thought that before dawn grief for Merrick and Lyman and Henry Corse and all of them came back.

I asked what he thought about before dawn. He looked at me.

"The Machine."

The Machine was the war and it was more than the war. The Machine regulated—Moreau's word—what you brought back and what you didn't. What you could stand and what you couldn't. It ground on. Nothing stopped it. Not men. Not guns. Not God.

"You seen it," he said. "You own it."

One morphine-deadened morning, I think, he realized it owned him.

We had talked about the woman nursing him after Second Bull Run. That helped, at first. Someone who didn't have to, had no family there, came. Stayed. Moreau now shrugged when I mentioned her. The wind howled. Chimney smoke blew flat down Railroad Street. People piled snow against their houses to keep warm. The sky was empty. The red-tailed hawks, crows and sparrows disappeared. The earth was numb.

At the end of March, Lorenzo visited for the first time. He couldn't speak. Uncle and nephew hugged. They were close. No words, but they were close. Death and something beyond death was between them. Touching Moreau helped Lorenzo. He let it. I saw. It didn't help Moreau. I saw that. I hadn't lost a brother.

Lorenzo left and Moreau said, "I pity Uncle and you. You never marched all night. Never shivered and prayed, shoulder to shoulder, with bayonets fixed." His eyes darkened. "I pity you."

Moreau
Moreau's Needle
March 7, 1863

65

Five a.m. I rise before the sun. No one is up. I go in the kitchen and light the lantern. Drink morphine. Heat water. Take needle and silk Mother left on table. I pull myself to the stable. Eight paces with the crutch. Path is icy but clear. Cold air on my face and hands.

Set lantern on trunk by the stool. Return to kitchen. Take boiling water to stable. John Brown neighs. Dogs stay in—don't like eight-foot snow. I set pan on varnished trunk by the needle and silk. Sit on stool. Pull off slipper, then sock. Remove bandage. Dip the cloth in water. Wipe wound.

No one sees. Not father. Especially father. He can't string. Father is a coward.

No matter.

Morphine numbs the cold. Lantern light dances in the corners, glitters off bridles, a whip, hoes, and rakes. If I scream, no one hears. If I flinch, no one sees.

Tie end of silk to end of needle. Put needle in wound.

Push.

Hurts.

New scar tissue, torn. Fresh blood soaks sock.

Pull silk through ankle. Pull to end. Pull the other way.

Hurts.

John Brown snorts. Opens and shuts an eye. He doesn't want to watch. Cold covers smell of leather, hay, horse dung, urine. My nostrils freeze. Tiny fine crystals hold membranes together. I like it.

Silk touches raw flesh. Hurts. Like fire.

Wind pushes doors, cuts into the stable. I see John Brown's breath.

I squeeze my nose. The lantern light is dancing yellow fire. Shadows are warm with cold. Warm with cold? Morphine and words don't mix.

Pull. Stop. Look. Pull.

My fucking life goes through that hole.

Hurts.

Pull out silk. Bloody. Put on varnished trunk.

Wet cloth—water is cool—sponge each side.

Wrap with fresh bandage.

Hurts.

The ritual. Dig under trunk. Take out .44. Father got it in Frederick from Frank Fay, politician. Father thinks it's with Helen's letters.

Why give it? What for?

Cold, solid weight. Invisible smell—cold metal. Pain in ankle. Drink morphine.

Gun in my hand.

I put gun in my mouth. Yes and no snap to attention. Clarity. No confusion…no frantic, crazy elephant, but the rigor of the parade ground... no pile of... Pools… Curdling… He looked at us... We watched... Did nothing... Nothing… Where's Betsey, Miss Bird… boy or girl... Merrick... Merrick... Merrick… in stable... cold... Are pictures thoughts or thoughts pictures? Feelings words or words feelings? Dreams words or pictures? Feelings? Heads? Laugh. Madness?

Like it.

Gun in mouth. The world does the bidding of metal.

Needle and silk can end.

Forever.

Mason

Iron Spring

March 17, 1863

66

Mary watched our son fail as he got stronger. "Disappearing," she called it. She was worried now. All of us were worried. Mary believed in the Lord and trusted in is His love, but this smacked of Hell. *None of us believe in Hell. Why is our son alone with the devil?* Was it Mary? It couldn't be. Helen? Was the woman not the girl he'd dreamt of? Wasn't her love pure? Mary judged it so. Was it me? The child? *Moreau had always seen the devil. He called it the heads.* Was home not the place the soldier dreamt of? Had the soldier stopped dreaming? *Don't call it madness.*

Moreau lived with silk and morphine. "My companions," he called them. He didn't complain. He was nicer, but... going away. Mary felt something apologetic in the distance creeping between Moreau and everyone. This troubled her more than baiting and anger.

One day Helen said, "He doesn't love me." Her eyes filled with tears. "He talks about whores."

They were in the kitchen, faces flushed with the warmth of the stove, freshly stoked with wood to cook dinner. Mary put her hand on Helen's shoulder. "No, child. No. It's not you. It's..."

Helen was sobbing, could barely get the words out. "I tried to be his whore. It didn't work. He said I didn't know how."

Mary hugged her. "It's not you, child. It's the wound. It will pass. Those things will take care of themselves."

"I'm so frightened," said Helen.

"Men talk like that to push us away. He can't love right now because he's hurt, so he takes it out on you. You have to be strong. He'll come back to us. He will be whole again. You must believe that."

On the Ides of March, I returned late from Oswego. I was now paymaster and enrolling officer for the Union Army. I couldn't string my son's wound, but I would help the Cause. I owed that to Ro and Merrick, to all the boys. It was good to be away from Railroad Street, away from apprehension about stringing, and guilt about not stringing. I was glad to be busy visiting mustering stations and wounded men. I wouldn't give speeches, but I would help. It was a balance, like morphine and coordination. I would help anyone who wanted to fight, but in God's name, I wouldn't talk a man into it. That was my filter, or was it my dodge?

I knew about morphine. I had asked Dr. Letterman, McClelland's Chief Surgeon, myself. I knew the balance of pain and dexterity. Why did Moreau insist on cleaning the wound? What did it prove? Why did he want pain more than love? *Is this madness?* I feared for him.

That night, snow piled high along Railroad Street, drifts reaching first-floor windows, ground frozen, wind cold enough to kill anyone foolish enough to be out, Mary spoke. All winter she had prayed for spring, for earth and creek to thaw, Merrick to be buried, Lorenzo to start planting, and Moreau to marry Helen.

It wasn't coming.

I returned after dark and stood by the fire a long time. Snow melted on my boots and beard and dripped on the old orange Persian carpet. Mary sat in the battered Cromwellian chair and stared at the fire, waiting for me to speak.

"There are reports," I said. "Lorenzo sits by the casket and talks to it. No one comes near enough to hear. They say he puts a gun in his mouth."

"I don't believe it," said Mary. "Lorenzo gave us his word he would bury Merrick."

"They say my brother talks all night," I said. "They say a woman visits."

Mary looked me in the eye. "Maybe someone comes to pay her respects to the dead."

I nodded. What Merrick had done in life, what women he had known, what secrets he had kept, should be buried with him.

"It's the Ides, Mason." Mary's tone changed. "'Oh thou bleeding piece of earth.' Do you remember?

> Between the acting of a dreadful thing
> And the first motion, all the interim is
> Like a phantasma or a hideous dream?"

"Yes."

"I looked up phantasma in the big *Webster's*," said Mary. "It means vision of things not seen. *Webster's* used the quote from *Julius Caesar* as an example. The circularity troubles me."

"'Dews of blood, disasters in the sun,'" I said. "*Hamlet*. I can not drive that from my mind."

Mary looked up from the fire. "Our son is going away."

"The wound is better," I said.

"Do you feel his going?"

"Yes." I looked at an uneven pattern of moonlight on an ice-covered window.

"We've drawn closer, Mason. You and I and Helen. But Moreau is far."

"I fear his sadness," I said.

"He speaks of Gib when he thinks we don't hear. Gib has authority, Mason. Authority we don't have."

I sat on the sofa and felt the weight of fear denied. Mary couldn't say it out loud, but I knew. She was afraid Moreau would kill himself. I almost told her about the child. It would have made her feel better, less helpless—I knew that—but it would have been another betrayal. *Was Moreau this close to disaster?* I looked at the jagged circle of moon on the iced-over window. I had never felt so wretched. Was I betraying Mary by not telling? Betraying Moreau by not revealing what I knew? If there were another way, any way, I would take it. Could that be Gib? Could the ex-slave complete the soldier's circle—believe, kill, be hurt, stop believing, believe again? The circle started with a shivering runaway who made Moreau a soldier, gave him the Cause, but being a soldier unmade him. When Moreau's fever broke, the circle should have been complete. Duty was done. For country, God, father. Gib. Moreau did right, like his letter said. Right as any man. But…the soldier survived; our son had lost Cause, God, and family.

Could Mr. Watkins repair the circle?

"Finding Gib might be impossible," I said. "It would be looking for straw in a haystack." I didn't say needle. I didn't like saying needle.

"The last straw, Mason."

"The last straw," I said, and smiled at Mary's wit, but Mary wasn't smiling.

"The wound is not just in his ankle," she said.

I nodded. The change. His going. It wasn't personal, and that frightened me. Moreau didn't blame me, the slaves, or God. What was wrong was beyond words. Beyond meanness and a child. Beyond mother, father, and Intended. *Don't call it madness.* Moreau was going to his comrades, Merrick, other dead boys, Why not? More men had died in one day at Antietam than in all the wars America had fought until this one. My son had seen the worst of the worst.

"He needs a different kind of physician," said Mary.

"It may not be possible."

"You found Gib once, now find him again."

I looked at Mary. Her cheeks and mouth were drawn in judgment.

"That day by the Creek," said Mary. "You took Moreau to rescue Gib. You had a plan."

"Yes, it was my plan. A design. I told Moreau this. I told him I am a coward and he is not."

"What does he say?"

"He says 'No matter.'"

Mary's face got tighter. Deeper worry.

"I haven't left Moreau's side since Keedysville. I have done right, Mary."

"Do you think you are helping him here?"

I had no answer. Wind beat on the windows. The moon's image shimmered on an icy pane and candles flickered. Winter was rising.

"You must find Gib, Mason. It may be the only way, and the only way to forgive yourself."

"Will you forgive me?" I asked. "If...?" I couldn't say it.

"We are beyond that," Mary said softy, "and we aren't there. Yet."

"It's a fool's errand. It's winter. The man is in Canada." I rubbed my forehead and eyes.

"You sent Moreau to war, Mason. Now you must bring him back."

"I saved his leg. I argued with the surgeon. You can't imagine that day."

"Moreau is not saved." Mary trembled. I got no sweet words. No hug. No touch. Her determination made me shiver.

"All right," I said at last. "I will go to the Underground Railroad office in Rochester. If anyone knows, it will be someone there. If there's anyone they'll speak to about Gib Watkins, it will be me."

"Thank you, Mason. Thank you."

67

That next day at dawn I stood at the station, waiting for the train. Without delays, mean weather, mechanical failure, track obstructions, or other unseen problems, the trip should take twelve hours. I would get to Rochester at six p.m., stay in a hotel, and visit the Underground Railroad office the next morning. Snow blew around my boots. My nose and cheeks stung with cold. My beard caked with snow. I couldn't smell the wood smoke from the building. Wind tore it away.

My destination was 25 Buffalo Street, the office of Frederick Douglass' *North Star*, the Abolitionist newspaper. I would go in person. The information I sought wouldn't be committed to paper or telegraph or given a stranger. I wanted to know the whereabouts of an escaped slave. As of January 1, 1863, the man was free, but the Underground Railroad's habit of protecting its network and human cargo was still in practice. I knew men in Rochester. And I was known. If they'd give this information to anyone, it would be me.

The day was bitter when I boarded the train, and the car was brutally hot, heated by an over-active stove. I removed my coat, spoke to no one, and looked out a sooty window at snowy woods. Mary knew I denied the perhaps fatal sorrow in our son. *It may be the only way to forgive yourself.* Like the daily cleaning, I wanted it to pass. I didn't know what to do. *The poet says: I am the man. I suffered. I was there.* I am here. My son suffers. I am afraid.

I doubted I would be able to find Gib.

I waited three hours in Rome for the next train, which the stationmaster informed me had been delayed by the storm. I walked out of the station to check the weather. Snow whirled, tumbled, and made a white circus. We were in for a good one. I stood in a rising wind and remembered the day the boys left, when right here, this very spot, I came to a makeshift podium, the last speaker, an afterthought as the families left. All day we had heard talk of sacrifice but there had been no sacrifice. Just bands, pies and speeches. I could have harangued—I was unflinching then—but instead recited the Twenty-third Psalm.

That had been the beginning of honesty. I didn't know it. The honesty of valley and shadow. The honesty of sorrow. If genius ever visited me, it was then.

It was noon before I finally got on a train going west. There was no rail line from Sandy Creek to Syracuse, so to get to Rochester I had to go east to go west. I was only partway there and already the journey was long. I kept looking at my watch, a handsome piece with "New York State Assembly 1860" engraved on its back in robust lettering.

The snow was thick, the woods outside the window a looming presence, the Erie Canal a dark parallel suggestion. The harder it snowed, the fewer telegraph poles were visible in the driving swirl. A thing too dreadful to speak of haunted me. I felt it like the steady, strained pounding of the train. A vicious and fatal circle. Send your son to war. He survives. You rejoice. You are proud, you love him, you want to help him. He has survived, but something is not right. You didn't know war comes back with the warrior. He is in a circle of Hell. I didn't recognize the valley or see the shadow cross his face, didn't know what killing kills. I had made sure Moreau met Gib, and Gib had enflamed Moreau's conscience. Now I needed Gib again. Gib was part of the circle. Somewhere out there, blown from our sinful nation into a Canadian wind. If I found him, would he be able to break the circle? By now Gib was probably in Western Canada with a job, maybe a wife, a family. A new life. What did Gib Watkins owe America?

I watched red signal lights in the snow, closed my eyes, and thought of Salisbury heads on stakes. I had always discounted the story of the heads—discounted any connection between my ancestors and me. Let the dead bury the dead. I discounted nothing now. The country was full of ghosts and those who were turning into ghosts. Snow pelted the sooty window and melted in black rivulets.

I told Moreau he used the heads to make himself feel important. A mirror to see an inflated, tragic image. Now it was my turn to see the devil. The heads were back. They were waiting. Moreau might be dead when I returned.

When I was a boy, my father used to threaten me with the old story, though in calmer moments acknowledged Salisburys had little to fear from Indians. Even as a child, I thought killing an unarmed man and dying for it was brutal, but just—and far removed from the optimistic, booming America I knew. Those were dreadful times with dreadful justice. King Philip's head was put on a pole and his severed hand shown for a shilling. Little Moreau told us the Salisbury heads watched him. "Someone's always watching," I told him. "That's why we try to behave honorably."

We told Moreau the heads couldn't talk or see. They were dead. Mary even said the story wasn't true, but the child knew it was. *Something that awful had to be true.* I told him he wasn't responsible for the old killings. None of us were.

"Are Salisburys cursed?" little Moreau asked.

"No one is cursed and no Salisbury has died in a war since 1675."

But Salisburys went to war. My father a lieutenant in 1812. His father a militiaman called to the Revolution. A Salisbury survived the Plains of Abraham. Nine bullets in his coat. Stories. Wars distant and heroic, or distant and awful, but distant. No one died.

Until now.

As the hours dragged on, I tried to sleep, but failed. Who can sleep surrounded by ghosts? I remembered two North Country men, shades now themselves, who went on fools' errands to Rochester—Charles Finney, the evangelist, and daredevil Sam Patch. Finney went to save souls for the Lord, Patch to leap a hundred and twenty feet off a tower into the Genesee River. Neither succeeded, though Finney survived. Finney preached that nothing is predestined. Talk to God directly. Save or damn yourself. He didn't shout like the preachers who see the devil at their heels and yours. Finney argued a case. Finest talker in the North Country.

Talk.

I traced an M on the window with my finger. Then another. My son was beyond talk. So was my brother. My nephew was dead.

Visibility from the train window was only a few hundred feet. The "burned-over district" of central New York was under sheets of snow and sleet. I stared at the storm and thought of men I knew as boys, now under the ground or waiting spring burial. I remembered little Jackie Barney pulling the tail of our cat Rufus. Major Andrew Jackson Barney of the 24th New York Volunteers was dead. The boy visited by a dyspeptic mathematics professor was killed at Second Bull Run. His uncle's former patient recognized him among the dead on the field of battle.

In times of peace, sons bury their fathers. In times of war, fathers bury their sons.

Maybe Reverend Finney was wrong. Maybe all is determined and all are damned. Maybe pleasing God isn't arguing a case or cutting a deal.

Burning cinders raced through the snow and blackened in the white swirl of the storm.

68

I arrived in Rochester an hour before dawn. The city still slept. The station was empty, and I napped on a hard bench until the sun rose, and then headed out to find the *North Star* office. The building was so small, I walked by it several times before noticing the number 25. The door was unlocked.

I was surprised by the place. From here issued the cries of the wounded—the wounded who must do their own crying, Frederick Douglass said. Here free men organized, publicized, directed forays south. They had a network that ferried human beings all over North America, yet in this tiny place there was no place to sit. It was cramped, smelled of ink and the packed closeness of rolls of paper, stacks of newspapers, pamphlets, barrels of ink. It was busy, vigorous, urgent. And uncomfortable.

At first I saw no one and I stood for a moment, wondering how war and the Emancipation Proclamation had changed the struggle. What would become of Douglass? What would become of the freed slaves? What would become of any of us?

"Have you come for the *Appeal*?" asked an old Negro, appearing suddenly from behind several rolls of newsprint. I suppressed the urge to jump. How had I not noticed him in a room so small? The Negro wore a white smock, stained with so many shades of ink as to be a catalogue of black, gray and white, analogous to the colors of his tightly curled hair.

"The *Appeal*?" I said.

"*Men of Color, to Arms*."

"No. I read it in the newspaper. My paper, not yours. *The Sandy Creek Times*." Small talk. Pointless.

"Who would have thought Massachusetts would raise the first colored troops? When we have sounded the trumpet so long and so loudly." The man was polite but strained.

"It is a mistake," I said, "which I regret."

"How may I help?" asked the Negro, his tone betraying a trace of impatience.

"I'm looking for a man." Now, perhaps, we might get somewhere.

He looked skeptical.

"A man my son and I helped to Canada."

The Negro crossed his arms over his chest.

"A man named Gib Watkins." I crossed my own arms over my chest.

"You come from northern Oswego County to ask for him?" The old man shuffled a pile of paper. "I hope you find Mr. Watkins."

"I took him to Gananoque myself," I said, not to be dismissed.

"Perhaps you might seek him there."

"I thought someone here might know," I said, raising my voice.

"Who are you?"

"The Honorable Mason Salisbury." I rarely used the title. I used it now.

The Negro paused and looked at me for the first time.

"Have I heard you speak?"

"I have spoken for the Cause."

"One of many voices," he said, and went back to shuffling papers. After a long minute, he shook his head slowly, and said, "You come as an Assemblyman?"

"I come as a father."

Snow melted on my beard. The old man wiped his hands on his smock and gave me a towel. He removed a pile of pamphlets from a loop-backed Windsor chair and said, “Sit down.”

I was tired and hungry. The train had arrived at four a.m. Now it was barely seven.

“Is Mr. Watkins in trouble?” he asked.

I shook my head no. I didn’t like his forwardness or his lack of deference to the Assemblyman who had travelled such a long way for his son. Though I had his attention, and perhaps his sympathy, I doubted the Negro would tell me anything.

“Why do you seek this man, Honorable Salisbury?”

“He is my son’s friend and my son needs his friend.”

“Where is your son?”

“At this hour, passing a piece of silk through a hole in his ankle made by a rebel Minié ball. Antietam.”

We talked for an hour and sure enough, I learned nothing useful. The old man did not know Gib Watkins, or at least said he didn’t. He brewed a pot of coffee and produced two stale rolls. I felt put off, patronized, possibly lied to, but when he said, “Let us get on our knees and ask the Lord Jesus for help,” I did it.

69

I didn't wait in the hot, high-ceilinged waiting room of the New York Central Railroad Station. I stood outside by the tracks, overcome by deep desperation, a desperation as hopeless as the snow racing through the railroad yard. I had failed. The errand was a mistake. Gib was gone. He was lost in the winter in another country, if even alive. I walked among sidings and tracks, not bothering to shield my face. Men loaded and unloaded cars. Snow howled in gusts. I went behind a boxcar, sank to my knees, got the derringer out of my carpetbag, and put it beside me. I tried to pray:

I sent my son to war. I cannot help him.

The old man made a fool of me.

What can I do?

My knees froze in the snow.

I looked around. What was I doing? I wanted to be seen. I wanted to be seen kneeling between cars, between God and pistol, praying for my son. I wanted it reported how the Honorable Mason Salisbury agonized in the snow and suffered. I wanted it known, if my son killed himself at home, in my care.

Tears came.

Why, what an ass am I! An ass! An ass! Nothing but an ass.

My son braved unspeakable minutes in an unspeakable cornfield, and I was on my knees, hoping someone would see.

"Be his father," I said out loud.

It was as if someone else had spoken.

The snow stopped as I reached Rome. I thought of telegraphing that I hadn't found Gib, but why send bad news? If there were bad news at home, I didn't want it. I waited in the station. I didn't want news or memories or gestures. I sat on a bench thinking, I'm not a hero. I'm an actor. I touched my wet knees. There's providence in no one seeing you be a fool. I remembered Moreau denying he was a hero.

"I'm not a hero," he told me. "Heroes are dead. Like Lyman, who the Rebs hung for breaking parole."

"Merrick is a hero," I said.

"Until he's forgotten."

"A hero, then a ghost," I said.

"We're all ghosts."

I had panicked in Rochester, but from Rome to Sandy Creek, I began to plan. I stared at the white fields and snow-canopied trees and decided to take the .44 back from Moreau. It had been stupid to give it to him. I was not his comrade—I was his father. I worried that taking the gun might not be enough. Men die in other ways. Hang themselves in barns. Die in the woods. Drown in Lake Ontario.

What would I tell Mary?

No Gib. No God. Only an actor.

I tormented myself the long way back with what I hadn't done. I hadn't confronted Moreau. I hadn't gotten angry. Hadn't said hard things about him or myself. Hadn't fought. I'd been proud and loving. I'd hoped—we'd all hoped—Moreau's pride in being a soldier, in not being me, would make it right. Make him love us. Trust us.

Now I knew it wasn't enough. I'd have to mention the child. I'd have to show the letter. I'd have to say I lied, but had told no one. Say I'd string. I had to do what I hadn't. What I feared. If that wasn't enough, Amen.

And take care of Mary and Helen.

The ghosts will care for themselves.

I got off the train at Sandy Creek. The sun set into a gray winter sky, leaving a momentary glow over the fields. The snow was blue and the wind promised a harsh night. A red-tailed hawk circled, then disappeared. I raised my collar and walked the three-quarters of a mile up Railroad Street.

There was one last hope and it was me.

Moreau

Bottom

March 19, 1863

70

In the stable. Five a.m. I look down the barrel of the .44, cock the hammer, and see horses, steaming pan, needle, silk, fresh bandages, good foot and bad foot. I look up. The lamp swings like a hanged man. Wind creeps and finds tiny cracks in the walls. Thoughts creep too.

Does air freeze?

Blood?

I put the gun by the pan and think of Lake Ontario. Frozen, white. Gray ice trapping light. Killing day.

The stable door opens. Shuts. Quick blast of freezing air. The lantern swings. John Brown neighs.

"Are you going to kill yourself, Moreau?"

I sway, sit up. Surprised. "Gib?"

"Father."

I close my eyes. "Get out."

Father looks at the .44 sitting by the pan. He's wearing his long black coat with the purple collar. Like a politician or an undertaker.

He moves closer. Out of the shadow into the lantern light.

I raise my hand and shake my head.

We look at each other. Why is he here? He can't string. He sent me to war.

I look at the gun. Father looks at the gun. A yellow halo surrounds the lantern. Father won't do anything. He moves closer. I want the gun. He wants the gun.

I reach for the .44, but my hand doesn't go straight. Father moves. A halo around his hand moves. He hits me on the side of my head. I crash onto the straw. Face hurts and I can't see out of one eye. My ankle stings and my face bleeds. He never hit me before.

He picks up the .44.

I sit on the hard, frozen straw. I rub my head and squint out of one eye. The light is swimming. Ankle throbs. "Shoot me."

Father looks at me and shivers.

"Shoot!" I yell.

"It isn't that easy, Moreau."

"Then give me the gun!" I shout. "It's easy enough for me!"

"Why are you doing this, Moreau?" He puts the gun in the straw by John Brown's stall.

"I'm already dead," I say.

"You're not dead," says Father. "You're hurt. You're a soldier. And a good man."

I spit. John Brown neighs. "Merrick is dead. Major Barney. Balch. Henry. Philo. Lyman."

"You've gone over to the heads, Moreau," says Father. "Come back. It's time."

I look away. Shadows dance on the varnished chest and saddles. "I've seen the elephant."

"The war isn't over, Moreau. Don't surrender."

"I'm not a good man."

"Do you think I am?" Father takes a letter out of his black coat. "This is yours. It was pinned inside your uniform."

"You said you didn't find it!" Liar. Judas. "You son of a bitch!"

"I have not betrayed you," Father says. "Your letter remains private."

He hands me the letter. I rip it up and drop the pieces in the straw.

"I never saw the child."

"Was the child yours?"

"It was mine," I say, angry. "With a whore. Should I bring Betsey here and show her off?"

"I told no one." Father picks up the pieces and drops them in the lantern. Quick red flame turns to black smoke that disappears in the draughty cold air. "I didn't tell anyone when I thought you'd kill yourself. I didn't tell anyone when your mother thought she'd lost you. I didn't tell anyone when Helen despaired of getting you back."

"You think that makes me trust you?" I say.

"What you do is up to you, Moreau. But as long as it remains secret, I will keep your confidence."

"The Honorable Mason Salisbury doesn't care that he has a bastard grandchild?"

Father speaks quietly. "Is the child not cared for?"

"Not by me."

"Moreau, a father can only do as much as he can."

I snort.

"Could you even find this woman? Would she let you see the child?"

I look at the needle, the silk, the cooling water. The yellow bottle. I hate it. I hate what I have to do every morning. I hate everything.

"You're alive, Moreau," Father says. "That's what matters. What would Lorenzo give to see Merrick again?"

I take a drink of morphine. "God damn Lorenzo and Merrick. And you."

"Your mother prayed every day and night for you, and this is how you act?" At last, Father is angry. His eyes narrow. His beard quivers. He is as angry as I've only seen him before a crowd. "Can't you think of anyone's pain but your own? No matter how you hate the war, or me, you have no right to treat your family like this."

I take another drink. I don't want to listen, but he keeps talking.

"Merrick is dead. That can't change. Your son grows up with a man who isn't his father. Sons have to live with the sins of their fathers. Who doesn't live with that? You have a family here, Moreau. Take care of the people who love you. I know I hurt you. I accept that shame for the remainder of my life. You may forgive me, or not. We may never speak, if you wish. But stop hurting your mother and Helen!"

I drink. The stable begins to waver and the lantern light dances. Thin smoke dissolves in the rafters.

"If you kill yourself," Father says, his voice steely, "you prove yourself the coward."

I drink again. I'm warm with morphine and full of easy, bright freedom. "Coward?" I laugh. "Who's the coward, Father?" I spit the word out like a curse. "Who can't string the wound of his only son?"

He looks like he knew this was coming. He stands straighter, slowly takes off the black coat, and lays it over the gun. His white breath comes quicker. "All right, let's try." He picks up the needle. The silk is attached. Mother did that last night. He rinses his hands in the water, which already has a jagged skim of ice. I drink from the yellow bottle. "Okay," he says, and lifts my leg carefully. He unwraps the bloodstained bandages. It doesn't hurt. The morphine makes the freezing stable almost pleasant. Father looks at the wound, a red pucker surrounded by yellow-white scaring, small in front, bigger behind.

"Nasty," he says. He positions the needle against the wound and pushes, tentative. It doesn't hurt much. He pushes it through. The wound bleeds. He pulls the needle out the other side, unties the silk, puts the needle on the table, and holds each end of the silk. He takes a breath and pulls the silk through. It turns red. He pulls it the other way, blood on his hands, staining his cuffs. He pulls slowly, steadily. He does not flinch.

I think of the child, whose life I shall not know, look at Father, and think of Helen.

"You're no coward," I whisper.

"Not today."

He pulls the silk back and forth as my wound bleeds. The ankle throbs. The lantern swings in a yellow, morphine halo. Father works the silk back and forth for a full minute, then wipes the ankle and bandages the wound.

He doesn't do it well, but he does it.

71

I hobbled into the house. Father steadied me. Then he went back to the stable for the needle, silk, and pan. When Mother came in, I was leaning alone against the door, looking at the fire in the kitchen hearth. She saw the bruise on my swollen face but didn't say anything. Father returned, and put the pan with needle and silk in it in the pantry. He probably had the gun in the pocket of his coat, but I didn't see it. I noticed how old and tired he looked. Mother looked tired, too. I probably looked and smelled like a wild animal. I shook my head and sat at the kitchen table, leg propped on a chair. Everything was slow and warm. The dogs came in to be fed. Waldo licked my hand. Governor Tompkins put his paw on my good leg. Mother said, "I shall make breakfast." Father nodded, and added wood to the stove, which warmed the kitchen and melted ice on the windows. He fed the dogs. The house filled with the smells of eggs, coffee, bacon, warm dogs, and toasting bread.

Helen came down, a blue robe wrapped tightly around her, her hair pulled back, covering her ears. She also looked tired. She looked at me, and said, "Isn't it early for so much morphine?"

"Father strung me," I said.

Mother and Helen stared. I don't know if they believed me. Mother looked at my fresh bandages. Helen looked at my swollen face.

"I want Dr. Bulkley to do it now," I said.

"Are you sure?" Helen asked.

"I'm sure." I got up and dragged myself to her. I whispered, "I love you," into her hair. She said nothing, just hugged me. She trembled and I felt hope and worry in her shiver.

"We'll see," she whispered.

I kissed her. I was like Waldo and Governor Tompkins. Happy and slobbering and stupid. I was full of morphine.

Mother hugged me. I felt her relief and her love. The enormity of my cruelty to her and to Helen, began to filter through the morphine haze. I didn't want to feel it. I would feel it a long time.

Father washed his hands in the sink.

Mason

Escape

March 19, 1863

72

Mary prayed that night. I listened to her give thanks, and heard the power in the words "our Lord" invoked for Moreau and Merrick. Mary asked for mercy for Lorenzo, prayed for Merrick's soul, and asked that Moreau let Dr. Bulkley attend him always. She prayed for Lyman Houghton, Henry Corse, and Jack Barney, for all the boys and their grieving parents. She prayed for Mr. and Mrs. Lincoln who had lost an eleven-year-old the previous winter. She prayed for me too.

I lay on the bed and watched a solitary candle. It sputtered and finished and I was in the dark, remembering the surgeon and his knives, and mulling over how everything could change in a minute. I was there. I spoke. I chose. This morning in the stable was no different. I was there, I spoke, I hit my son as hard as I could. Maybe it saved him. Maybe it saved me. I shall hope. There was nothing, absolutely nothing, nothing else I could have done. There's divinity in that.

Mary lay beside me, eyes open. "What happened in the stable?"

"I fought for him."

"You hit him."

"I hit him. There was no other way."

"You surprise me, Mason."

"We came to the end of words."

"Is that when men hit each other?"

"It was the only way to break Moreau's loneliness."

"Has Moreau been so alone?"

"Moreau has been alone with the devil," I said.

"I thought he'd been alone with you."

Mary smiled. You can feel a person smile in the dark.

"He was terribly alone," said Mary. "Even with his mother." She touched my face. "A father's love is different. It demands and judges and it must. That's why there are mothers and fathers."

"It is also love," I said.

"And hard to give," Mary said.

"Very."

"But necessary." Mary sighed. "It's why I wanted you to go to Rochester."

"Rochester? I went to find Gib."

"You might have, but I hoped you would fine something else."

"What?"

"A plan. A design."

Some things are easier said in the dark. Easier to hear, too. I knew what she had wanted me to find.

"I believe Moreau will stop eating his own heart now," Mary said.

"If Bulkley cleans the wound, our son will be fine."

"Perhaps we shall all stop eating our hearts."

Mary kissed me and put her finger to my lips. "There is more you are not telling me. More was said and more done in the stable, but I don't want to know." Mary put her finger to her own lips. "Some things are between fathers and sons."

There's always more that doesn't get said.

"I love you, Mary. That's all we can know. The rest is hope."

Mason

Thaw

March-May

1863

73

Two years, two weeks, and two days after the Rebels fired on Fort Sumter, Moreau and I finally started speaking again. Moreau asked for a walk, so I put off a trip to Oswego. We went to the creek, near where we had found Gib. Moreau used a cane but walked with a firm step. We took no guns and expected to see no one. The day was sunny but cool, unlike the day we "found" the runaway. Bright North Country April. Clouds high, fast-moving, and very white. The creek was partly frozen after the hard winter. We came to the place where Gib had awaited us, concealed in the brush, waiting to help send my son to war. Moreau leaned against a leafless oak and looked at the creek. Water flowed around and under uneven ice. The ice, too thin to support a man, was jumbled and held branches and rocks and the grit of winter. The wind off the creek was cold.

"She'll melt," Moreau said.

I nodded.

High overhead hawks, the color of old barns, circled. A murder of crows eyed us from a dying oak.

Moreau looked at me and said, "What do we owe the dead?"

I went to my haunches, Indian-style, and looked at the leafless tag alders, last year's tall, yellow grass, branches and wooden vines hanging over scraggly brush. The snow was gone, clumps of leafless bushes looked thick as palisades and trembled in the wind. Once again, this wasn't the conversation I expected.

"Burial," I said.

"Those Salisburys, William and John, were they buried?"

"In a pit. They got no stone."

"Merrick wouldn't have got one, if you hadn't come."

"William and John Salisbury," I said. "Are they buried, Moreau?"

"You mean, have I buried them?"

"Yes."

We stared at the rapid water.

"The night before Antietam," said Moreau. "Merrick said the heads would be gone after what was coming. He was wrong. But they're gone now."

"And the newly dead?" I asked.

"I can't bury the new dead. But they don't scare."

"What we owed," I said, "you paid."

"Merrick paid."

I lowered my head. When I looked up, I noticed my son's color. His face had regained some of its old, ruddy luster, his dark hair was combed, he was clean-shaven. Moreau was becoming a young man again.

"It started here," I said.

"Yes," Moreau said. "And no. It started before Gib."

"All right," I said.

"I reckon it started with the heads," said Moreau. "They were something I had to answer for."

We looked at each other, the creek, crows, hawks, fast clouds, the large sky.

"Do you still believe in the devil?" I said.

Moreau looked at me, the creek, me again. "Devil is a name for things I don't understand. Never understood."

"Is war the devil?" I said.

"War is war."

I looked at him. "War doesn't stay away long. Killing Indians, fighting Mexico, stopping slavery. For me, the heads, the devil if you will, say, 'This place began in violence and is violent still. Take your stand.'"

He steadied himself. "I didn't go for you."

I turned. High clouds streamed east.

"Never liked slavery," he said.

"Families get caught in history," I said. "Born at the right or wrong time, young when the world goes to war. Lucky or unlucky."

"It's bigger than the heads," said Moreau. "Bigger than me and you."

"Killing Indians," I said. "Profiting from slavery. North and South are both part of it. Both are being punished. Slaves pulled America out of the wilderness and the wilderness got in America."

"The Salisbury debt is paid," said Moreau.

I wondered if he was thinking of his son, the child he'd given up. I looked at him. "I hit you." I was afraid I wouldn't say it. "I'm sorry."

Moreau looked at the creek. "I thank you, Father. I do."

I looked at my son, lowered my head, and wept silently.

74

Spring came and Lorenzo found peace. Not a happy peace, but peace. I didn't believe it, but Catherine said so. Yes, a woman visited and sat by the casket at night. The woman found peace, too. Catherine said, "Please don't tell anyone." It was private. Merrick's secret made his death easier for Lorenzo. Merrick had found another mourner in the woods.

In May the ice in the creek broke, ploughs returned to the fields, sparrows left the barns, and Merrick was buried in Stevens Cemetery on the Orwell road. Lorenzo dug the grave. On a warm Friday, he drove the casket and the stone in the cart drawn by the two white mules. He cemented the stone into a granite block so "nothing might knock it down till long after no one remembers Merrick Salisbury."

A procession formed behind the cart. Lorenzo told only Moreau and me, but people came, and many walked behind the cart. Lorenzo let me and a half dozen Salisburys carry the casket and lower it into the grave. Moreau walked behind using his cane. Sometimes he touched the casket.

Moreau didn't weep. He looked at the trees, alders, oaks, elms, maples, beeches, ash, and said, "I hope they get tall."

That's all he said.

Moreau

The Lesser Wilderness

June-July

1863

75

Once I talked to God. Now I would talk to a woman.

Everything else was smooth. Pretty smooth anyway. Father and I said what we had to say. Sometimes words do the work they should. There's a little acting in speaking—all of us, not just father, are making speeches when we talk—but there comes a time to accept it. Making Father feel good made me feel good, which was a surprise. I supposed I needed Father's best. I couldn't tell you why.

Mother was getting rested, and that was good. I drank morphine every morning. I had gotten used to sweats and crankiness and not sleeping. Dr. Bulkley strung and watched me get better. One morning he told me, "You got to stop drinking it sometime. I'm not telling you to stop, but I'm telling you that." I started drinking less. That was hard.

Things got easier, but I still hadn't set everything right.

In the spring Helen became beautiful. Her cheeks were ruddy, her walk more confident. She had come to a decision. I could tell. Sometime over the long winter Helen discovered a strength in herself she hadn't known she possessed. She was tired of being a sweetheart waiting for a soldier. She was ready to be a wife. Father noticed, Mother noticed, and people in town noticed. I remarked on it. Helen said, "That's just talk."

More than talk was coming. After worry, anger. Helen showed it, though quietly. She had reason.

On the Ides of June, Helen and I took the buggy out. I brought a cane and a blanket. Helen brought lunch. John Brown would have preferred to sleep. We went to the place by the creek beyond Woodville. We hadn't been there since I left for war.

The morning was clear, but not warm. Big-shouldered hawks, crows, and gulls circled new-plowed fields. We went through Woodville, passed the Woodville Hotel, Woodville General Store, Baptist Church, carts and wagons, and the McTavish place. I waved to O. B. Scott by his shanty, and Nathaniel Wood of the Woodville Woods in front of the Wood place, then crossed Woodville Bridge. The creek ran high and wide and bright and splashed the limestone flats and ledges. It swirled in pools, broke over branches, carried sticks and pebbles and sand. The noon sun danced up and down Big Sandy as it ran to Lake Ontario.

We didn't talk. We went to parts unknown. Helen had thought this out. She didn't smile. Her mouth was tight, her lips compressed, her eyes narrow. She didn't look at me.

We found our place, tethered John Brown, and spread the blanket. The creek ran muddy between banks populated by oak, tangled tag alder with tiny speckled flowers, gray ash, green willow, tall slippery elm, red sumac, balsam, poplar, new leaves everywhere, high grass and vines not yet knotted and woody.

"Lie down," she said.

I half sat, half fell, my cane beside me. The creek was smooth and quiet.

Helen climbed on top of me, pulling her dress out of the way. She kissed me roughly, putting her tongue in my mouth, and bit my lip until it bled.

"Forget your damn whores."

She squeezed my ear, pulled my hair, tongued me, tongue against tongue. Then her tongue was in my ear. She licked and bit an earlobe. My ankle throbbed. My member throbbed. Helen was someone else, a woman who didn't like me.

She pulled my beard, rubbed my chest. My ankle bled and she let it bleed. She rubbed my pants. Grabbed me. If you've never done something, you do it too easy or too hard. She undid my belt and I got bigger. She pulled at it. Either she didn't know how, or she wanted to hurt me. I didn't make a sound. She didn't make a sound.

She tore at the buttons of my pants. I reached to help and she pushed my hand away. "I'll do it." I raised up to make it easy. My ankle hurt. She pulled down my drawers and put her mouth on it. No looking first, no discovery, no pleasure. She gagged and pulled back and wiped her mouth with the back of her hand. Put her mouth on it again.

Her hand went around my balls and squeezed. Her finger dug around my fundament. I almost said, "How do you know about that?"

Sucked. Fingered. Sucked.

I got harder.

She nibbled. Bit.

My member hurt.

I heaved and gasped.

"Not yet."

She massaged my thigh, raked her fingernails down the inside. She kissed my ear. She rubbed my balls. Would she make me come and keep her clothes on, like a ten-penny whore? You get this. You don't get love.

She straddled me. She still wore her shoes. Her skirt was up like an umbrella. No underwear. No lacy tease. She took my member, put it against herself. It didn't go in. I didn't move. She pushed against me. She moved up and down. We were silent.

Helen held me. Moved slow. It didn't last long.

I cried. Couldn't help it. She tried so hard. Needed so much.

She cried. I had been afraid she wouldn't.

"You will marry me," she said. "You will stop talking about whores."

She slapped me.

She was bloody. As was my ankle.

She had brought bandages.

My wound bled and Helen bled. We bled by the creek in the place the Iroquois call the Lesser Wilderness, where Americans ambushed the British and the Indians say the world began.

Helen will be my wife and bear our child. Children will make it easier to think of the child I lost. Maybe having children with Helen, raising them together, providing what a father should provide, will make my guilt fade. Or maybe not. But if that guilt helps me to be a better father and better husband, then I will welcome it.

Helen said she wants a little girl, one who looks like her.

I'd welcome that too.

76

Uncle Lorenzo came to the wedding. He sat in the wagon drawn by the white mules. Then he and Catherine came down and joined us. July fourth. Some of the 24th came. Like me, they had mustered out on May 29. A few would go back.

There was a fight at Gettysburg. Some say worse than Antietam. No one says worse than the cornfield. After Gettysburg, the swift sword went south.

I couldn't do it again. I say I could, but I couldn't.

The brothers are brothers again, but different. We like to be together, but don't talk much. We don't mention Keedysville. It made us different from what we had been. Jesus, we're all different—Father, Mother, Helen, the brothers, all of us.

77

I am a miller now.

I'm happy in the village and wouldn't be anywhere else. Helen is happy too. The war, in a strange, awful way, wedded us to Sandy Creek. It took many, and now that we're back, the quick and the dead, I won't leave again. I like the creek, the smell of the mill, the sound of horses and carriages and carts on Main Street—even winter that drives us to our fires and close beds. I like the Baptist church, though I don't have anything to ask of God. Let that be for others. There's a time to question and a time to recognize answers. You just have to sort them out. I like Sandy Creek—the answers and the sorting out are here.

I was wounded and Mother and Father and Helen were wounded, too. Who gave us our wounds is not so important now. When I came back, the war was in me, and for a long time I couldn't get it out of me, but finally I did. Most of it, anway. Helen says, sure, we were wounded, but wounds heal, and scars are for show to those who don't have them. We have those too.

We asked Father to stand for re-election, but he says he's too old. I know what he means. We're too old for old things. We're ready for new ones. Helen says God's newest thing is children.

Helen is expecting.

I won't tell our child about the heads. I won't tell about the cornfield or Keedysville or the stable. I don't want our children thinking they must find a war, make fatal choices, or suffer impossible mornings.

Let them find what they must by the creek.

Mason
Sandy Creek
Christmas Day
1870

Epilogue

My part of this story is true as I can make it, but truth is complicated. So is memory.

The war is remembered differently from what it was. It's clouded by Lincoln's death, which somehow becomes the final word, the last lilac in the dooryard. Simplified, sanctified. If ever people needed a death, solemn and public, it was the American people, and the death was his.

The cemetery across Main Street has new graves. Bodies buried at the battlefields were exhumed, identified, and brought north after the war. Most of Sandy Creek's lost sons lie here.

For some of us, memory stays fresh. For others, it's already become something else. Terrible things get remembered soft. It's also a kind of forgetting.

Acknowledgements

A historical novel needs much guidance and information, and I was very fortunate. Margaret Kastler, former Sandy Creek Town Supervisor, and Charlene Cole, Town Historian, were wonderfully helpful. David K. Parsons and Marie K. Parsons' *Bugles Echo Across the Valley: Oswego County, New York, and the Civil War* was invaluable and a fine work of local history. I couldn't have made so many trips to the North Country without the incredible hospitality of Bonnie Bliss, and the friendship, advice, and insights of Barb and Frame Chamberlain, who are the best. Civil War re-enactor and historian Brian Codagnone let me fire an Enfield rifle and introduced me to his regiment's medical re-enactor. I have held a capital saw.

The people who tend the Woodlawn and Stevens Cemeteries, where Moreau and Merrick Salisbury lie, are always to be thanked.

Editorial assistance was generously given by Mari Black, the world champion fiddler, who is a world-class editor. Eleanor Goodman is an excellent editor and was a great help.

My grandfather, Lucius Albert Salisbury, first told me many of these stories. My late father, Lucius Albert Salisbury Jr., added more, and as a combat veteran of World War II, provided incomparable details and insight into war.

Ace Salisbury added much technological help and more patience with the author's shortcomings. Barbara Salisbury was, and is, the center of all things.